A SOUL INCARNATE

THE CREATURE SANCTUARY

CHRIS ANDREWS

This book couldn't have been published without the help of some wonderful people. I would like to thank:

- The members of the Canberra Speculative Fiction Guild's Novel Critique Group who offered invaluable feedback
- My incredible beta readers: Megan Crossin, Jenn Garza, Karen Roberts, Dar Baker, Alisa Aiken, Elizabeth Close
- Robert Porteous, who went above and beyond with advice, feedback, and so much more
- Nicola Semmler, for an amazing cover
- My wife and kids, of course

Hand over her mouth, Allura staggered through the bathroom door to the toilet, half shoving her head into the bowl as she retched. For a moment she felt better, but then the cold sweats came on once more. Trembling with the familiar, horrid, sickly feeling in her gut, she tried and failed to hold it in.

After several more bouts, she rinsed her mouth at the basin, weak and trembling. "Why do I keep doing this?" she asked her reflection in the medicine cabinet mirror.

She'd forgotten to pull her blonde hair back. It was filthy. "Crap."

Because you're an idiot?

Allura glared as her reflection changed into Sparrow's appearance. "Screw you, Sparrow."

You wish you could.

"Eww. You're supposed to be my imaginary friend, not my lover."

Oh, I'm far from that. I'm thousands of years of experience rolled up into a bitter ball of frustration and simmering resentment. I'm everything you deserve.

He was probably right on the last part. After showering and washing her hair, Allura pressed her aching forehead to the tiles and let the water-saving showerhead's jets punish her neck until the hot water ran out.

After drying, Allura wiped the fog from the small mirror with her hand, grimacing at the dark circles under her eyes. Her reflection changed once more, only now Sparrow sported unkempt hair, probably to mock her appearance. "What's with the goatee?" she asked when she belatedly noticed it.

She'd gotten good at imagining him over the last couple of years. Why she imagined him to be a slightly dishevelled college professor who criticised everything she did, she couldn't say. Probably her subconscious speaking the truth.

You're too old for this. You're a mother of three. Grow up, Allura.

And there it was. Advice she didn't need or want. "Mother of two," she corrected bitterly, the old, painful heartache threatening to overwhelm her once again, even half a decade after Piper's death. "Hey! What do you mean, I'm too old?"

Ahh, three thousand years of trying and failing to resolve your issues, only to fail once again. At least we're persistent, aren't we? Maybe it's time you gave up and moved on? A new incarnation would suit us.

What was all that supposed to mean? "A new incarnation?" she asked. Allura honestly couldn't tell if she was insane or if her imaginary friend was.

Sparrow's image vanished, replaced with her own. Glaring at his infuriating disappearance, she towelled her long blonde hair dry and left the bathroom to get dressed for work.

A thrill of fear rushed through her when she found a man sitting on her living-room mattress.

"Quicksilver?" she asked as she breathed a sigh of relief. She glanced at the apartment's door and then back at Quicksilver, trying to remember anything from last night. He was dressed in a suit minus the tie, his back to the wall. "Did...?"

"Of course not," he said, clearly struggling to keep his eyes on hers.

Allura abruptly remembered she was naked and with a rush of embarrassment ran for her office door, peeking around the corner when she was suitably hidden. "What are you doing here?"

"You called me at two this morning. I found you in the carpark across the street from the casino, passed out against a tree. Very becoming. There was a delicate pile of half-digested carrots next to you. Probably a gift from a passing drunk."

Allura flushed as foggy memories returned, and wished they hadn't.

She ducked back into the room and opened the single wardrobe door, grabbing her last fresh shirt with the casino's tiger logo on it. It took her a minute more to find the matching pants in the corner of the room.

As well as her desk and laptop computer, neither of which she'd used in months, the office contained two filing cabinets, bookshelves, and her clothes, mostly second-hand from the local op-shop.

The filing cabinets guarded the overburdened bookshelf holding dusty cameras, telescopic lenses, and disused surveillance equipment. She hadn't taken an actual investigative job in nearly six months, not since she'd started working at The Menagerie Hotel and Casino. There wasn't enough space for a bed in the room with everything else, so she'd dumped her mattress, minus the broken bedframe, in the living room. It was currently Quicksilver's seat.

Allura dressed before looking around for her clothes from last night. She opened the office door. "Did you undress me?" she asked.

Quicksilver, still sitting on her bed, stared back, his expression carefully blank. "They were a bit manky thanks to the carrots and whatnot. They're washed and in your dryer."

Allura flushed again. She really needed to stop drinking.

Quicksilver held up her apartment's keys and tossed them to her. "You almost threw up in my car, too. I'm surprised you had anything left by this morning."

"You're just jealous," she said with a forced smile, hoping he'd appreciate the dregs of her humour.

His steady stare said he was anything but jealous. "Shall we play this game again tomorrow? How about one-thirty this time, just to mix it up?"

Allura dropped her eyes. "I should thank you for bringing me home."

"Yeah," Quicksilver agreed. "You should."

God, she hated apologising. "Thank you," Allura said as she walked to the kitchen bench. It was piled up with dirty dishes, few matching, and some beginning to waft an aroma rodents might appreciate. "I should have married you when I had the chance," Allura added.

"Wendy and our kids might not agree," he replied.

Allura smiled. "They're good kids, and Wendy's a keeper. Letting you go might have been the biggest mistake of my life."

"The biggest of many."

She laughed. "True that."

She dumped three teaspoons of instant coffee in her last clean glass, filled it with hot-ish water from the tap, and drank it straight. For a few seconds she kept a hand over her mouth as the coffee threatened to come back up.

"This brings back fond memories from when we were dating," Quicksilver said. "Worst week of my life." His voice was heavy with... something. Nostalgia perhaps. Did he really miss the person she'd been back then?

Allura gave him an uncertain look, but when he met her gaze, she was the one to look away. "Why?" Allura asked.

He frowned. "Why what?"

"Why... Why keep looking after me? Why be my friend? I'm a mess and—"

"You know why."

"Because you feel sorry for me?"

"Yeah," he said with heavy sarcasm. "That's it."

"Seriously, why are you always there for me? You're still a cop. I'm an alcoholic deadbeat working for someone you think's a mobster. He's not, by the way."

Quicksilver released a long sigh. "I wish I could pretend to be someone else, too."

She flushed angrily at that, fighting off unwanted memories. "You don't owe me anything and I've been trouble for years. Why do you keep pulling me out of the gutter? Seriously, I want to know."

His shoulders slumped, and he gave in. "Because Piper would have wanted me to."

Pain and hurt almost shut Allura down. She had to force herself to take a deep breath before she could speak. "Piper's dead. She doesn't want anything anymore."

"Allura—"

"I've begged, borrowed, and stolen every cent I could in order to track down the bastard who bought and murdered her, only to come up with diddly squat. I've got nothing left, Quicksilver. Just let me drink myself to death. Please."

"You have two other children."

She gripped the empty glass, the dregs of her coffee pooling in the bottom. Her white knuckles threatened to shatter it. "They're better off without me."

"No, they're not."

She put the glass down with the rest of the unwashed dishes and indicated her apartment with a wave. "It's not like there's anything here for them, even if Greg agreed to fly them across the country to see me."

The awkward silence stretched. To cover it, she took a bag of dry cat food from under the sink, put a handful on a metal plate, and opened the kitchen window to place it on the sill. She couldn't afford to keep a cat of her own, but feeding a stray or two gave her something to care about, at least. Everyone wanted to feel wanted, and stray cats were all she had.

"Oh god," she whispered with unwanted realisation. "I'm the neighbourhood's crazy cat lady."

Quicksilver laughed at that. "You want a lift to work?" he asked.

More than a little embarrassed at her realisation, she nodded. "Yeah. That'd be good. Thanks."

You can feel it, can't you? The inevitable? It's about to happen all over again.

Allura glanced at Sparrow's reflection in the car window. She certainly had a strong feeling of déjà vu, so maybe Sparrow was reflecting her own anxiety. "Yeah," she agreed.

Quicksilver gave her a curious glance as he drove, but

Allura ignored his unspoken question. At least it was only a short drive from her apartment to the Kingston Foreshores, so there wasn't much time for small talk.

He found the time anyway. "I want you to promise me something, Allura."

Not this conversation again. Inwardly, she groaned, though she didn't let him see it in her expression. "What?"

"Stop drinking."

She rested her aching head against the cool glass window. "That's against my religion."

He sighed and pulled the car over, turning the engine off.

She sat up straight and gave him a frown. "What are you doing?"

He twisted in his seat to face her, squaring his shoulders, chin up a little more. "Promise me you'll stop drinking."

"You've asked me that before," she replied.

"I'm serious Allura. I can't keep doing this. Promise me you'll stop."

"Oh, come on..." Allura began in her best wheedling voice. "You know I don't make promises. I..."

He held up a hand to cut her off. "Because you've never broken one as far as I can tell. You're my best friend, my first love, and the mother of my first-born child. You've always had my back and I've always been there for you, too. But... Wendy's threatening to divorce me if I keep running out at all hours to help you through your latest mess. Promise me you'll stop drinking. Please."

He sounded serious. "Quicksilver—" she tried, but again he cut her off.

"Make the promise and keep it, or find someone else to call. Please. You're killing me and my marriage. You know I've got your back, but you're not reciprocating. One day, I may not be able to help you out, and we both know it. Please stop drinking."

Angry, she reached for the door handle, expecting him to stop her. He didn't. Allura hesitated, looking over her shoulder. "You're serious?" she asked.

His eyes were steady as he nodded. "I should have been at home this morning helping Wendy get the kids ready for school. Instead, I was making sure you didn't die in your sleep or something. How you're even conscious I don't know."

Allura slowly let go of the door handle. She needed Quicksilver more than she needed to drown her pain every night. Sparrow gave her a single nod from the window.

"Fine," she whispered. "No more grog." It wasn't exactly a promise, more like a lofty goal, but it should be enough to get him on side again.

"Not good enough," he said.

Damn. How did he know her so well? She closed her eyes, shaking her head slightly. "Fine," she whispered, unable to look at him. "I'm sorry for needing you so badly and for everything I've put you through. I'll sort myself out. I swear it. No more alcohol. I'll even make it a pinky promise." She held her hand up, pinky outstretched.

He wrapped his own pinky around hers, as if not quite certain he'd expected her to agree. They shook, and a chill ran through her as if she'd just done something momentous. A sensation of tightness closed over her skin as if her words were actually binding. She shivered.

"You better follow through with it." Quicksilver turned the engine on again and pulled back into the traffic.

Sparrow broke the silence inside her head as Quicksilver drove past the Old Bus Depot Markets.

He's a keeper. You should have married him when you were pregnant with Piper. She was his daughter too.

"Get stuffed," she replied.

"Me or Sparrow?" Quicksilver asked as he turned left.

"Sparrow." She'd spoken to Sparrow too much lately.

"How about you call that helpline number? The one they're always promoting on television? It's free."

"Ouch," Allura said as Quicksilver slowed the car at an intersection as they approached The Menagerie. "You think I can't give up the grog on my own?"

"I was referring to your conversation with your imaginary friend," he replied as the car picked up speed again.

"I wish I'd never told you about Sparrow."

Ahead, police cars had cut off access to the area between the back of The Menagerie and the Jerrabomberra Wetlands.

Quicksilver pulled up as a uniformed police officer directed him to stop. He put the window down. "Hey Jim, what's going on?"

"A murder. Real weird one."

Jim bent a bit lower until he could see Allura. He smiled. "Cassie! Been a while. How you been?"

Allura gave him a genuine smile. "Hi Jim. My name's Allura now. I changed it a couple of years ago."

Jim raised his eyebrows. "That's uh... Okay. Allura it is. You consulting with Quicksilver now? I'm assuming you've still got that side business photographing marriage cheats and whatnot?"

"Something like that."

Jim nodded. "Go on through, then. They could use your help."

Allura no longer had a security clearance, which meant

no more access to crime scenes, even as a consultant or photographer. She'd never officially been registered as a private investigator either, so she really shouldn't be allowed through.

"Thanks Jim," Quicksilver said. "You coming to drinks this Friday?"

"Hell yes, and thanks for the invite."

2

Quicksilver killed the engine.

Time to bail.

Allura glanced at Sparrow. "Why? We just arrived."

Don't you recognise trouble when you see it?

Quicksilver gave her a look. "Your imaginary fiend still giving you sass?"

Fiend. That was appropriate. "Yeah. But he's making about as much sense as me when I'm drunk."

Sparrow made choking sounds as Allura opened the door, his protests disappearing when she could no longer see his reflection.

"I should get to work," she said, frowning at the commotion ahead. "Dragging me into that chaos could get you into trouble."

Several of the Menagerie's security personnel were being interviewed on the sidewalk across the road at the rear of the twenty-storey hotel and casino. An ambulance waited nearby, too. There were uniformed police everywhere.

"Pretend I'm interviewing you. That'll fly considering you work at the Menagerie," Quicksilver said.

Allura brushed aside a lone hair tickling her nose, curiosity fighting to the surface. "I don't want to get you into trouble."

"Come on. You've helped me out on a dozen cases over the last couple of years. More. How's this different?"

She gave him a look. "I let you bounce ideas off me over a beer or two. In confidence. Nobody knew. Having me here is..." She indicated her work uniform. "Just turning up with me could cause you problems. Everyone thinks I work for a mobster in a pinstripe suit, remember? Including you."

"You're about the only person who doesn't believe that," Quicksilver said as he shrugged and began walking toward the commotion. "You're a potential witness. Come on." He gave her a follow me gesture. Curiosity finally got the better of her and she hurried to catch up.

They entered the cordoned-off grassy area behind the tall building. Allura squinted against the mid-morning sunlight reflecting from the windows of the twenty-storey Menagerie. She recognised a few faces in uniform, but not as many as she'd expected. Lots of newbies on the force.

Allura kept close to Quicksilver's back until he stopped at a mummified corpse hidden by tall grass about ten metres from the road. The woman's flesh was dried out, while her long dark hair framed a skeletal face even her family wouldn't recognise. "Holy shit," she whispered in shock.

"This isn't possible," Quicksilver said as he started reading the report on his computer notepad. "She's..." He looked around as if seeking whoever was in charge. "It has to be a hoax." He walked around the corpse until he stood opposite Allura. "This can't be Jingyi Lee. At least a dozen people saw her alive last night."

Allura crouched, careful not to touch anything. "Body switch?"

"Maybe."

"What does a hoax accomplish?" Allura asked, running through possibilities.

He didn't seem to hear the question as he continued studying the report. "The long grass and nearby shrubs hid the body, so it was only pure chance a man walking his dog discovered her this morning. The dog did, at least." He sounded distant.

"The body's too close to the Menagerie to be a coincidence," Allura said. "You think this is a setup?"

Quicksilver brushed dark hair from his eyes. His hair was cut a little too long, though it suited him in a roguish kind of way. He claimed it helped him blend in with Canberra's less affluent communities. The jacket belied that. How he could wear a jacket in summer, she had no idea. She could use a bit of shade herself.

Quicksilver kept reading through the report. "Her parents confirmed she was at dinner with them last night." He glanced at the body and then back at the report as if trying to reconcile them.

"If this is Jingyi Lee, how'd she get mummified in hours?" Allura asked.

He shrugged and kept reading. "She had a fifteen-year-old sister who went missing about four years ago while they were holidaying in Malaysia. Nobody's seen the girl since. Could be connected."

"A kidnapping in Malaysia connected to Australia? How?" She looked around. "The area's been stomped on pretty good. I assume it's all been photographed, and forensics are done with everything except the body?"

"Yeah," he said absently. "We're late to the party." He continued reviewing the report. "The father and mother don't speak English, so they used an interpreter. Mister Lee is a business executive. He and his wife arrived three days ago from China with Jingyi Lee. The missing daughter's name was Bo. Officially, Jingyi Lee works for the Chinese government, but we've got no details about what she actually does. Did."

"So, she's a spy?" Allura asked with a smirk, not entirely sure if she was being serious. "Get the feeling this is out of your depth? Maybe you should take a walk with me to the Menagerie, and I'll buy you a drink?"

Quicksilver gave her a frown. "You promised."

Allura grimaced. "I'll have a soft drink. Did Jingyi Lee have a job title?"

He flicked the screen to the right. "She is... was, qualified as an interpreter. No job title. Her parents were vague on the details."

"How the hell do you desiccate a corpse?" Allura wondered aloud. She looked around as if a clue would materialise nearby, like a guy holding a placard saying *I did it*.

She stared in surprise when she saw Slade Mills, her old boss and former lover, talking with another cop near the road.

"Shit," she whispered under her breath, turning away and hoping he didn't see her.

Quicksilver caught her glance. "These days Slade runs the people smuggling and modern slavery division," he said, filling her in.

And Jingyi Lee's sister went missing about four years ago. Slade's presence was unlikely to be a coincidence then.

Quicksilver returned to reading his tablet. "Jingyi Lee ate lobster with her parents in the High Roller restaurant before going for a walk along the foreshore. Her father played roulette in the casino while her mother visited the spa. Everything's verified. There's even CCTV footage outside the casino."

Allura did a slow turn. She'd never actually stood at the back of the Menagerie. The twenty-story glass-fronted building contrasted oddly with the bush and lake setting. Apartments to the right. Bushland and the lake behind her stretching all the way to Fyshwick.

Built in the decade before the Kingston Foreshores precinct was commercially developed, there'd been almost nothing in the area then. Now, there was a sprawling complex of apartments and restaurants nearby, all built to take advantage of the lake, the casino, and the location.

Her boss, Lawrence Shaw, owned the land they stood on, the Menagerie, and half the apartments and commercial premises in the area. That was just the tip of his reach, though. He owned half of Canberra as far as Allura could tell. He also owned her, depending on how she looked at it.

"I think someone's sending a message to Shaw," Allura said, feeling an odd loyalty to the man who'd helped her get back on her feet. Shaw had lots of enemies and a dangerous reputation, but he'd always been good to her.

"Or Shaw stuffed up," Quicksilver countered. "One of his minions was probably on his way to dump the body in the lake, but got spooked."

Minions? Allura worked for Shaw. Did that make her a minion? She tried not to feel offended, but it was hard.

Why the city needed two casinos she didn't know, but the Menagerie was the only one with poker machines, a significant advantage over its rival. The poker machines were limited to a floor that had been sub-let to a local club, so officially the club owned them, not the casino. Casinos weren't allowed to own poker machines in Canberra, just tables of broken dreams.

The partnership attracted a lot of people to the casino, though. For that reason and a dozen others, more than a few people would have been happy to see Shaw take a hit of the lethal variety. Causing trouble for him by dumping a body near his casino probably only came in at the high five level.

"You want my opinion? I think it's a setup," Allura said.

Quicksilver scowled. It clearly wasn't what he wanted to hear. "Care to say why?"

"Remember that massacre about a year ago?" Allura asked. "The police officially put it down to a gangland war in Mitchell, not that the public bought the explanation."

Quicksilver nodded. "The one that came complete with torn-apart bodies and no explanations that fit? I've tried to forget."

"That was messed up, and so is this."

"Messed up, sure, but I can't see a connection."

"Mummified bodies and corpses that look like they'd been torn up by hyenas? They're both off-the-charts weird. That's the connection."

"Which means what?" Quicksilver asked.

"Remember that car rebirthing racket a couple of months ago where that biker got shot and killed? Got a pretty good writeup in the news."

"Yeah. I wasn't involved, but of course I know about it."

"I overheard Shaw telling a couple of people to spread the rumour that he ordered the hit. He's all reputation."

"Yeah, I heard that rumour too. I'm inclined to believe it, though we've got no evidence."

"Exactly! He takes credit for stuff he doesn't do, because he knows you'll never pin it on him. Even if you believe Shaw ordered Jingyi Lee's murder, he's not stupid. He wouldn't dump a mummified body at the back of his own casino. He doesn't need that kind of attention. This is a message for him, not from him." Allura pointed at the Menagerie's external cameras. "I can probably prove it. If you're nice to me, I can ask for the footage. It'd save you a lot of red tape."

He raised an eyebrow. "I was nice to you last night."

She flushed with more than a little shame. "True. How about you forget about my promise in exchange for access to the footage? I'll even let you buy me a drink."

"Shall I invite Wendy and the kids? We could all get drunk together."

Allura laughed. "Of course not. Your kids aren't even teenagers yet. That'd be tacky."

Quicksilver offered a begrudging smile. "You really think you can help? If you can't, Shaw will demand a warrant like he did when I was investigating those girls who went missing last year."

"I can ask."

"I could ask with my gun drawn and handcuffs out," Quicksilver added.

Allura snorted back a laugh, at which point her former boss and lover Slade Mills finally noticed her. He frowned and began walking their way.

"Shit," Allura whispered, dropping her gaze as if pretending not to see him was the same as him not seeing her. "I hope you're not too keen on your job," Allura said to

Quicksilver under her breath. She looked up and forced a smile as Slade stopped before them.

Slade was still good looking for a man in his late fifties. He had an intensity she'd always found attractive, despite their falling out.

Lawrence Shaw was the only other man with that same presence, but he'd shown no interest in her beyond their professional relationship. That stung a little, but Shaw was the kind of guy who had a different girl in his bed every night, so it was probably a blessing.

Slade was still hard, fit, and lean. He had a sharp mind, too. "Morning Rabbit. Quicksilver."

Quicksilver did a double take. "Rabbit? I thought you hated that nickname," he said to Allura.

Allura clenched her fists. Quicksilver was right, but if she didn't play nice, Slade could make things very difficult for Quicksilver. "I prefer House Bunny," she replied with a smile she hoped didn't look forced.

Slade laughed. "House Bunny? Sure."

Grey at the temples and with a five o'clock shadow, she'd forgotten how good-looking Slade was for a man nearly a couple of decades older than her. She hadn't forgotten how she'd caught him in their bed with another woman, though.

"Why are you investigating a murder? Is it linked to human trafficking?" Quicksilver asked Slade, neatly changing the topic.

Slade offered a half-committal shrug. "Why are you here at all? You weren't called in."

Quicksilver met Slade's eyes. "I was just dropping Allura off, saw the commotion, and..."

"And you were stupid enough to bring a civilian along for a peep show?" Slade asked with raised eyebrows.

"Care to share any goss?" Allura intervened, hoping to

diffuse the situation. "Otherwise, I've got a bar to run. Happy to leave you two at it, though."

Slade gave her a speculative look. "What do you know about your boss, Lawrence Shaw?" he asked, eyes going to Allura's uniform.

Allura felt the conversation cross into dangerous territory. She didn't want to get involved in any kind of feud between Shaw and the police. "I have a loan with him, which is helping get me back on my feet. Working in his bar helps pay it off."

He gave her a doubtful frown. The awkward silence stretched as if he could get her to say more by not talking. She'd been a cop, though, and knew the tricks.

He gave up, putting a hand on her shoulder and guiding her away from Quicksilver.

When they were far enough not to be overheard, she pulled away, or tried to. He didn't drop his grip. "Please don't touch me. You lost that right when you invited another woman into our bed."

He gave her a long-suffering look. "And I've apologised a dozen times. What do you want from me?"

"What do you want from me?" she countered. "I'm not a cop anymore."

He looked around and leaned in as if not wanting to be overheard. "We're investigating a murder likely committed by your boss. I need inside information."

Offended, she stiffened. "I'm not risking my neck for you."

His hand tightened on her shoulder, pinning her in place as she tried to move away. "Then how about I release a report about an investigation I was a part of about five years ago? Two men involved in child trafficking disappeared. Your daughter went missing a few months beforehand.

Would you like to know who the evidence points to, and who didn't pursue the matter?"

Allura went cold. He knew. Shit. He really knew what they'd done. "You're blackmailing me?"

"Blackmail's a strong word. Let's just say I've been putting some coins into the bank of opportunity, and opportunity has finally appeared."

"I don't know what you're talking about," Allura said, nausea rising. She might have thrown up if she had anything in her stomach.

"I could show you my personal notes about that investigation, which I never filed," he added. "Very interesting reading. They mention both you and Quicksilver. A lot."

Oh god. Feeling whiter than the few small clouds in the sky, Allura swallowed down bile. "Leave Quicksilver out of it. He wasn't even there," she lied.

Slade smiled, but it wasn't a pleasant smile. "Then let me tell you what's about to happen. You're going to help with this investigation, understood? Afterwards, you're going to return to my bed. I want you back, Allura."

To protect Quicksilver, she'd do whatever he wanted. "Fine," she whispered, her voice almost hoarse. "You leave Quicksilver out of it, and I'll keep an ear out for information. You want my soul as well, or is having me back in your bed enough?" Allura added with all the bitterness she could manage.

He narrowed his eyes at her tone. "Let's just agree on the basics, shall we? We're going to return to Quicksilver now, and you're going to take him to the Menagerie and do whatever you can to help. Is that clear?"

"Yes," she repeated, not daring to say more.

"Good. Start looking for answers that prove Shaw's

guilty. I want him arrested within the week, got it? I'll be in touch."

His hand still on her shoulder, he guided her back to a very curious and somewhat nervous-looking Quicksilver.

Slade smiled as he released his hold on her. "Word is that Jingyi Lee was investigating an international people smuggling ring. Hear anything about it, Allura?"

"No," she said honestly, still shaken by Slade's threat. "But I can keep my ears open and pass any info through Quicksilver."

Quicksilver gave her a strange look at her tone, but she shook her head slightly. He got the message and didn't question her.

"I assume the Menagerie is as much of a rumour mill as anywhere else?" Slade asked. "Should be good pickings."

She smiled weakly. "I can probably get Quicksilver the security camera footage. That help?"

Slade nodded, smiling as if he wasn't blackmailing her. "You do that."

And there it was. He had a hook in her, and she had no way to get out. Was Slade dirty or just obsessed? He was certainly still the same asshole who'd broken her heart. If he was gunning for Shaw though, one of them was going to lose, and she was now in the middle. She might as well slit her own throat and be done with it.

Slade inclined his head as if she was fully on board with everything he wanted. "We suspect Jingyi Lee held a similar position to me on the other side of the Great Firewall of China. That, or she was dirty and using her job as cover. Maybe both."

"And you think Shaw's involved?" Allura asked. Quicksilver was decidedly quiet, watching Allura more than Slade now.

Slade glanced at the tall building across the road, the upper levels made up of apartments and hotel rooms. "I'll ensure the investigation's transferred to Quicksilver for now, but I'll remain involved. If you hear anything that implicates Shaw and it leads to his arrest, I'll make sure you get the credit for it. Fair, Allura?"

Fair? Shaw valued loyalty above everything else. If he didn't kill her after this, one of his people might, if only to prove themselves to him. She might have to leave the country to untangle herself from this mess, and she wasn't even sure that would be enough.

"Is it possible Jingyi Lee was investigating Shaw because of her sister?" Quicksilver asked when the silence stretched. "She might have been staying at the casino to poke around."

"Allura might be able to find out," Slade said. The words implied 'or else'.

"Anything more you can tell us?" Quicksilver asked cautiously, his tone implying he'd picked up on the tension and lack of ethics involved, but didn't know what to do about it considering Slade outranked him.

Slade let the question hang for a long moment. "Unofficially, I think Jingyi Lee was one of the good guys, which suggests Shaw didn't want her sniffing around his turf. What do you think, Allura?"

Another loaded question. "I think I should keep an ear out for anything out of the ordinary and tell Quicksilver about it."

"Good enough. For now." Someone waved for Slade's attention. "Gotta go."

Quicksilver chewed his bottom lip as he watched Slade walk away. "What the hell, Allura? Helping me out with footage is one thing, but Shaw's not going to be kind to you if he thinks you're passing information to the police."

"I'll be fine," Allura said without confidence. "I'm not going to do anything stupid."

She already had, and Slade knew everything about it. If she ran, Slade would make Quicksilver pay. If she did as Slade wanted, Allura would probably end up at the bottom of a staircase with a broken neck, or worse.

Slade had put her on a tightrope over a chasm, and there was no safety net.

3

Allura walked through the casino's reception and into the Atrium Bar, the large open area where drinks and food were served. The family-friendly space was filled with tourists and casino guests who'd gathered around a temporary stage next to the dance floor.

Directly behind the bar, a netted enclosure rose to the roof six stories above, the circular space full of butterflies. Potted flowers hung from a central chain, kept alive with a drip-watering system. Allura suspected some of the butterflies had migrated to her stomach after what Slade had asked of her.

On the stage, one of the Menagerie's massive Siberian tigers was on show for tourist photos, probably brought out from the zoo before dawn. The tigress's paws were almost as big as dinner plates, and she outweighed the biggest three men in the room, combined.

The Siberian looked Allura's way like a favoured pet desperate for help. Allura couldn't help a snort of laughter at the look on the tiger's face. Two tigresses currently took turns posing for tourists on different days, though she hadn't seen the third one, Missy, for a while. Apparently, Missi was pregnant, and the trainers wouldn't risk her.

Allura could tell them apart easily enough, but she doubted the tourists knew there was more than one.

"That's not legal," Quicksilver said as he stared at the tigress, his hand going to the missing gun under his jacket. He wasn't allowed to take his weapon home, and he'd spent most of the night looking after Allura before coming directly here. "It's got no muzzle or even a chain holding it to that stage. Nothing."

Allura put a hand on his shoulder. "Lotti's gentle. They wouldn't do this if it wasn't safe."

"But—"

"The casino puts this show on two or three times a week. It's safe."

Quicksilver glanced over people's heads as if hoping to find gun towers. "How's this safe? Seriously? If that tiger gets spooked, there'll be a massacre."

Luci Nguyen held Lotti's chain while four security guards stood at the corners of the waist-high stage. Each security guard concealed a Taser from casual view. They'd never needed them, though. The tigers had been raised with people and were professionally trained and well behaved.

Today, Luci was dressed in black leather, her ruby and gold choker tight about her neck. She wore fishnet stockings and a top hat with coat and tails. Sometimes she did the show in a feather-laden showgirl outfit or as a cancan dancer. She'd also done it as a clown, which was a little creepy.

Quicksilver frowned, but he clearly trusted Allura more than the tiger. "I did that meet-a-cheetah thing once. It was amazing, but the cheetahs were like big house cats. That tiger's big enough to eat a cheetah." He cocked his head. "Hey, is that Luci Nguyen?"

"Yeah," Allura said. Luci had never taken to Allura or anyone else as far as Allura could tell. She was rumoured to be Shaw's enforcer, the kind who would put a knife in your back or poison in your drink, not that she'd been anything but polite to Allura. If Luci caught wind of what Slade had demanded of her, Allura's new priority would be clearing town faster than a mouse in a python's sights.

Rumour had it that Luci had worked for both the Yakuza and the Hong Kong triads before switching her loyalties to Shaw. Allura had happily ignored the rumours. Luci was Vietnamese for a start, and she couldn't speak Chinese or Japanese. It didn't mean she wouldn't take a crowbar to the side of Allura's knees if she suspected betrayal. She certainly gave off that vibe.

Officially, Shaw employed Luci as an entertainer and a bartender in the After Dark Ladies' Lounge, a highly unlikely occupation for an underworld assassin.

Still, Luci wasn't just a bartender. The choker she wore was made of woven gold wire bound into a cord as thick as Allura's finger. The large ruby dangling from it was worth an absolute fortune on its own. She'd heard it was a gift from Shaw, implying her value to him. Allura had seen men more than twice Luci's size jump at her command.

Lotti continued behaving herself, a heavenly feat considering she was now being mauled by a chocolate-smeared toddler maybe two years old. Dozens of guests took pictures with their phones.

"How do they get away with this?" Quicksilver continued, still caught up on the likely legalities. People expected cops to know everything there was to know about the law. If only that were possible.

The tigress yawned, displaying frighteningly big teeth in a mouth that could close around a man's head. Lotti glanced at Allura again, her long-suffering look imploring help until her gaze settled on Quicksilver as if he were a threat to Allura.

Quicksilver noticed, and didn't look happy.

"I'll protect you from the big pussy," Allura said as she put her hand against Quicksilver's shoulder and guided him through the crowd.

"Bite me," he muttered.

As the people-barrier thinned, a massive mountain of a security guard moved in front of Quicksilver. Nicknamed Teddy Bear, he was Shaw's head of security and rumoured stand-over man.

Clean shaven with close-cropped, mousy-coloured hair, Teddy Bear was easily the biggest man Allura had ever met. He might have even given Lotti a half-decent wrestle. Teddy Bear stood about six foot eight and was built like a pro-boxer, his uniform tight across his chest. He could probably pick Quicksilver up with one arm, and Quicksilver weighed half again what Allura weighed.

"Allura," Teddy Bear said. "I thought we made it clear you weren't to drag any more refuse in off the street."

Allura snorted back a laugh, much to Quicksilver's disgust. "Mister Shaw about?"

Teddy Bear moved aside to reveal the man in question talking with Mia, the two of them close to the bar and the huge central net full of butterflies.

Mia was a tiny young woman of Chinese descent who ran the Cancan Coffee Bar and the evening shows. She was also heavily pregnant with her fifth child and married to Shaw's adopted son, Don Bencivenni. Mia smiled when she saw Allura and nodded to Shaw before leaving, as if knowing what this was all about.

The first time Allura had met Shaw, she'd felt déjà vu and a sense of imposing danger. Today was no different. She caught other women struggling not to glance Shaw's way as well. Allura imagined Sparrow laughing at her for no obvious reason.

Shaw looked Quicksilver over like a man bracing for a fight.

She'd read Shaw's file several times when she'd been a cop. The casino owner was a former street brawler and rumoured underworld figure, commonly known among police as a thug in a suit. It worked for him rather than against him. He'd taken a small empire and built it into a big one over the last few decades, a lot of it because no one dared to oppose him.

A little taller and broader than Quicksilver, if not nearly as big as Teddy Bear, he had a chiselled cast to his features and the kind of dangerous, bad-boy looks Allura usually went for. If his nose had been crooked, it would have suited him. It was disappointingly straight.

That magnetism which had first attracted her to him gripped her once again, but as before, he showed no interest in her, which stung as much now as it had the first time she'd met him.

Growing amusement in his expression made her flush when she realised he'd caught her checking him out.

Despite being considered one of the most brutal men in the city, he'd always been polite to her. Generous, just as he was to all his staff. With the exception of Luci and Mia, and his adopted son, Don, Allura had never met anyone with the courage to challenge him on anything.

"You look happy for someone hosting a murder," Quicksilver said as they reached Shaw.

Allura gripped his forearm, squeezing as hard as she could. "Don't be an ass," she muttered under her breath before releasing his arm.

"Allura. It's always lovely to see you," Shaw said, ignoring Quicksilver's barb. Probably to piss Quicksilver off, he took Allura's hand and kissed it as if she were royalty. Allura was so surprised she didn't protest, but the temperature in the room rose significantly.

Quicksilver tightened his grip on his datapad. "You going to kiss my hand, too?"

"If you wish." Shaw reached for Quicksilver's hand, but Quicksilver stepped back. It was enough to make Shaw smirk, the kind of smirk which suggested Quicksilver had better stop playing games or he'd find himself with a few broken teeth.

"Mister Shaw. One of our patrons died near these premises last night," Allura said, ignoring Quicksilver's discomfort and her own swirling insides. "My former colleague has a request I was hoping you could help him with."

Something changed in Shaw's expression. It was subtle, but despite his show of nonchalance, the murder clearly concerned him. She swore she caught anger in his eyes. "Several police orificers have already questioned me."

"Orificers?" Quicksilver asked.

"Slip of the tongue."

She'd been right, then. Shaw was the target, not the instigator. How was she supposed to tell Slade that? Who'd actually committed the murder, and why?

Quicksilver pursed his lips. "I need the footage from your CCTV system," he said. "Specifically, the back, front, and all entrances and exits to the Menagerie for the last twenty-four hours."

"A request that's been made several times already. This casino's policy requires a warrant." Shaw looked like he could have happily thrown Quicksilver out just then, perhaps in a body bag. "If you'd asked politely, I might have been inclined to break policy."

Quicksilver didn't back down. "I can get a warrant, and I'm sure the media will love to hear about it. All press is good press, right?"

Shaw gave Quicksilver a steady, flat stare, a signal Allura recognised from her long experience as a cop. Both men were spoiling for a fight.

Allura stepped between them. "Mister Shaw, it's going to cost you nothing to provide the footage, and it might help thaw relations between you and the police force. Please—"

Shaw raised an eyebrow. "Please? That's a word I haven't heard you use since you first came to me begging for money."

Allura flushed.

Quicksilver cleared his throat. "Do we need to get a warrant for the footage, Mister Shaw?" His tone was barely polite.

Shaw focused on Allura. "Ms Forsayeth, if you'd consent to having dinner with me here tonight, I'll gladly provide all the footage Defective Silver requires, no warrant required."

Allura caught her breath. What the hell? Was he asking just to piss Quicksilver off, or because he was genuinely interested in her? She didn't have a clue how to respond. Maybe someone had overheard her conversation with Slade and reported it to him. Crap. She must have gone white.

Quicksilver gave Allura a look which clearly told her to turn down the request.

Mouth dry with tension at being put in the middle of the issue despite her desire to be invisible, Allura ignored the look. "Dinner, and five grand off my debt to you." That should put him off. Hopefully, it didn't piss him off.

Shaw studied her as if seeing her for the first time. If anything, he seemed amused. "Agreed. Eight o'clock?"

Oh shit. Really? "Eight o'clock," she repeated weakly. She should have made it ten grand.

Shaw led them to one of the three glass elevators evenly placed around The Atrium, where one of his security people held the doors open for them. Women subtly glanced Shaw's way as he passed, as if he were magnetised, yet it was Allura who was having dinner with him tonight. That equally thrilled and scared her.

The elevator took them up to the sixth-floor balcony overlooking the Atrium. Shaw guided them through staff corridors until they reached the casino's locked security room. Allura had never been inside.

Banks of monitors displayed dozens of rooms and walkways, including the empty nightclub currently being cleaned. Mostly they showed lots of unused gaming tables. Only a handful were open this early. The system endlessly cycled through the cameras, all presumably being recorded. Two people were monitoring everything, though there was room for half a dozen more. The extras were probably only needed at night.

Allura caught sight of Sparrow's reflection in a turned-off monitor.

Leave. Cancel the dinner. Get out of town. He'll kill you again.

Sparrow then laughed and vanished, leaving Allura confused. When she looked up, she found Shaw staring at her, a frown betraying something she wasn't comfortable seeing from him. Curiosity. Had she responded to Sparrow under her breath, and not noticed?

"The footage?" Allura prompted.

Shaw approached the young woman at one of the monitor banks. She had red-dyed hair and an impish look about her. "This is Neednap," he said to Quicksilver. Allura had met the woman, but they'd rarely spoken. "Recently nicknamed when we found her asleep during her break. You may call her Polly."

The pretty young woman smiled, clearly not offended. "I had a hangover. I didn't think it was a good excuse not to show up to work and they haven't let me forget it since."

"Neednap, I need you to compile all the footage available from the back dock and casino entrances since yesterday, and provide it to this upstanding public servant."

"Of course, Mister Shaw." She turned to her computer and began tapping keys to call up the required footage.

"Leave out nothing relevant. We don't want my favourite defective trying to pin this murder on me."

"Defective again?" Quicksilver asked. He leaned closer to Allura as Shaw focused on Neednap's work. "Shaw's being far too generous with his information, and hitting on you has to be a distraction."

A little insulted, Allura ignored the comment. Her situation was weighing far more heavily than Quicksilver's unintentional insult. She had to make good on a dinner with Shaw for a start, not to mention Slade Mills was likely to ask her to do much more than report rumours. And if she didn't get murdered before it was all over, Slade wanted her back in his bed. She'd do it to protect Quicksilver, but there had to be another way out.

Shaw glanced over his shoulder. "Defective Silver, if you

insult Allura again, please note I won't stand in her way if she murders you with the pointy end of one of her stilettos."

"Can you hurry please, Polly?" Allura asked, hoping to diffuse the tension.

Polly nodded, a new screen appearing. "I'll drop the files into a cloud-based folder. Where should I send the download link?"

"My work email address," Quicksilver said, handing her a card with the details.

Shaw opened the door for them to leave. "Don't forget about dinner tonight, Allura. Meet me in the After Dark Ladies' Lounge."

"It will be a pleasure," Allura said with a smile that threatened to crack one of her molars. If Slade Mills heard about this...

4

Rather than returning home after work to change, Allura walked the ten minutes to the Kingston Hotel, locally known as The Kingo. Despite her promise to Quicksilver to give up the grog, it was time to drown her fears in a bottle of vodka.

She'd spent her entire shift feeling vaguely sick. Why did Shaw really want to have dinner with her? Why had she agreed? Was she doing it because Slade Mills was blackmailing her, or to help Quicksilver?

If she was honest with herself, it was both and neither. She wanted to have dinner with Shaw, and that equally scared and thrilled her.

She entered The Kingo and waited at the bar until the customer before her carried four beers away. Allura moved up. "Vodka and lemonade, please."

Realising she was more scared than thrilled, she intended to drink her emotions numb in the two hours before she had to return to the Menagerie. Shaw hadn't asked her to turn up sober, and being drunk would at least ensure she'd be able to get through dinner without her nerves getting in the way.

After paying for her drink with her credit card, Allura went looking for a table. Her pay was deposited into the linked account every fortnight. If she went over, it added to her debt with Shaw. If she underspent, it covered her debt. Simple.

Shaw had originally given her credit so she could search for her daughter's kidnappers, but with no work as a private investigator, she'd been forced to use it for everything, and the debt kept racking up. Debt slavery, she supposed. Calling it that was a lame way to justify her situation, but pretending it was someone else's fault felt better.

Allura left with her drink as a young woman took her place. She didn't want to be Allura Forsayeth tonight. Or anyone. She didn't want to be in debt, she didn't want to think about Slade's not-so-subtle blackmail threats, and she certainly didn't want to face Lawrence Shaw across a dining table while sober.

At least she could do something about that last problem.

Sitting, she wrapped her hands around the cool glass, condensation wetting her hands. Now she had it though, she didn't feel like drinking. Determined not to waste it, Allura lifted the glass to her lips, but the smell brought on nausea and she almost barfed. What was wrong with her? She tried again, but her stomach threatened full-on rebellion if she tasted it.

She placed the drink back on the table and stared at it for the better part of two hours, watching the ice melt and the condensation drip.

When she left The Kingo, she left sober, the vodka still in the glass.

The afternoon heat hadn't abated much, but the cool of

evening was doing its best to creep over the city and cast long shadows across the streets, while orange sunlight reflected off the massive flagpole over Parliament House.

She hated seeing the flagpole because it reminded her that politics attracted all the wrong sorts of people, and those people made the rules. People like Slade Mills and Shaw. Shaw owned her more-or-less, and Slade Mills wanted her.

Distressingly sober, she was certain it wasn't just dinner tonight. Most likely, Shaw wanted something from her. What?

The Menagerie's interior was blessedly cool and welcoming as she entered, but Allura felt no relief as she took the glass elevator to level four and made her way to the After Dark Ladies' Lounge.

Sparrow appeared in her multiple reflections in the elevator, laughing at her. Bastard.

SHAW SAT on the edge of his desk, staring at his sketches on the opposite wall. There were forty-nine sketches, each of a different woman with the same soul. Lovingly hand-drawn, they represented forty-nine incarnations across three millennia. If there were more, he hadn't met them.

Today he'd drawn a new sketch, but hadn't hung it. He wouldn't while she was alive.

Despite each incarnation's differing appearance and personality, they were all the same person. They always seemed to retain an echo of long-forgotten pain resonating in her soul, something that shaped them throughout each life.

Most of his sketches had caught her incarnations at a

point he thought of as innocence, a look they'd all shared, until realising what he was. That was when the conflict began. By keeping his distance, he'd managed to put that off so far. She hated herself more than him or anyone else.

Shaw held up the framed sketch, seeing the same soul behind the eyes, yet in this lifetime she carried more grief than any other of her other incarnations. More self-loathing, too. "What do you need from me?" he whispered. Whatever it was, he had no idea how to give it to her. God, he'd tried dozens of times.

Luci entered his office, still wearing her top hat and tails. She frowned when she saw him holding the portrait.

"Don't say it," he said.

Her scowl deepened as she sat on the desk beside him, slipping her arm behind his back. Her vampiric lifeforce seeped into him like the sour reek of sewage. He tried not to shudder at her touch.

"I'd never treat you with such contempt," she said.

He forced a half smile. "It's not contempt. She's broken, and I don't know how to fix her. Besides, you've only lived through two of Lumi's incarnations. You don't know her. Not really."

"Three incarnations, if you count the current one." Luci glanced at the portraits on the wall, pointing to the one on the top right. "In what century did she live?"

He tried not to react to Luci's tone. "Afia lived a thousand years ago. She was a slave, freshly in chains when I found her." He dropped his eyes to the portrait in his hands, trying to see the similarities. There weren't any beyond the eyes.

Afia had had thick, curly hair, and a toothy, too-big mouth. Beautiful in body, if not in looks.

She'd been born somewhere near the Mediterranean and wasn't ever going to win hearts, but she'd been compelling in a way he'd never encountered in any of Lumi's other incarnations.

"I was a trader at the time, visiting what's now the Middle East. Turkey, I think." He blinked, trying to remember, and failing. Had it been Persia, or the Ottoman Empire? Three thousand years were becoming a blur.

"Did she tear out your heart like all the rest?" Luci asked, her tone conveying her feelings on that topic.

He shook his head. "She stabbed me in the back. Literally." He'd bought her from her owner, intending to take her home and give her a life of luxury, but Afia had put a knife between his shoulder blades and stolen as much food as she could carry before running away. His rueful smile grew, and then faded. "I let her go," he said. "Not that it did her any good."

Luci was quiet for a long time. "Some people can't be fixed, Lawrence. You know this won't end well for her if you keep her around."

He stared at Afia's image. Lifetime after a lifetime, Lumi had returned to him. Was it a punishment, karma, or divine justice? She never remembered him, but he always recognised her.

"Lumi's the one who keeps appearing in my life," he corrected.

"Three thousand years should be enough to tell you something. Let her go," Luci said. "You have me."

"Yet we can never be together," he said softly. "We're different Creatures."

Luci stiffened slightly and took the portrait from his hands. He guessed she was considering smashing it. Instead, she crossed the room and hung it on the only available hook among the others, top and centre. Fifty portraits now, floor to ceiling, wall to wall.

"You need a bigger office."

He'd take it down once Luci left. "I need to know how to end this cycle." What did Lumi's soul want or need? Why did she keep returning to him?

His frown deepened as the question resonated through him. Maybe it wasn't him she kept returning to. Maybe...

Luci sat beside him again, the taint of her lifeforce like the faint reek of a rotting animal as her shoulder brushed his upper arm. Fortunately, he could only sense her lifeforce when they touched. Ignoring the feeling, he put his arm behind her shoulders and drew her close. "If only you'd had the good sense to have been turned into a succubus instead of a vampire."

Luci laughed, the sound bitter. "If only."

When she didn't say anything more, Shaw glanced down to see a sad smile flirting on Luci's lips, her eyes on the portraits.

The sad smile deepened, but she couldn't mask the pain in her eyes. "I'd give anything to be her, because then I could have you," she whispered.

Shaw pulled her closer. "No, you wouldn't. You'd hate to be her. Not knowing. Not remembering. She's been broken for thousands of years and nothing I do can fix her." Considering he was the one who'd broken her, karma was ensuring he suffered the consequences. Not just him though, he remembered, though he'd always shouldered the blame. She always returned to him, but not just him.

The screen on Shaw's phone lit up with a text message. "Allura's back," he said.

He stood, but Luci put a hand on his arm. "Let me go meet her," she said. "She's probably drunk by now. Maybe I can sober her up with a coffee or two before you arrive. I promise not to kill her before you get there." She shivered at her promise.

Shaw smirked. "A thousand dollars says she won't touch your coffee."

"A thousand dollars says she passes out drunk without touching tonight's dinner," she countered.

That seemed like a safe bet. "Deal."

5

Somewhat nervous to be having dinner with her boss, quite aside from Slade's demands to betray the man, Allura pressed her palms to the polished mahogany doors leading into the After Dark Ladies' Lounge, and pushed. They opened easily.

The churning feeling in her stomach intensified when she found the low lighting was set to sensual. A single candle burned on the only table in the room, the table draped in lace. The rest of the tables and chairs had been removed, leaving only the fixed booths around the walls.

This wasn't a meeting place. It was a seduction room. Shit. Shaw really wanted to annoy Quicksilver, probably expecting her to tell him all about it later.

Caught between Slade Mills, Lawrence Shaw, and a romantic dinner she didn't want, Allura wasn't sure how to deal with the situation. She felt used.

A dribble of wax ran down the candle's side, its pool of light reflecting from the polished cutlery. The emotions keeping Allura wound tight slowly softened. She hadn't been wined and dined in years. It felt nice, even flattering, and made her feel important. She hadn't felt important since she'd been a cop.

All this for her, though? It made her wonder if Shaw had a deeper agenda.

The After Dark Ladies' Lounge was big enough for about a hundred and fifty people, including the private booths around the walls. Now, it was empty except for one table and two chairs.

"Screw it," she muttered under her breath. This had to be an ambush disguised as flattery. Shaw wanted something from her, just as Slade did. Time to cut and run before Shaw arrived.

The staff door behind the bar opened and Allura's hopes for a quick escape suffered a catastrophic implosion.

Luci walked in, her gaze freezing Allura in place. Still in her tiger taming outfit from this morning, she smiled, but it wasn't a warm smile. It was more the kind of smile a woman reserved for a rival she wanted to murder.

Luci brushed her red-fringed dark hair aside. "You look stunning," she said, her expression like a cat who'd discovered a wounded bird. "I like what you've done with your hair."

Allura couldn't remember the last time she'd put more than a token effort into her appearance. She was still in her work uniform too, and probably smelled like spirits and stale beer from working behind the bar all day.

She faked confidence. "Was Shaw expecting to see me in a long black dress and my hair professionally done?"

Luci raised an eyebrow at the tone, her hair and makeup immaculate, cherry red lipstick the exact opposite of anything Allura would apply. "Couldn't have hurt."

Allura looked away briefly. "Touché," she muttered.

Luci pursed her red lips, a frown betraying

disappointment. That didn't make sense. Why disappointment?

"I could organise something now," Luci said, an oddly hopeful tone in her voice. "Shaw won't mind the delay."

Luci helping her? Seriously? "I'm good, thanks."

Luci cocked her head in curiosity, her top hat threatening to topple. "You're sober?" she asked. It sounded like a question. "You are sober, aren't you? You look sober." She sniffed, as if trying to smell alcohol from across the room.

Trying not to feel even more offended, Allura walked to the table and pulled the nearest chair out, allowing her to face the bar, and Luci. "Why are you here, Luci? I thought I was supposed to meet Mr. Shaw."

"Lawrence is finishing something up. Can I get you a coffee?"

Allura sat. There was a pitcher on the table. "I'm good." She poured herself a glass of water. The water tasted cool and fresh, filtered, with no hint of chlorine.

Luci stared at the water as if Allura were drinking acid.

"Seriously Luci. I do drink water sometimes."

Luci shook her surprise off and collected a bottle of red wine and two glasses before approaching the table.

"No wine for me, please," Allura said. It felt awkward to say that, but she really didn't feel like drinking. A drink would take the edge off her nerves, though.

Luci glanced at the doors as if expecting the real Allura to walk in at any moment. "You sure?"

Allura nodded. "How long will Mr. Shaw be?"

As if she'd summoned him, the staff door behind the bar opened again and this time Shaw entered. He approached Luci, putting a hand on her shoulder as he spoke softly. "Kyle and Zannah have arrived. You need to prepare."

Prepare? That might be something Slade would be interested in. If it was juicy enough, it might even get her out of his clutches. "Who are Kyle and Zannah?" Allura asked.

Shaw and Luci turned to her as if moving in unison. "Friends," Shaw said cryptically.

Luci glanced at Allura and muttered something under her breath. The news seemed to have annoyed her even more. "The meeting room? I'll go find them."

As Luci left, Shaw sat opposite Allura. He glanced at the single wine glass, and with a sigh he filled it before sliding it in front of Allura.

"No thanks," she said, passing it back.

"Huh?"

She didn't think she'd ever seen him surprised before. "My liver's having its yearly day off."

He looked from the glass to her and back again, as if trying to figure out a puzzle. Was she really that bad? Yeah, probably. She'd intended to come here drunk, after all.

A waiter entered, his back to them as he pulled a small cart through the service door. He was a tall young man with a mop of thick, mousy hair. On the cart were two covered plates. He stopped beside them and picked up both plates, only realising at the last moment who sat with Shaw.

"Allura?"

Great. Now everyone would be gossiping. "Yes Axel, it's me. I'm here to serve dinner for you and Mr Shaw. Please, sit." She stood and indicated her chair.

Axel glanced at the chair without moving, the colour draining from his face.

"She's kidding," Shaw said with an exaggerated sigh. "Continue, please."

That was probably the only bit of fun she'd have tonight. Allura sat back down.

Axel placed one plate before Allura and the other before Shaw, lifting the metal covers to reveal a dozen oysters each, the shells nestled on a bed of sea salt. Half were Kilpatrick-style, the rest mornay. Allura's stomach rumbled, reminding her she hadn't eaten all day.

"When would you like the mains, Mr Shaw? Twenty minutes?"

"That will be perfect, Axel. Thank you." Axel left with his cart.

Allura stared at the plate. "Who doesn't need a good aphrodisiac when dining with their staff, right?"

"You don't like oysters?" Shaw asked, his tone curt.

Allura picked up one of the Kilpatrick oysters, speared it with her little fork, and ate it like it was the last meal she'd ever get. She almost moaned. She hadn't eaten oysters in years. She ate two more before she realised Shaw was watching her.

She put her fork down. "Did I do something wrong?"

Shaw waved a hand, indicating she should continue. "It's nothing. Another time, another... friend who loved oysters. Forget it." He picked up his own fork.

She was certain he'd been about to say another woman, and that irritated her for some reason she couldn't quite define. She certainly didn't have any claim over Shaw or he over her, particularly as he seemed to share a bed with a new woman every night.

Allura quickly finished her oysters, finding they were more filling than she remembered. It was a good thing the mains weren't ready yet.

"Why are we doing this?" she asked after Shaw had finished eating. Time to stir the pot and get some insight into his intentions. "I mean, this is all nice and romantic, but it seems a bit harsh to use me to piss off Quicksilver, if that's your game."

Shaw coughed and had to use his napkin to cover his mouth. He cleared his throat as he put his two-pronged fork down. She couldn't read his face. Maybe amused. Maybe pissed-off.

"What do you want, Allura?"

Odd question. She shrugged. "My debt to you cleared, a million dollars in the bank, and a swanky apartment of my own high up in the Menagerie's tower, preferably with views across the lake." She hoped her sarcasm wouldn't get her into trouble. Nobody wanted trouble from a man like Shaw, but he'd asked.

"Anything else?" he asked, one eyebrow raised.

Allura had the impression she was in dangerous territory, but backing down now would be worse than meeting the challenge in his expression. "How about my murdered daughter brought back to life, alive and well?" Piper would be sixteen now. The burst of regret, grief, and loss overwhelmed her at the thought. She had to look away.

"No. I can't. I'm sorry."

She took a deep, calming breath. "No. I'm sorry," she said. "I didn't mean to say that."

"I've lost people too," he said, sounding sympathetic. "Let's start again, shall we? Same question. What do you want?"

She wanted to know if this dinner was merely a means of annoying Quicksilver, or if he had a genuine interest in her. The second option scared her the most.

Allura studied his expression and found genuine curiosity there. Okay, actual interest then. She decided to play it straight. "Considering this dinner came out of a murder investigation where you're the prime suspect, how about you put me at ease? What happened to Jingyi Lee? Do you know who killed her?"

His expression relaxed at that, to her relief. "Are you asking for yourself, or Quicksilver?"

Allura stiffened at the tone, as if the mention of Quicksilver was an afterthought. Did he know about Slade? His people must have seen them talking. "Me. Surely you have some idea."

He gave her an assessing stare, as if he didn't believe her. "I can only guess. Jingyi Lee came to me for help and I did what I could. She was a good woman. Dropping her body nearby was a message to me to mind my own business, I suspect."

She watched his face. If he was lying, he was bloody good at it. "Who wants you to mind your own business?"

He frowned, eyes narrowing as he stared back at her. "Very dangerous people. Why do I get the impression you're fishing for information?"

She looked away as a rush of fear spiked through her. "Quicksilver believes you're a crime lord, but he wouldn't use me like that."

"I'm aware of his perceptions."

Oh shit. He genuinely suspected someone else was involved then, only he didn't know who.

She pointed at the empty oyster shells, hoping to change the topic. "It would have been nice to have a choice about what I ate," Allura said, realising too late how ungrateful that sounded.

Shaw pushed his plate aside, his shoulders stiffening. "What would you like to eat, Allura? Pick anything and I'll have the chef send someone to buy the ingredients if they're not on hand."

A burger with a side of wedges would be an

improvement over her regular diet of two-minute noodles and vodka. She tried to look contrite. "I'm sorry. What's prepared?"

He gave her a look. "Lamb shanks in a red wine jus, garden vegetables, and freshly baked warm sourdough with garlic butter. Lamb shanks are an old favourite of mine."

He had a favourite? She tried for humour, though she couldn't remember having eaten anything that sounded so good in years. "Lamb shanks are hardly lobster, but I can live with it."

He pulled out his phone. "How would you like your lobster prepared?"

She didn't actually like lobster all that much, and he'd clearly missed the attempt at humour. "Forget the lobster. Please. I didn't mean to annoy you."

"Really?"

Had she? The question hit home in a way that hurt. How the hell did he know her better than she knew herself? "Yes. Please, forget the lobster. I was being ungrateful." In truth, he'd done more for her than anyone she'd ever known, except Quicksilver. "Thank you for such a nice meal."

He sighed and put his phone away.

"Can I ask you a personal question?" Allura asked, once again hoping to change the topic.

Wariness crept back into his posture, though he kept his expression neutral. "Okay."

"Why have you been so good to me since I came to you? You gave me a job and an open line of credit to search for Piper's killer. You wouldn't have done that for too many other people, I suspect."

Strangely, he looked like he'd been caught out doing something he shouldn't have.

Shaw was spared from explaining as the main doors to

the lounge opened behind Allura. She glanced over her shoulder as the hum of outside conversations and music spilled in.

A woman entered. Tall, young, and stunning, she could easily have been a model. She had exquisite Polynesian looks to go with her height. As young as she was, maybe twenty, she was also heavily pregnant.

Shaw frowned at the intrusion, but the woman continued into the room as if she hadn't noticed.

"There you are," she said with a bright smile for Allura.

Allura raised an eyebrow. "I think you're in the wrong room," she replied. She'd never seen the woman before.

A man followed the pregnant woman in. Short but broad, he had shaggy hair, a close-cropped beard, and a no-nonsense demeanour. He didn't look like he belonged with the young woman, more like he was her too-short bodyguard, but despite that, Allura got the impression they were a couple.

The doors closed, the sounds outside receding, and the two approached the table like they'd been invited.

Shaw scrunched up his napkin and dropped it on his plate. "You're supposed to be meeting Luci," he said, his tone annoyed.

Allura sat a little straighter as the tone of the room changed uncomfortably.

The woman hesitated for a heartbeat before forcing a smile. "We heard you had a hot date and wanted to put in a good word," she said with a wink at Allura.

Allura felt like she'd been put in a spotlight.

The young woman wasn't quite at the waddling stage of her pregnancy, but definitely prepping for a big lifestyle change. And soon.

The man with her was... well... plain. He had broad

shoulders, powerful arms, and seemed uncomfortable with his short-cropped beard by the way he scratched his jawline. He had an instantly forgettable face, too.

The man held out his hand to Allura. "I'm Kyle," he said in a surprisingly rich baritone. "My wife's Suzannah, but she goes by Zannah." He had an old-school American accent with a hint of English or Scottish buried deep. Allura couldn't quite place it.

Didn't Shaw mention Kyle and Zannah when talking to Luci? She guessed Kyle was in his early thirties, maybe ten years older than Zannah.

Kyle's grip was solid, his hand thick and meaty. Zannah shook Allura's hand next, her fingers long and slender. Allura winced at her grip.

Zannah's face immediately became apologetic. "Sorry, I'm still getting used to my new strength."

"Pregnancy ramping up the testosterone levels?" Allura asked, hoping her humour hit the mark this time.

Zannah laughed. "Nah, it's a werewolf thing. Happens at night."

"A werewolf thing...?" Allura echoed with a doubtful glance at Shaw, who looked like he was trying not to murder the couple. "I'm glad it's not a full moon then," Allura added. At least the woman had a sense of humour.

"We're trying to have a meal," Shaw said tersely, breaking the awkward silence. "And you're supposed to be meeting with Luci."

Zannah again gave him the kind of smile that would turn any man into putty. Any man but Shaw, it seemed. "A mutual friend suggested we introduce ourselves to Allura. I believe you know her. Kimbriel?"

Allura had never heard of the woman, but Shaw

suddenly seemed more alert. Anyone who could make Shaw take notice had to be important.

After a moment and a deep breath, Shaw responded. "In that case, perhaps you should make an appointment with Allura tomorrow?" he said.

"How far along are you?" Allura asked Zannah, hoping to head off a murder.

Zannah smiled brightly. "Got about two months to go, but they'll come early, I'm told. I think I've got a football team in here." She placed a hand on her stomach.

Kyle held up two fingers. Twins.

Allura smiled, the memories of her own pregnancies returning, tainted now with Piper's kidnapping and murder. "Congratulations."

Zannah gave Kyle a challenging look. "There's at least four," Zannah contradicted Kyle's unspoken tally. She smiled, a gentle, doting smile. "I can't wait to meet them."

Kyle looked pleased with himself, too. How the hell had these two hooked up? Was it a case of beauty and the billionaire?

"You've introduced yourselves," Shaw said, glancing pointedly at the doors. "Luci's waiting for you."

"Ready, love?" Kyle asked.

Zannah arched her back, a hand on her stomach as if she could support the weight there. She leaned in close and gave Allura a hug like they were best friends. "If you ever need us, just call. Okay? I mean it. And don't mind Captain Grouchy Pants there. Believe it or not, he means well." She glanced backward at Shaw and gave him a winning smile. "She's a keeper," she whispered theatrically, giving him a wink.

Shaw's expression darkened.

Just then Luci burst in from the main doors like a murderous Valkyrie, glaring at Kyle and Zannah as if she'd been stalking them for hours.

6

Dinner wasn't a total loss, at least not for Allura. She couldn't remember the last time she'd eaten so well.

Afterward she sat back, far too full, staring forlornly at the remaining half of her butter-soaked sourdough. There was just enough gravy left to tempt her into using the bread to mop it up, but she'd probably be sick if she tried.

"I think this is the first meal we've had where we haven't hated each other by the end," Shaw said.

Allura raised an eyebrow. "We've never eaten together."

He gave the barest hint of a frown. "I was thinking of... Someone else. Sorry."

Allura tried not to rise to the unexpected jealousy she felt. Instead, she pushed her plate back and dropped her linen napkin over it to remove the temptation. She wasn't sure if this was the right time, but when was? "I have a favour to ask," she said as her mind went back to their conversation before they'd been interrupted.

Shaw met her eyes, and she couldn't blame him for the wariness in his expression.

53

"Which is?"

"Can I work somewhere else in the casino? I don't want to manage the Atrium Bar anymore."

He blinked as if she'd just clapped her hands in front of his face. "What exactly are you asking for? A job in security? Are you looking to use your skills as a former police officer?"

A chill ran through her. Did he have some insight into what Slade Mills had said? Best to avoid security. "No. I deal with enough drongos at the bar. Could I maybe train as a croupier? Or work in one of your shops? Even an admin job would be fine. Just not the bar."

He held his breath for a long time, an assessing look in his eyes. "Are you looking to earn more money to pay off your debt sooner?"

She'd only been working directly for him for the last half year, but she'd been borrowing money off him for much longer. Her debt was substantial to the point she doubted she'd ever be able to pay it off, even with a significant pay rise. "Anywhere. I just don't want to be around alcohol anymore."

He seemed relieved, if anything. "I'll organise something tomorrow."

"Thank you," she said, meaning it.

He stood. "Unfortunately, I have more work to do tonight. If you'd excuse me?"

"You're leaving already?"

"You're asking for favours. It seems like an appropriate time."

"But..." She indicated the room with her hands. "You invited me to a candlelit dinner. I was expecting..." She wasn't sure what, but more than just a meal and an implied interrogation.

"Dancing? Romance? Seduction?"

"Coffee?"

He walked around the table, lifted her hand and kissed the back like a lord farewelling a lady. That did all kinds of unexpected things to her insides.

"I would like nothing more than to spend the entire evening with you Allura, and as many more evenings as you're willing to give me." He straightened, still holding her hand. "Perhaps we could have dinner next week?"

"Okay?" she said before her brain could run through the implications.

He smiled, perhaps regretting the uncertainty in her tone. "I'll ask Sunshine to organise a time. Perhaps she could even provide something for you to wear in place of your staff uniform."

She looked down, flushing. "Sober's a good start though, right?" she asked, both nervous and liking where this was going.

He hesitated, but inclined his head. "Very welcome." He released her hand and left the room via the staff door behind the bar.

Allura stared after him. He'd shown absolutely no interest since she'd first come to him begging for money, not to mention the last six months of working directly for him, and now this? What the hell had changed?

Slade, that's what. Was Shaw playing a subtle, long game with her, or was he genuinely interested in something more than a working relationship?

The double doors behind her opened and Allura glanced over her shoulder. Luci and Kyle entered, followed by Zannah and Mia, the two women appearing to be trying to outdo each other in the pregnancy department.

Allura raised an eyebrow when Charlotte and Mary walked in behind them. Both worked with Mia in the CanCan Coffee Bar, and being of the same height and ethnicity looked so much alike that Allura had confused them for the first few weeks she'd worked at the Menagerie.

Luci had changed into something appropriate for a ninja. All black, minus the face coverings and sword. Kyle was similarly dressed.

"I didn't think he'd ever leave," Zannah said as she took Shaw's seat. She picked up Shaw's untouched glass of red wine, put it to her nose, and inhaled. "How could anything that smells this divine be bad for babies?" she asked.

"I'm not pregnant," Charlotte said hopefully. Zannah regretfully handed it to her. Charlotte sipped, and then moaned in delight. Allura felt jealousy rise up. Now was a fine time to give up drinking.

Zannah held her hand out to Luci. "Pay up."

Kyle laughed, as did Mia and Charlotte. Luci glowered. "Do you think I've got five grand stuffed in my bra?"

"What did you bet on?" Mia asked as Mary came over with a chair for her. "Thanks hon," she said, sitting next to Zannah.

"That Allura would be sober."

"What?" Allura asked. "You don't even know me!"

"I got it right, though, didn't I?" Zannah asked, unperturbed.

Mia cleared her throat, drawing everyone's attention. "Would you like to help some people tonight?" she asked Allura.

Wariness seeped into her. "Help?" Allura asked cautiously.

"There's an establishment in Fyshwick, a massage parlour, officially. It's a trap for overseas girls and street kids, many of which eventually end up being forced into sex work and porn films, or worse." She leaned forward. "Would you like to help us free them tonight?"

A thrill of fear and excitement rushed through her. The fact that they'd clearly waited for Shaw to leave said this wasn't something he'd sanctioned. "Why are you doing this behind Shaw's back?"

A ripple of discomfort went through the group.

Luci looked particularly uncomfortable considering she wouldn't meet Allura's eyes when she spoke. "Shaw planned the whole thing. Just not your presence. He wouldn't allow you to help if he knew."

Mia leaned forward. "You used to be a cop, Allura. You know how to deal with traumatised people. Your presence would be helpful when Luci starts bringing the girls out. Possibly a few young men, too."

They were all staring at her as if expecting agreement right then. "If you have any evidence of abuse or modern slavery, you should hand it over to the police," Allura said, determined not to get on Shaw's wrong side without need.

Kyle cleared his throat and put a hand on Zannah's shoulder, but he addressed Allura. "I need someone to watch my back. I don't want Zannah there for obvious reasons, and a friend recommended you."

A friend? Who the hell did they know in common? Did he mean that Kimbriel person he'd mentioned before? Allura focused on the heavily pregnant Zannah. "You want me to watch your husband's back?"

"*We* need you," Charlotte countered before Zannah could reply. "Mary and I are useless at night and don't have your experience or training. Mia too, even if she weren't pregnant. If you want to help these girls, please say yes."

"I'm sorry. It's illegal," Allura said.

"Of course it is," Zannah said. "That's why we need you."

What the heck was this woman on? "No."

"Ten grand," Zannah said. "Yours if you say yes right now. You can keep my ill-gotten gains from my bet with Luci too. That makes it fifteen."

Luci narrowed her eyes.

That got Allura's attention. Fifteen grand? "And I'm supposed to do what, exactly?" She glanced at Kyle. "Comfort traumatised girls while making sure you don't get stabbed in the back?"

Kyle nodded. "Pretty much. Mostly be helpful as Luci and our wolves bring them out. You're only there as backup."

"Wolves? Is that your nickname or something?" Allura asked. Zannah had alluded to werewolves in their previous conversation, and it sounded even more ridiculous now.

Zannah snorted and smirked, sharing a knowing glance with Kyle. "Yeah, it's our nickname."

Allura wasn't sure why that came across as patronising. "And you're keeping my potential involvement from Shaw because?"

Nobody met her eyes. "You in or out?" Mia finally asked. "If you're in, I'll add five grand myself. Twenty grand total. All cash."

Holy crud. "Twenty grand?"

"For one night's work," Luci added. "A couple of hours really, and Shaw never needs to hear you were there. Not now. Not ever."

Allura hardened her expression. "Surely you'd prefer a big burly guy capable of dealing with trouble?" she asked. She looked from face to face, finally returning to Mia. Something was up and they weren't willing to explain it to her. "Well?"

"Please don't look at me in that tone of voice," Mia said.

Allura raised an eyebrow, her expression not changing.

Mia gave her a long-suffering sigh. "Fine. Our friend who said we need you with us tonight. She's a psychic."

"Right..." Allura said with all the sarcasm she could manage. "Does she live around the corner from the local prophet?"

"No," Luci said with annoyance. "She said we'll fail if you say no," she added. "Please?"

Please? From Luci? She actually believed this nonsense?

"Twenty grand, Allura. Going once, going twice..." Zannah added.

If she could see Sparrow right now, she was certain he'd tell her to run. Although her stomach was doing nervous flips, twenty grand was a lot of money. "Fine. I'm not buying into your psychic crap, but for twenty grand I'm in. If Shaw gets wind of it though, I'm stepping aside and letting the bus flatten you all. Fair?"

"Fair," Charlotte said.

What the hell was she going to tell Slade Mills about all this? Hopefully, he'd never find out.

A NOISE WOKE ALLURA. She jumped and her heart raced when she realised someone was looming over her in an unfamiliar bedroom.

"It's just me."

"Mia?" Allura blinked in the gloom, her heart still thumping and her head foggy from a lack of sleep, though the fog was rapidly vacating. It had taken an hour or more to get to sleep, but once she had, she'd slept more heavily than she had in years, and felt groggy now.

"It's Mary, not Mia. Time to go."

Allura scowled, but the look was lost as Mary left the room, giving Allura privacy to dress in the dark clothes left for her. She glanced at her phone. It wasn't quite three in the morning and her eyes felt gritty. God, she needed a shot of something to wake up. Vodka, preferably. Allura quickly tied her hair back and left the hotel room, following Mary to another room on the same floor.

Kyle, Luci, Teddy Bear and Mia waited for her, the four of them seated on the bed or in chairs, talking softly. Teddy Bear frowned, the big man clearly not happy to see her. For the twenty grand they were paying her, he could suck it up. She wasn't turning down money like that.

She hesitated when she saw a handgun and two clips on the desk against the wall, as well as a large, sheathed knife and belt. "What's that for?" she asked a little nervously. One of the clips was adorned with silver squiggles.

Kyle handed her a hefty vest. "Body armour. Just in case."

The bad feeling she'd started out with got worse. "Nobody said anything about guns or body armour." She pointed to the weapon. "And that's illegal."

"You want to back out?" Teddy Bear asked hopefully.

If he didn't want her there, it probably meant he cared about what happened to her, or at least the consequences if things went wrong, which in turn implied she wasn't being set up for a fall. That was good.

"No," Allura said. She put the vest on, surprised at how well it fit. She'd forgotten how heavy they were though, which brought back memories of her early years as a cop.

"The gun's for you. Use it only as a last resort," Kyle said in his old-school accent. "If regular bullets don't work, use the silver clip, but not otherwise. Understand?"

Don't work? "Armour piercing?"

The group shared odd glances with each other. "Something like that."

She looked about, more than curious now. "Why am I the only person with a gun?"

"Because you're the most vulnerable," Mary said. "And I insisted."

Mary had insisted? Between Mary, Charlotte and Mia, or Huey, Duey and Louie as Allura sometimes thought of them thanks to the similarity in their looks and heritage, Mary was always the one who'd looked after her when she'd been at her worst. "I don't get it."

Luci pointed to the group in general, her finger finishing on Mia. "Shaw will skin everyone alive if we let you get hurt. So, you get a gun, and we expect you to use it if necessary. Got it?"

The bad feeling got worse. "This is more than just a raid, isn't it?" Allura asked. "If you lot don't spill the details, I'm walking. Why is this so important and why aren't you telling Shaw about me?"

Luci gave her a flat stare as Mia spoke. "We're after a specific girl. She's like me."

"Chinese?" Allura asked. "Or short?"

Luci smirked, though she wasn't much taller than Mia. Allura could see over Mia's head. Luci's too. Just. Teddy Bear scowled.

"She's a relative of mine," Mia said.

She hadn't known Mia had any relatives, excluding her own children. "So, this is personal?" Allura glanced around the room, seeking confirmation.

"Yeah," Teddy Bear said. "Kinda."

Clearly, they weren't going to tell her anything more than what she needed to know. He stood, picking up the belt with the knife already attached, and tossed it to Allura.

"Time to go. Try not to shoot me. You can shoot Luci, though."

"Screw you," Luci said, her words emphasised with her middle finger, though she had a slight smirk, as if they often played this game.

Allura put the belt on and holstered the gun. The knife's sheath, she realised, was designed to rest horizontally across the belt at the small of her back, easily hidden. The spare clip marked with silver went into one of the vest's pockets.

"This is getting weirder and weirder," she muttered. She raised her chin. "Why me? Really? Surely there are better people for this?"

"I told you she'd be trouble," Teddy Bear said.

"Kimbriel said we'd fail without her," Kyle muttered as if trying not to let Allura hear. "We can't leave her behind."

"Kimbriel?" Allura asked. "The prophet?"

"Psychic," Mia said.

The entire group gave each other strange looks. Mary put a hand on Allura's arm. "Kimbriel said you needed to be there."

Allura raised an eyebrow. "A psychic said you'd fail if you didn't drag me along, and you trust her so much you're willing to pay me twenty grand and give me a gun? Why didn't you just say so?" Her sarcasm may have been lost on them, judging by the fact Teddy Bear and Luci left the room.

The rest filed out after them, except Mary.

"I wasn't finished," Allura said lamely as the room emptied. "Seriously?"

What the hell was she getting involved in?

Mary caught her arm again, her touch gentle and caring. "Watch yourself, Allura. Kimbriel, the uh, psychic, is never wrong, but she rarely tells anyone everything either. She often has her own agenda. If she says you need to be there, then I trust it's true, but it doesn't mean everything will go smoothly or that she has any interest in your wellbeing." She glanced at the door with a frown. "Or anyone else's."

This was wrong on so many levels. "I'll watch my back," Allura agreed, and meant it, trying to ignore the bad feeling in her guts.

ALLURA and the raiders of the evil massage parlour took the elevator to the Menagerie's private basement carpark, stopping near three black vans.

Excluding Teddy Bear and John, a man almost as tall and solid as Teddy Bear, and Austyn, a skinny tech specialist only a little taller than Allura herself, Allura didn't know any of the other dozen people gathered and waiting.

All in their mid-twenties, the six men and six women could easily blend in on an average city street. Three of the men were of mixed heritage, part Asian, part Caucasian, she guessed, and two more might have been Maori. The last man reminded her a little of Kyle, though he was about a foot taller.

Two of the women, possibly sisters, had long red hair, while the other four didn't stand out in any way except for being taller than Allura. You could pass any of them and never take a second glance.

Maybe that was the intention.

Still, there was a similarity about them, possibly more attitude than appearance, like they belonged to a religion Allura hadn't been indoctrinated into.

She glanced at Teddy Bear, John and Austyn, and realised they gave off the same vibe.

The unfamiliar group stared back at Allura with equal

measures of distrust and what she could only ascribe to disdain, like Allura wasn't good enough to be a part of their clique.

"I thought..." she began, feeling uncomfortable. "Who are they?" Allura asked Luci.

"You can trust them," Luci said. She didn't sound convinced herself.

"Not an answer," Allura replied.

"They're my people," Kyle said. "You can trust them."

"Your people? I only just met you. Trust is a little way off yet. Who are they?"

"Later," Kyle said with a frown and a 'leave it alone' stare.

Allura gave him a look, but it slid off him like water on oil.

She checked the black vans. The number plates were from different states, none local. Stolen? It added another level of illegality that made her even more uncomfortable than she already was, but she'd agreed to go and they'd already paid her.

As the only person with a gun, Allura really hoped she wasn't being set up, the gun possibly used in a crime and potentially traceable to her. Maybe she could accidentally drop it in a drain?

"Phone," Mia said, a hand out to Allura. "If anyone asks, you were here all night. I'm your alibi, along with Charlotte and Mary. Your phone can be tracked here, and the hotel room booking's in your name."

Allura hesitated. She might need her phone.

Mia pursed her lips. "We've got your back, Allura. I promise." Mia shivered as if someone had walked over her grave.

Teddy Bear put a big meaty hand on Allura's shoulder.

"Mia wouldn't make a promise like that if she didn't mean it."

"Even so, it seems like I'm doing all the trusting at the moment," Allura said.

Several of the women snorted. "You've got that wrong," said a woman with a solid build and short cropped dark hair. "We don't know you. Teddy Bear and Kyle vouched for you."

Teddy Bear had vouched for her? She glanced at the big guy, who nodded gravely. That made no sense at all.

"Humans," another said disdainfully, her red hair pulled back tightly, giving her a severe look.

Allura raised her eyebrows. "Humans?" she asked. "And you're what, werewolves?" She was seriously getting over this crap.

The woman who'd spoken glanced at Teddy Bear with a look of surprise. "She's been told?" she asked, her hands on her hips as if preparing to take on Teddy Bear by herself.

"Told?" Allura asked. Was their nickname supposed to be a secret?

"Later," Kyle repeated. "Give Mia your phone. We're in the far van. I'll explain the plan on the way."

"You bloody-well better," Allura muttered, slapping her phone into Mia's palm with more force than necessary. Gently nudging Mia aside, Mary gave Allura a hug. "Kyle's a good man. He'll watch your back."

"I hope so," Allura replied softly before following Kyle to their van. He took the driver's seat, leaving her to ride shotgun.

The others divided up into the remaining two vans, Kyle following them out of the basement.

"Okay, spill," Allura said once the Menagerie was in the rearview mirror, tension mounting and the lack of answers only contributing to it. "There's too much weirdness to all this. What gives?"

Kyle sighed. "They're all friends of mine. You can trust them."

Allura gave him a flat glare.

He returned her look with a frown. "Just use the weapons if you need them. Fair?"

"You promised answers," Allura said with all the annoyance she could dredge up. "If you want me to help—"

"We do," Kyle said, cutting her off. "Tonight, we're specifically after a girl being held against her will. She's related to Mary."

"Which I've already been told. Is this about Jingyi Lee's murder? She was Chinese, and so are Mia, Charlotte, and Mary."

"Yeah, something like that."

That was a long way from convincing. "So, we're looking for a Chinese girl. What else?" Allura pressed.

"Actually, we think she's Caucasian," Kyle said.

Think? Allura gave him a look that conveying everything she was thinking. "This girl's related to Mia, but Caucasian? Care to explain?"

"It's complicated," Kyle said. "Cousins."

"Complicated? So's this conversation," Allura muttered in exasperation, giving up.

They were only a few blocks away when Kyle spoke again. "You and I will head into the rear car park. The others will park up the street, enter the premises from the front and send the people we're rescuing out the back. It's our job to collect them and get them safely in the van. If we don't have enough room, we'll put them in another van. You okay with that?"

"Yeah," Allura said curtly. "As long as I don't accidentally shoot you from irritation, I'll cope. Actually, I'll probably cope better if I do shoot you."

He seemed amused at her tone. "This is a rescue operation, okay? We're the good guys, and you and I aren't getting into the fight. Just don't get the clips mixed up if it doesn't play out the way I hope it does."

Jenna stumbled headlong into Cheri's office and fell, hitting the raw floorboards and skinning her elbows. She giggled.

Penelope hauled her upright, keeping Jenna steady until she could stand again. Jenna's stilettos kept her off balance for a moment, but she smiled over her shoulder at the tall werewolf. "You've got pretty eyes."

Penelope gave Jenna an exasperated sigh and pushed her a little further into the room.

Jenna looked around. "Cheri!" she said enthusiastically.

Cheri glanced at Penelope. "How much did you give her? She's off her nut."

Penelope shrugged. "It's nearly dawn, and she's not restrained. Better to be safe. She'll burn through the high in an hour, anyway."

It took Jenna a long moment to realise she was standing beside the new girl from the Philippines. Ali? Alsi? Alma. That was it. Such a nice name.

She could see over Alma's head even without the heels,

just as Penelope could see over Jenna's. Penelope didn't have heels, though. She had boots an army officer would be proud of, white fishnet stockings, and a short black skirt. She looked beautiful.

Cheri stood, her thin strawberry-blonde hair falling across her freckled shoulders. Her lips pursed like she'd been sucking sour worms as she looked over at Jenna.

Jenna smiled as Cheri walked around her desk. "I like your hair," Jenna said.

"Shut up, Jenna. Speak again and I'll cut your tongue out, got it?"

Jenna nodded. She wanted to sit down. It had been a long night on the film set and tomorrow night they'd shoot her death scene. That'd be a short night at least, and she'd get a few days off until she revived and recovered.

She felt tension growing inside her as she thought about it. She didn't want to be killed again, and this one was going to be brutal. She'd be getting stabbed to death with a screwdriver. It would take hours for her to properly die, according to the script, and they planned to film it all.

She grimaced and tugged at her silver collar, her fingertips stinging at the contact. They'd filled the lock with solder so it couldn't be removed, but at least it had a thin silicon lining to prevent direct contact with her skin. Touching the outside still hurt though, while some of the silicon had come away and her neck underneath was scarred from it. At least the scarring meant it didn't hurt much anymore.

"Alma," Cheri began. "You tried to run away again."

Cheri was even shorter than Alma, not that size made much difference considering Cheri was a vampire.

Alma glared back, defiant.

Maybe Alma didn't know Cheri was a vampire? Oh. That would be bad. "Alma—" Jenna began, but Cheri silenced her with a glare.

A fresh bruise was swelling across Alma's left cheek, the shine catching the light.

"I come Australia to work. You keep me prisoner and..."

Cheri backhanded Alma's other cheek so hard the little woman staggered into Penelope. The werewolf's near-black skin contrasted sharply with Alma's, which was only a couple of shades more tan than Jenna's. Penelope righted Alma and pushed her forward again. The tall woman kept her expression neutral, though Jenna could tell Penelope didn't like seeing the abuse.

Alma touched a hand to her cheek, eyes tearing up, but her glare could have stripped paint from a moving car at a hundred paces.

Jenna tried to go to her, but Penelope put a hand on her shoulder. "Sit this one out, kitten."

"Kitten," Jenna repeated. Nobody had called her kitten before. She liked it.

Cheri gripped Alma's jaw, forcing the little woman to her tip-toes with a surprised squeak. "You're whatever I say you are, understand? Until you pay back your debt, you're staying here. Say it."

Alma gripped Cheri's wrist, trying to break her hold. Her eyes widened when she couldn't. "I no slave," she said through gritted teeth.

Cheri's eyes narrowed. "Would you like me to send a note to your family in the Philippines telling them you've lost your job and won't be sending them any more money?"

Alma gave the slightest shake of her head, fear in her expression. "I, no—"

Cheri hauled Alma to her desk, pressed the woman's

right palm flat to the timber, and drove a knife through the back, pinning her to the desk.

Alma screamed and might have collapsed if Penelope hadn't caught her.

"That's not very nice," Jenna said as blood began seeping from Alma's wound. "She's human. Humans don't heal well."

Cheri pointed a warning finger at Jenna while Penelope leaned forward, her face beside Alma's. "I suggest you be quiet, Alma. Very quiet." She released Alma's shoulders, leaving the woman to stand on her own.

Alma was already several shades paler. Trembling, she grasped the hilt and tried to pull the knife out. All she managed was a gasp.

Cheri moved closer to Jenna. "And you, you little bitch, cost us a lot of money tonight."

"Huh?" Jenna asked in surprise.

"You almost clawed out the client's right eye!"

Jenna looked down at her red-painted fingernails, trying to think back through the fog of heroin. It didn't affect her as much as a human, but it still made it hard to think. "The director told me to fight back."

"He said struggle! Push the client off or slap him. Not scratch his fucking eye out!"

"She is a tiger," Penelope pointed out. "What'd you expect?"

"You want your jaw broken?" Cheri asked Penelope.

Penelope looked down, shaking her head slightly.

Jenna realised there was blood on her fingernails and more on her palm when she turned it over. "I didn't mean to hurt him," she said. "I just wanted to make it look real. Be a good girl."

"Put your tongue on the desk," Cheri said, already

holding another knife. This one was silver, the caustic tang of it filling the room now it had been unsheathed.

Jenna swallowed, her high from the heroin burning off on a rush of adrenalin. She backed a step. "It was an accident." Her voice made her sound small and weak, like she was begging. She was.

"Kneel and put your bloody tongue on the desk or I'll cut out your eyes with this blade, and then your tongue and all your fingers."

"What's that noise?" Penelope asked, turning to the closed door. She cocked her head, listening. "There's a fight out there." She inhaled through her nose. "I can smell smoke."

Penelope opened the door. Distantly, someone cried out in agony, maybe on the floor below. It was a man's voice. Penelope drew a silver blade from the small of her back and rushed out.

Cheri swore under her breath, ripped the blade free from Alma's hand, and pointed the blood-streaked weapon at Jenna. "Take Alma back to your room, lock her and yourself in your cage, and stay there. Understand?"

Jenna nodded, too afraid to speak. Alma was almost too weak to stand on her own, so Jenna wrapped her arms around the older woman's shoulders and guided her toward the door. She froze. An Asian woman Jenna had never seen before stood there, a longsword in her hand, the blade slender and double edged. She had long, dark hair fringed with red tips, and she was glaring at Cheri.

"Get out," the new woman said to Jenna without even looking at her.

Cheri held up both knives, the one in her left hand turned backwards as if to use as a shield against her forearm, the other pointed at the new woman. "Go to your cage like I told you, Jenna. This is between me and Luci, and it's been far too long in coming."

"Agreed," said Luci. She moved into the room and made way for Jenna.

With permission from all sides, Jenna guided Alma out, but the way ahead was blocked by a man and two women fighting in the corridor. She didn't know the women.

Despite fearing she'd get in trouble for not going to her cage, Jenna took the only option available to her and steered Alma into the stairwell.

As Jenna hauled open the door to the fire stairs, two werewolves, both in wolf form, tumbled over each other from another room and into the corridor.

Jenna pulled Alma to her chest and hugged her close as the werewolves crashed through the opposite wall. She pulled open the fire door and ushered Alma in.

Jenna and Alma were barely down to the first landing as the werewolves crashed into the door above them, the hinges tearing away and the frame splintering inward.

"Hurry," Jenna said with a rush of fear as the door gave way and the two werewolves tumbled through, ripping into each other with vicious snarls. Blood sprayed and Alma cried out, trying to cringe into the corner, but Jenna forced her down the stairs.

"Don't look," Jenna said, her own heart thundering as Alma tried to turn around. They'd barely made it to the next fire door before the werewolves tumbled down the stairs. Glass shattered beyond the door where Jenna stood, suggesting more werewolves were fighting on this level too.

As Alma began to pray, Jenna steered the terrified

woman further down the stairwell to the bottom landing. Jenna had been killed dozens of times, but she recovered when she died. Alma wouldn't.

Jenna slammed her shoulder into the fire door leading to the shopfront, but bounced off. There was one more door down the last half flight, so she guided Alma down to ground level, the pair taking the stairs so fast Jenna almost missed her footing.

Hearing the snarling werewolves tumbling further down the stairs with savage snarls, Jenna dragged Alma to the fire doors and shoved her hip against the bar. The doors opened to fresh pre-dawn air, the pair of them stumbling out and down the three outside steps to the rear carpark.

"Are you okay?" Jenna asked. Alma was trembling, tears streaking her mascara down her cheeks.

Alma gripped Jenna's hand. "We run, yes?" It wasn't really a question.

A window shattered at the far end of the building on the middle level, grey smoke billowing out. The smoke was backlit by the building's internal lights and illuminated from the three external floodlights, showing a single dark van near the rear entry.

At Alma's insistent pull, they stumbled into the mostly empty car park.

Alma was paler than fresh linen, holding her bleeding hand close to her stomach, her good hand squeezing Jenna's in a death grip. Her determined expression told Jenna the woman had no intention of returning to the building, no matter who won the fight.

"Hey!" It was a man's voice, calling from the far end of the building as he ushered two women toward a van. Jenna squinted. Sophie and Emma, both former street kids like

Jenna, looked scared as the man guided them from the building. A woman, easily twice Jenna's age, was holding the van's rear doors open.

"I'll get them," the woman called to the man, and began jogging toward Jenna.

For a moment Jenna felt hope, but then she saw the woman carried a gun and a knife, and there was every chance she was armed with silver.

"Run," Alma cried and dragged Jenna into motion, pulling so hard Jenna stumbled, her stilettos tripping her up. She would have fallen if Alma hadn't supported her. Two more steps and Alma fell, her hand slipping from Jenna's grip.

"Run!" Alma yelled. "I catch up."

Ingrained obedience sent Jenna stumbling into a run, but her heels made it hard. She kicked them free and broke into a sprint, ignoring the armed woman's yells to stop as Jenna reached the car park's fence and turned down the driveway to the street.

"Stop! We're friends!" The woman's voice followed Jenna.

Jenna didn't have any friends, and if Alma feared these people, then so did Jenna.

Jenna turned left at the street and ran from the chaos like a scared kitten. Two buildings down the road, she looked back over her shoulder. The woman was following, though she didn't look fit by the way she scrunched her face up as if already winded. She was fast, though, but all Jenna had to do was keep ahead and she'd be okay. Hopefully. As long as the woman didn't shoot her.

Hoping Alma would be okay, Jenna took a risk and ducked between two buildings, the alley emptying out into a small delivery yard. Cornered, Jenna clambered up a stack of old pallets against a brick wall about three metres high, got to the top, and jumped over just as the woman rounded the corner. "Stop!"

Dropping heavily, Jenna ran down the driveway, almost stumbling into the chain wire fence separating the buildings and a second driveway. As soon as she made the street, Jenna turned right, running further from the fight.

She took several more turns to try to confuse whoever was chasing her before crossing a main road and skirting the traffic lights at a four-way intersection.

Ahead, a huge concrete bridge crossed the road she was on, the bridge lit with overhead lights. Breathing heavily now, Jenna stumbled to a stop, holding her stomach against the cramp trying to force her to double over. At least she couldn't see or hear anyone chasing her anymore.

After taking half a dozen deep breaths, she forced herself into a stumbling run until she made it to the far side of the bridge. She stopped again and looked back. If anybody was following, she couldn't see or hear them. Sucking in deep breaths as her panic slowly subsided, she started at a fast walk, the approaching dawn a sliver of orange on the horizon.

Jenna saw a street sign in the gloom, Dairy Road. It didn't mean anything to her, though she knew the names of some of the major streets in the area. Scattered streetlights made pools of ghostly illumination through a hint of fog across the road, the lights revealing more commercial buildings to her left and unused land to right.

She might find shelter amongst the buildings, but she wasn't far away enough yet, and so she kept walking. Dairy Road curved around to her right to run parallel with the overhead road she'd just passed under. The area ahead was dark, and the road had an abandoned feeling. She continued walking until she reached a gate barring the road ahead.

"Hey! Wait!" It was the woman who'd chased her out of the car park.

Jenna spun as her heart raced with newfound fear.

8

After seeing the girl climb the stack of pallets and scramble over the wall like a mountain goat, Allura hoped she hadn't broken an ankle when she landed on the other side.

Determined to check, Allura clambered up the pallets herself, but when she got to the top of the wall, the other side was empty. Swearing at her own stupidity in persisting, Allura lowered herself over until she was gripping the top with her fingertips and let go.

A moment of vertigo preceded a jarring thud. She rolled backwards with a wince, but at least she hadn't broken anything. With gravel sticking to her palms after pushing herself to her feet, Allura dusted her hands on her pants and ran down a driveway to the road. Taking a guess, she went right, away from the massage parlour.

By the time she got to the end of that road, she was huffing like an old steam train. She put her hands on her knees, doubled over, and sucked in deep breaths. Twenty years earlier, she'd regularly jogged ten kilometres a day.

She doubted she'd run more than ten metres at a stretch since then.

Squinting into the predawn gloom, Allura couldn't see the girl. Wisdom dictated she return to Kyle since she was supposed to be watching his back. She could almost hear Sparrow laughing at her stupidity when she decided finding the girl was more important.

Going right would circle back into the industrial area. Left would take her toward the main road through Fyshwick, and further from Kyle and the others. Allura banked on the girl wanting to get as far away as possible and forced herself to jog towards the lights at the next intersection.

The horizon was brighter, at least. If it had been a shade darker, she might have missed the hint of movement under the Monaro Highway bridge. Someone was on foot, heading toward the wetlands and the lake beyond.

Wishing a taxi would swing by, Allura began jogging again, staggering really, though it felt like an epic attempt at a dead sprint.

And that's when the universe finally smiled on her.

Just off the road and half hidden by a tree lay an abandoned BMX bike, sized for an early teenager. She stood it up, finding it in working condition, if a little rusty and small. It had air in the tires, at least. She hopped on and began pedalling, struggling to keep her balance, having not ridden a bike since she'd been a teenager. She crossed the road at the lights and silently coasted downhill toward the bridge.

The road flattened out at the bridge and she had to pedal again. As she rounded the corner she could just see the girl in the darkness, almost at the vehicle gate which barred the way to anyone but people walking or riding through the gap to the left.

"Hey!" Allura cried out as she got closer.

The girl spun, looking over her shoulder, long dark hair cascading down her back. She froze, and even in the gloom, Allura could see her dread.

"It's okay," Allura called as she got closer, puffing from the exertion of pedalling.

"I'm not going back!" the girl said, crossing her arms and backing up until she hit the gate. "I won't." She sounded like she was about to cry.

Allura dismounted a few metres away.

"That's good," Allura said. "I don't want you to go back. I'm with the people who came to rescue you and the others."

The girl stiffened at the word rescue, clearly not believing Allura. She moved sideways as if to make her way around the gate.

"You were with the werewolves." It was a flat statement, and full of distrust.

Werewolves again? No doubt a metaphor for all the bad people in the world. The girl probably thought being rescued could only dump her into a worse situation than she'd been in. Better the devil you know. "I'm just a girl like you," Allura said. "A woman."

The girl's stare suggested Allura was an idiot, but then she frowned. "You're human? You smell human. I'm not human, not anymore," the girl said, and clearly regretted it. She looked like she was about to break into tears. "It wasn't my fault!" she crossed her arms under her breasts as if to hug herself for comfort.

Allura put her hands up, palms out. "I know it wasn't," Allura said, whatever that meant. "I'm here to help you and the other girls."

The girl took another step toward the bike path. "Leave me alone."

Allura stepped in time with the girl, moving left toward the dirt car park. "It wasn't your fault," Allura tried again. "What's your name?"

The girl glanced at the brightening horizon over the Monaro Highway. "Stay away from me. It's nearly dawn. You'll regret it if you try to take me back."

"Jenna!"

Allura spun to see a woman jogging toward them, her midnight skin almost hiding her in the gloom. She was only visible thanks to her white singlet top and matching fishnet stockings.

Allura, not prepared to take any risks with the kind of people who'd abuse children and vulnerable immigrants, drew her gun. "This is a police matter. Turn around and leave." A decade earlier, it *would* have been a police matter. Now it was just Allura with an illegal gun on an illegal raid. In for a penny...

The woman stopped, hands up. She was tall enough to see over Allura's head and looked like she could arm wrestle most men and win. If she didn't work out seven days a week, Allura would buy drinks for the entire bar the next time she stood in the Menagerie.

The woman sniffed the air, frowning. "You're human," she said in surprise.

Again? "And you're a unicorn?" Allura asked.

The woman narrowed her eyes as if trying to figure something out. "You got silver bullets in that gun?"

All the talk of werewolves and other creatures began to give Allura doubts, which formed into a sickly feeling in the pit of her stomach. For the first time, she honestly began to wonder if she needed to use the clip marked with silver.

"Don't let her take me," Jenna said, sidling up to Allura as a pleading sound entered her voice, clearly making a decision about who to trust. "I don't want to go back."

Keeping the gun trained on the woman, Allura stepped back slightly and put her left arm around Jenna's shoulders, guiding her toward the cycle path. There was nowhere for them to hide, but the gate was a barrier if the woman charged. "I won't let her take you. I promise. You're safe with me." She shivered with the morning chill but kept her gun trained on the woman. "You need to leave," she told the tall woman.

She gave Allura a smile that was all white teeth. "There're worse things than being shot, human. Walk away and leave Jenna with me."

Keeping the gun on the woman, Allura met Jenna's desperate eyes, the girl shivering with fear now. "I swear it on my life. You're safe with me. I'll look after you."

"Promise?"

"I promise," Allura said, meaning it.

The entire universe exploded in white light, and Allura staggered.

She shivered and felt Jenna shiver in response as something monumental passed between them, deep and vital. For a moment she felt dizzy, the entire world fading away. "I promise," she repeated in a dazed whisper.

Jenna whispered in return, the word as vast and perfect as Jenna herself. "Mum?"

The word filled the shattered hole in Allura's soul, mending the broken part that had been torn out of her when Piper had died.

The Earth felt like it had stopped spinning while time itself came to a halt. Jenna met Allura's eyes, wonder in her own, and smiled. The universe brightened with that smile. "Mum," Jenna repeated, only this time with confidence.

It seemed as if they'd been searching for each other all their lives. "Jenna," Allura whispered.

The crunch of gravel under boots sent fear through Allura, jolting her from whatever spell had held her. She turned, bringing the gun around, but too late. The woman swung, the right hook catching Allura across the jaw and sending her sprawling.

She hit the ground, skinning her forearm as she crashed to the bitumen with an explosion of sound. Dazed, it took her long seconds to realise she was still holding the gun.

Jenna screamed, the sound a stab of anguish through Allura's heart. She forced herself to her feet, bringing the gun up, dizzy and struggling to aim it.

"Leave my daughter alone!" Allura yelled, finally finding the woman holding Jenna to her chest, the pair of them facing Allura.

"Mum!" Jenna cried, and to Allura's surprise, the timid girl kicked backward to catch the taller woman's shin.

The woman cried out and staggered back. Jenna struggled free from her grip and got away.

"Run!" Allura cried to Jenna, keeping her gun on the woman.

The woman grimaced before bending and gripping her calf, blood glistening on her fingers when she stood again. Allura must have shot her when she fell. She was lucky she hadn't shot herself.

Allura staggered a half step toward the cycle path and the direction Jenna had run. The woman's punch had felt like a freight train. If Allura didn't sit soon, she'd fall. Pain was beginning to thump through her head in rhythm with her pulse. She might even have a concussion.

"Walk away," Allura said, completely missing the huge man approaching to her right until he grasped her wrist and forced her to point the gun at the sky.

Allura cried out as he lifted her off her feet with one hand, his grip hurting her wrist. Her gun clattered to the ground.

Desperate with fear, Allura drew the knife at her hip, swinging, but he slapped the clumsy swing away with his free hand. The knife fell to the road as fear thundered through her heart.

"Go get the girl," the huge man said to the woman.

"The bitch shot me in the leg!"

The bones in Allura's wrist broke as the man gripped harder. Allura gasped and struggled to stay conscious, only dread for Jenna preventing the pain from sending her into oblivion.

"Then crawl."

The dark-skinned woman swore, but began going after the girl, hobbling but moving quickly despite the damage.

Still holding Allura off the ground with one arm, the man met her eyes. "You don't mind taking a message back to Shaw for me, do you?"

Allura was certain the message would be her dead body. She mustered all the defiance she could manage and spat in his face. "Actually, I do."

"JENNA!"

Spurred on by a fresh rush of fear at Penelope's distant voice, Jenna glanced over her shoulder and almost stumbled. Recovering, she ran towards the brightening dawn, obedient to her mother's order even if that made no sense.

She didn't have a mother anymore, yet now she did. She didn't have time to question it. She sprinted.

If she could make it to dawn, she'd be strong again, and something strange filled her at the thought. Hope. The collar would prevent her from changing, but she'd still be strong. Far stronger than Penelope. Stronger than Noah, even.

The bike path soon converged with a bridge spanning a river about fifteen metres across. Putting a hand on her side to ease her growing stitch, she crossed over and followed the bike path toward the city centre.

The path continued between the river and a new road, both meandering as they followed the river and hills. Jenna paused when she heard a car approaching, but it went past without slowing, followed by three more, their headlights illuminating the area in the brightening pre-dawn.

After the cars passed, Jenna began running once more, her stitch a little better for the moment's rest. The path threaded through trees and mowed lawns, water on the left, a main road to her right.

With hope blossoming as the sky brightened, she gave into thirst and staggered to the muddy river, cupping a mouthful and sipping. She made a face. Very muddy. Still, it was water, and not likely to kill her. She drank a few more mouthfuls before she returned to the bike path, half walking, half running, following it until the river opened up into Lake Burley Griffin, the ornamental lake at the centre of Canberra.

Light from the apartments and casino across the lake reflected off the water, a fine mist rising and obscuring any details. Beyond the apartments, Parliament House's huge flagpole caught the first rays of the morning's light.

"Jenna!"

Jenna spun, fear rushing through her once more. She backed across dry grass toward the water, sharp sticks and rocks biting into her bare feet. "Please Penelope. I don't want to go back." Jenna got all the way to the water and backed into it, almost slipping on the mud and roots.

Penelope's dark face was hidden in shadow thanks to the growing dawn behind her, but she limped forward with a grimace. Blood ran freely down her calf, the exercise preventing it from healing.

Penelope stopped a couple of metres from the edge of the water, pain in her expression. "Jenna, I swear if you make me go into that water to drag you out, you'll regret it. I've always been good to you, haven't I? If I say something, you know it's true, right?"

Jenna nodded, but took one more step back, regardless. Her mother had told her to run, so that was what she was going to do. Run, or swim, if she had to. Get away. Already knee deep in the cool water, she took three more steps backwards until it reached her thighs.

Penelope stopped at the water's edge, fists clenched. "If you don't get out of the water and come with me, you know they'll find you anyway. Noah will hurt you so bad you may not recover for weeks. If you come back with me now, I'll protect you. You know I will."

"I don't want to," Jenna said, taking another step backward, her feet squishing into thick mud. "Noah promised he'd look after me, but he kept me prisoner instead. He let people hurt me. They're always hurting me."

Penelope looked down and away, shame in her expression. "I know, Jenna. I know. And I'm sorry. If not you though, then it'd be another girl. A human girl. Humans die. You won't. You're saving those girls."

The emotional blackmail hurt, but Jenna didn't give in. She backed another step until the water reached her waist. There was a good five metres between them now. More.

She glanced up. Sunlight had touched the top of the hill on the opposite side of the road. A minute more and Penelope wouldn't be able to stop her. Just one more minute.

Something slithery brushed her thigh and Jenna cried out, hugging herself. She looked around as a ripple moved across the glassy surface and circled back.

"Mermaids! Get out of the water now, Jenna!" Penelope yelled. Penelope splashed into the lake to drag her out, but a blast of water struck the big woman in the chest and threw her back to the shore in a rain of muddy droplets. She coughed and rolled to her side, kicking and scrambling away from the water's edge.

Something encircled Jenna's left ankle. "Help!" she squealed before it pulled her under.

9

Shaw's upbeat ringtone woke him up. Sunshine had set it up for him, and he didn't know how to change it. He squinted at the dim glow around the edges of the blinds and groaned. Dawn.

"Can you turn that off?" Simone asked sleepily, startling him.

He'd forgotten she was still in his bed. Simone was a petite ginger about twenty years old. Her pale freckled skin had been spray-tanned, giving her an over-cooked appearance.

She turned towards him, revealing dark circles under her eyes. She seemed to lack the energy to open them properly. This was the second night in a row she'd slept with Shaw. If he let her stay again, he'd risk killing her.

Shaw picked up his phone and glanced at the screen before answering. "What is it, Luci?" Luci was even less of a morning person than he was.

"Get to room twelve–ten. Now." She hung up.

Shaw blinked at the phone. Orders? From Luci? It took him a moment to remember what she'd been doing last night, at which point he kicked the covers back and got up. Something must have gone badly wrong.

He pulled on the first clothes he got his hands on before leaving the apartment. Simone wouldn't be stirring for hours yet. Maybe not today at all.

Teddy Bear opened the door as Shaw got to the room. The big werewolf wouldn't meet his eyes, which didn't bode well.

Luci and Kyle seemed reluctant to meet his eyes, too. Someone lay on the bed, but all he could see were dark boots. One of the werewolves had probably been stabbed or shot with silver. Damn.

Teddy Bear left the room, which was good. The space was barely big enough for the people in there as it was. Kyle and Luci glanced at whoever was on the bed at the same time as Shaw moved in.

His chest tightened when he realised it was Allura. Shock almost kept him silent. "What happened?" he asked coldly.

Luci flinched.

Allura lay on the bed, her heavily bandaged stomach soaked in fresh blood. Her face was pale. Too pale.

Her right wrist had been splinted and bandaged as well, and it looked like they'd been in the process of tending to her other wounds. Every finger and joint on her left hand looked like it had been broken or dislocated, the skin badly bruised in shades of purple and black. Her wrist and forearm were swollen too, suggesting the bones had been shattered. Fingerprint-sized bruises darkened her skin.

"What happened?" he repeated.

Allura sucked in a painful breath, grimacing in her sleep. Everyone tensed. Shaw thought she was about to wake up, but then she went limp again, drifting back into unconsciousness.

He glared at Luci. "You took her with you? Why?" He clenched his fists. "And why isn't she at the hospital?"

Luci spoke, but wouldn't look at him. "If we took her to the hospital after what happened last night, how soon do you think it would be before we were being investigated?"

"So, you'd rather let her die instead?"

Luci finally met his eyes. "You could save her."

Lawrence glanced at Allura's blood-soaked bandages. She was breathing, but shallowly. "I don't think she's in the mood for sex," he said coldly. She'd likely die before he could turn her anyway, assuming that was Luci's intention.

Kyle spoke. "People died at the brothel, Lawrence. It wouldn't take much to tie her to the scene."

Allura opened her eyes, sucking in a pain-filled breath as panic filled her expression. "Jenna?" she asked. "Where's my daughter? Where's Jenna!"

Shaw moved toward her bedside, but Allura subsided into unconsciousness before he could get there.

"Who's Jenna?" Shaw asked.

"The shapeshifter girl we went to rescue," Teddy Bear said. "The tigress. Her name's Jenna."

Shaw fought for calm, but it slipped from him. "Why was Allura there?" he asked again, his voice cold and soft. Deadly. Allura shouldn't have been anywhere near the raid. "Why is she confusing Jenna with her daughter?" Dead daughter, he amended silently.

"Can you save her?" Luci asked in a clear attempt to distract him.

He gave her a flat stare. "I'm an incubus, not a vampire. I can't just drain her to the point of death and feed her my blood."

"You've had Simone in your bed for the last two nights," Luci replied. "You're flush with lifeforce, so it wouldn't require much sexual stimulation—"

Shaw cut her off with a glare. "Not without her consent," he said.

Despite being a vampire, Luci flushed.

Shaw touched fingertips to Allura's upper arm, careful to avoid the dark bruises there. Her lifeforce, though always vital, felt weak. She was holding on, but barely.

"You or Kyle better explain Allura's presence at the raid, and if you try to divert me again, I'll throw you both out the window." He meant it.

The silence lasted several seconds before Kyle spoke. "We took her with us on Kimbriel's advice," he said.

Shaw looked up sharply. "Kimbriel told you to take her?" Why the hell was Kimbriel interfering?

Kyle nodded. "She said we'd lose Jenna if we didn't."

"And the tiger girl is... where now?"

"Gone," Kyle admitted. "She ran away. Noah's wolves are out searching, too."

Mia burst into the room, stopping sharply when she saw Allura on the bed. She paled. "Nobody said it was Allura!" She rushed around to the other side of the bed and sat, leaning close. "Allura?" she asked softly. "Allura?"

Shaw met Kyle's eyes. "Does Noah know where the girl went?"

Kyle shook his head. "Allura chased her. We found her like this, along with scents of two werewolves. One was Noah's, the sadistic bastard. He probably tortured Allura while the other one went after Jenna. We lost the girl's trail at the lake."

Mary followed Mia into the room, eyes widening when she saw the bloody bandages. "We think Jenna took to the water to escape the wolf," Mary said, having obviously heard enough of the conversation to join in.

Even Mary knew? Shaw felt his fury mounting. Other than calling an ambulance, he could only think of a couple of ways to save Allura, neither of them good. "Are the mermaids in the casino?" he asked. They could save her, though they'd have to sacrifice another human to do it.

"No. They were out last night," Mia said softly. "They won't return before nightfall."

A ghoul could turn Allura and save her life, but he doubted Allura would consider that a kindness. He took a deep breath. "Wait outside, please, all of you."

Kyle seemed to be about to argue, but when he saw Shaw's expression, he nodded and followed Luci and Mary out.

"You too, Mia."

"Are you going to try to turn her?" Mia asked. "Please say yes."

"No."

"Then I'm staying."

A flash of anger heated Shaw's blood. He clenched his fists, releasing his breath slowly before speaking. "Don't defy me, Mia."

When he met her eyes, he saw resolve there, not fear. "Allura's had a terrible life, Lawrence. If you're going to end her suffering, at least let me be here with her."

If there was a god, they were punishing him. "Fine," he said as he moved to the end of the bed. "Kimbriel!"

Mia jumped at the name, eyes going wide as she realised who he was calling.

"Kimbriel! Get your skinny little ass here right now! This shitstorm's your fault and you need to fix it."

A short blonde woman appeared in the room, coming

into view like a ghost growing solid. "Hello, Lawrence." She didn't appear any older than twenty.

Shaw clenched his fists. "Help her, Kimbriel."

She raised an eyebrow at the command. "No."

He felt the blood rush to his head, momentarily blinding him with anger. "You can shatter mountains and part the sea, but you won't fix a knife wound to the stomach? She's dying. Help her."

Kimbriel, though half his size, gave him a dangerous stare. "I can't heal her without her permission. You know that."

"She wouldn't have been there without your interference," Shaw said. "Do something else, then. Fix her the old-fashioned way. With surgery. Stop the bleeding, at least."

Kimbriel glanced at Allura, then Mia, and back to Shaw, her expression hard. "You've had three thousand years and fifty incarnations to fix your relationship with her. What's one more lifetime?"

"Kimbriel," he began warningly.

The short woman raised a hand, forestalling his protests. She glanced at Mia instead. "What do you think Jenna's going to do when her mother dies?"

Mia blinked at Kimbriel, her confusion clear. "Her mother? Allura's not her mother."

Kimbriel pointed at the dying woman. "Jenna bonded with Allura when Allura promised to protect the girl. She's her mother now. You know how it works."

Mia, already pale with shock, paled even further. "That's impossible. Allura's human. She can't bond with a tiger."

"And yet she did."

Mia shook her head. "How?"

"You know how."

Mia still seemed confused, but not nearly as confused as Shaw felt. "Allura has tiger ancestry?" Shaw asked, putting the pieces together before Mia. How had he never known?

Kimbriel nodded. "Yes, on both sides of her family. Why do you think Piper's death shattered her so badly?"

Mia closed her eyes. "Because Allura bonded with Piper?"

"It almost destroyed her. Bonding with Jenna has healed that tear in her soul. Why do you think I sent her with you?"

Mia glanced at the unconscious woman, a sheen of perspiration on her deathly-pale face. "I've never heard of a tiger bonding with another tiger's cub outside of family, let alone a human doing it."

"Your children are human," Kimbriel countered. "Just as Jenna once was. They may yet become tigers, just as Jenna did."

Mia frowned, clearly trying to figure things out. "If everything you say is true, Allura and Jenna would have to share the same close ancestor. They're related? Cousins?"

Kimbriel inclined her head. "Something like that. Do you still want to save Allura?" she asked Shaw.

Shaw nodded. "And keep her human?"

Kimbriel glanced at the door. "Ask Luci. She has the means. She was holding out in the hope a better solution arose." With that, Kimbriel faded away like a ghost.

10

Jenna coughed up muddy water. It came out of her nose and mouth, stinging her sinuses. She thought she might suffocate.

Sucking in deep breaths, she coughed the final dregs out before rolling onto her back and breathing luxuriously, the oxygen perfumed with the scents of grass, trees, and distant city life.

Water lapped over her legs, but her upper body rested in dappled sunlight filtered through willow leaves.

She'd escaped Cheri's establishment and Penelope's pursuit, only to be dragged under water and drowned. Any Creature who'd do that wasn't likely to leave her alive, yet she was. Why?

Long willow branches reached all the way to the water just beyond her feet, screening her from anyone who might be swimming or paddling on the lake. Whoever or whatever had brought her here wanted her isolated.

Cautiously sitting up, she found herself on a small island in the middle of Lake Burley Griffin, the murky water hiding anything deeper than a metre. Black Mountain wasn't far away across the water, the massive tower atop it just visible through the willow branches.

She could have been dead for hours or days, she could never tell. The more brutal the death and physical damage, the longer it took to revive and recover. Unlike stab wounds and worse, drowning rarely affected her for too long. She hated being drowned, though. Mostly she hated the panic and fear that always came with it, and there'd been plenty of fear last night.

"You're awake. Finally."

A fresh rush of fear jolted Jenna to her feet so quickly that water splashed about her. She spun, calf deep with muddy water swirling around her legs. Four women in bikinis stood among the island's willows, all watching her. Were they dryads? She'd never met one, but they were rumoured to be beautiful.

No. Why would a dryad wear a bikini? Mermaids then? If so, one of them must have drowned her.

These women all had dark skin and long dark hair falling past their waists. The one on the left looked like she was from India, the one to the right from the Middle East, while the other two were probably from the Pacific Islands. They all seemed to be in their late teens or early twenties. Definitely Creatures. They could have been thousands of years old, despite their youthful appearance.

"What are you?" The taller of the islander girls asked. She was classically beautiful, with wavy hair and looks that could have made her a movie star.

Jenna took half a step deeper into the water, not certain the water was safe after last night, but they were on land and she had nowhere else to go. "Please don't hurt me."

The daylight might make her strong, but there were four of them and she didn't know what they were capable of.

Mermaids were elemental Creatures. Neither day nor night gave them an advantage, but close to water, they would be far more dangerous than Jenna.

"I asked you a question."

"My name's Jenna. I'm looking for my mother," Jenna said quickly, almost stumbling over the words.

Her mother? The thought rushed at her with fear and relief. Yes, she had a mother now, and the feelings that brought up filled her with hope and desperation. What was her mother's name? She was alive, but that was all Jenna was certain of.

"Can you help me?" Jenna asked without much hope, but it certainly wouldn't make her appear threatening. The women hadn't killed her, after all. Well, not in a permanent way, and they could have. Easily.

The woman who'd spoken stepped forward, her feet bare and her stride casual and unhurried. "Why was that wolf after you?"

They weren't allied with Noah, at least. "Her pack had me caged. I ran away." She pointed to her collar, careful not to touch the exposed silver on the outside.

The woman moved closer, eyes narrowed at the realisation the collar wasn't simply decorative. Claws protruded from her fingertips and she stopped a little more than a metre away, anger in her eyes. The remaining three women moved to flank the first. "Why?"

Jenna glanced at the claws. "Please don't hurt me. I don't want to be killed anymore."

The woman raised both eyebrows. "Killed anymore?"

Jenna nodded. "They made movies where people would pay to kill me. When I wasn't making movies, they kept me in a cage."

The woman looked over her shoulder at the other three

as if gauging their reactions. They gave nothing away, but one of them nodded slightly, as if accepting Jenna's story. The closer woman turned back. "We'll take you to shore," she said. "We have friends—"

"No!" Jenna said with a fresh rush of fear. That's what Noah had told her when she was living on the streets two years ago, and there'd been a lot of getting killed since then. It was how she'd become a tiger. The stress of her first death had triggered something inside her, even though she'd been human until then. "I need to find my mother."

The woman considered that and pointed across the water. "That's the Australian National University. We can take you there. Cross the campus to the city centre and leave town. Steal the money if you have to. You can make enquiries about your mother when you're away from here."

Jenna nodded with relief, though she had no intention of leaving. "Thank you."

11

Allura grimaced at the taste in her mouth, scraping her tongue against her teeth to try and get rid of it. Sap. She shivered in disgust. She'd tasted sap from a tree in her yard as a child, thinking it was maple syrup. It had taken hours to get the foul taste out of her mouth.

"Allura?"

She opened scratchy eyes at Mia's question. "Where am I?" she asked, her voice husky. Everything hurt, particularly her stomach and hands, which ached, though the discomfort seemed to be fading.

Mia smiled as if her prayers had been heard. "Alive. You're home."

Home? This wasn't Allura's apartment. It was the same hotel room she'd used before she'd been stabbed... She swallowed, a cold sweat breaking out over her entire body.

"You're safe," Mia said quickly, sitting on the edge of the bed and gently taking Allura's hand.

Allura began to pull away in fear of the pain she'd experienced, but her hand was only tender now. She squeezed Mia's warm hand experimentally. Her wrist and forearm didn't hurt beyond muscle soreness, and more surprisingly, she still had all her strength, as if there'd never been any damage.

She glanced at her other hand, where that bastard had taken pleasure in dislocating and breaking every joint there. She held it up, flexing tender fingers, but there wasn't even any bruising.

"How long have I been in a coma for?" Months, at least. How many operations had it taken to set her hand right? Why hadn't she lost her strength? Why weren't there any scars?

She wiggled her fingers again to be sure this wasn't some self-induced delusion. Like her other hand, her fingers were tender, but they all worked just fine. Her hands should have taken years of physio to get right if that were even possible, but they were barely sore, like she'd had a good workout and had forgotten to stretch afterward.

"How long have I been unconscious?" she repeated. She flexed both hands above her face, staring in wonder. No hint of any trauma.

Her stomach felt fine, too. A sickly feeling went through her at the memory of that bastard slowly forcing the knife into her guts, his other hand over her mouth to prevent her screaming. That was the last thing she remembered.

"You're healed," Mia said, taking Allura's hand again. "Everything's fine."

The evidence agreed, if not her mental state. She ran her free hand over her stomach but couldn't feel a scar. They must have organised a seriously good plastic surgeon. "How long have I been unconscious?"

"The entire day."

"Huh?" Allura tried to sit up, but a dizzy spell put her on her back again. She felt Mia's hand on her right shoulder.

Soothing. "You mean a year?" Allura asked after the dizziness had receded.

"It's a long story."

"Why does my mouth taste like sap? Why do my fingers work?" They should be damaged for life.

"Easy answer, lifeforce. Think of it as magic," Mia said.

Magic? That probably meant that whatever they'd done to save her was illegal. Perhaps an experimental drug? She was alive and recovered beyond all hope, so she shouldn't complain. Still, nothing came for free or without consequence.

Something was missing. She looked around, trying to figure it out.

"What's the matter?" Mia asked.

That's when Allura's heart constricted. "Where's Jenna?" she asked, dread filling her. "Where's Jenna? Where's my daughter!"

She began to sit up, but Mia gripped both Allura's shoulders and held her in place. "We were hoping you could tell us."

Panic rising, Allura pulled away, or tried to. She was still pitifully weak. "Let go of me!" She tried to shove Mia's hands off.

"Calm down!" Mia was six months pregnant and considerably smaller than Allura, so Allura shouldn't have any trouble breaking her hold. She couldn't.

"Let go!"

"Settle down and I will."

Allura glared, and with a supreme act of willpower, stopped struggling. "Happy?" she asked.

Mia nodded. "I want to help you find Jenna, but you have to listen first. Okay?"

Fighting down panic at the possibility Jenna was in

worse trouble than before, Allura nodded, though she kept testing Mia's grip. Was the woman on steroids?

"I'm not human," Mia said. "Sort of."

That had to be the dumbest statement ever. "Chinese people are human," Allura said sarcastically. "Trust me, I learned it in school."

Mia smirked. "I'm a shapeshifter. Charlotte and Mary too. We're like werewolves, but feline. Siberian Tigers, actually. Our species came out of northeast China or southeast Russia, depending on the century you happen to be pointing at."

Allura didn't have time for this stupidity. "If you don't let go of me in three seconds, I'm going to..." She remembered how strong Mia was and backed down from her lame threat. "Say things I'll regret."

Mia's smirk broadened into an actual smile. "Why don't you go check the mirror in the bathroom?" She released Allura's shoulders. "Go. We can talk after that."

"The bathroom?" Allura echoed a little uncertainly. "What's in the bathroom? A subscription to *You've been pranked*?"

"Go."

She got up, watching Mia in case she tried to restrain her again, but the woman didn't move. The hotel room door was beside the bathroom door, and as tempting as it was to make a break for it, Allura needed answers. She turned on the bathroom light and entered.

When she glanced at the mirror, a different woman stared back at her. Not younger exactly, but not the gaunt mess she'd been before, either. The woman staring back looked healthy, her cheeks no longer painfully hollow and her skin smooth and perfect, unworn from grief and self-abuse.

Allura swallowed. Her reflection swallowed too.

She tentatively touched the mirror, thinking it had to be an actress on the other side of the glass. If so, she mimicked Allura's movements perfectly.

Her reflection changed into Sparrow's appearance.

You have an imaginary friend you can't explain, but you won't accept magic is real?

"Piss off," she muttered, wanting her own reflection back. Sparrow surprised her by fading away.

It took her a full minute to accept the fact that she was staring at herself, poking her cheeks several times to be sure. "What the hell?" she whispered.

She returned to Mia, who was still sitting on the bed. "What did you do to me?"

Mia patted the bed. "Magic, like I told you."

Allura refused to sit. "And you're a shapeshifting tiger? Tigress?" Allura amended. "You expect me to believe that?"

Mia nodded. "Has it never occurred to you that I have four children with Don, the oldest in first grade, yet I barely look like I'm twenty years old?" Mia asked.

"No," Allura said honestly. She glanced down at Mia's growing stomach. "You started young?"

"Thirteen?" she asked. "I'm over six hundred years old, Allura, and I'm not the only one around here who's different."

"Different?" She glanced at her healed hands. "By different, do you mean you did something to me?" she asked, a new kind of fear beginning to rise inside her. If magic was real and Mia really was a were-tiger, was she the same now? "Did you bite me?"

Mia looked offended. "Why would I bite you? I'm not a werewolf. Shapeshifters are born, not made."

Allura stared at Mia like they'd never met. Little Mia.

Lovely Mia. Mia the inhuman shapeshifting Siberian Tigress who talked about werewolves like they were real. Allura began to speak, but the words trailed off. How was she even entertaining the possibility it was true?

Allura touched her fully-healed stomach as if seeking proof. "If you're a were-tiger, was that you in the lobby the other day, posing for photos? The tigress?" Did she just admit to acceptance?

Mia shook her head. "That was Charlotte. She and Mary take turns. We can't shapeshift when we're pregnant, at least not if the baby's human. It would kill the baby. I have to stay human until I give birth."

Allura touched her cheeks, the skin softer than she could ever remember it being. "How did you fix me?" Her fears formed a knot in her stomach. "Did you change me into a... something?"

Mia shook hear head, but there was an edge of hesitation to it. "We gave you concentrated lifeforce. Luci calls it nectar. It's something the dryads make, though they're very selective about who they trade with. It heals and restores health. If you're not sick, it'll make you younger instead. You would have died without it."

Allura studied Mia's face. "Why do you look guilty? What did it cost?"

"Luci paid for it. You don't have to worry."

That didn't sound good. "What was the price, Mia?"

Mia sighed. "Someone's life. A very bad person."

She stared, shocked. "You killed someone to save me?"

"It wasn't like that. Luci traded him to the dryads for nectar, months ago. The asshole was selling drugs to kids. The bigger question is, how did you bond with Jenna considering you're human? Jenna's a tigress. You're not."

Jenna was a were-tiger too?

"I'm guessing you have an answer?"

Mia nodded. "You have tiger ancestry, just like my children with Don. You might have even become a tigress yourself under the right circumstances."

She wasn't sure how to respond to that. "So... I might become a shapeshifting were-tiger one day? How?" The thought was exciting.

A frown touched Mia's features, and she shook her head slightly. "Humans with shapeshifter ancestry can only become shapeshifters during puberty." She met Allura's eyes. "It takes a traumatic experience like a life-threatening accident, emotional devastation, or someone trying to kill you. We're guessing that's what happened to Jenna. Her shapeshifter ancestor could have been generations back. All we know is that you share the same ancestor. You couldn't bond otherwise."

"So, how did we... bond?"

"I'm guessing you had a traumatic experience when you were a child. Before puberty. It probably changed you enough to let you bond with Jenna, just as you bonded with your firstborn daughter, Piper. The bond can be one-sided. Are your feelings for Jenna almost the same?"

Piper's name brought a familiar, devastating ache to Allura's heart. "Yeah," she whispered. There wasn't any point in denying it.

"Jenna's your daughter now. Genuinely your daughter. Understand? You bonded with her. Nothing can ever change that. I envy you. I've never bonded with any of my children. It takes someone special to form a bond, because you have to give yourself over to it entirely. I've never been able to do that. I guess I'm just too selfish."

Allura wasn't sure if she'd been complemented or told she'd been cursed. "Jenna's alive. I can feel it." Jenna being missing felt like a hammer blow to her chest, reminding her of all the horrors she'd experienced when Piper went missing.

"If you can sense Jenna's lifeforce, then the bond goes both ways. She bonded with you, too." Mia gripped Allura's hand. "That's even more special. She could have rejected you and you'd have been stuck with a one-way bond."

"Of course," Allura said, not really understanding.

Mia sighed. "Shaw has a dozen Creatures out looking for Jenna right now, and Kyle's pack is helping too. That's over two dozen werewolves. They're trying to catch her scent, though in an urban environment it's hard. If Jenna's out there, she should be safe enough during the day. After dark's the problem, but our wolves are out in force. Noah doesn't have the numbers to search widely, so they'll stay clear of us."

Werewolves? What else was real? "Is Noah a werewolf?"

Mia nodded. "Yeah. But Luci's also out there, even though it's still daytime. They'll find her."

Even though it's daytime? "But—" Allura began. "Luci? She's like you too?"

"A vampire."

Allura closed her eyes, trying to get her head around it. If it weren't for her miraculously healed body, she wouldn't have believed it. "I need to help."

"There's nothing you can do but hinder them, Allura. Come nightfall, Jenna will find somewhere to hide, and you don't have a werewolf's sense of smell to help find her. Bonding with her doesn't allow you to hone in, only to know if she's alive. Mary and Charlotte have volunteered to escort you around the city tomorrow if the wolves can't locate her by dawn."

"But I need to be out there." She turned towards the door, but Mia's grip on her hand tightened.

"You're a target, Allura. Noah has your scent, along with every wolf who visited the place where you were tortured. Do not leave the Menagerie without an escort. I'm serious."

"I want to help, though. I need to." Mia's logic made sense, but Allura couldn't leave this to others. Jenna was too important to her.

"If you go out there, Teddy Bear's going to have to assign at least one wolf, maybe a couple, to look after you. If they're looking after you, they can't be looking for Jenna. Trust the people here, Allura. Trust me."

Allura didn't care about her own safety as long as Jenna was safe, but she wouldn't survive another encounter with Noah if it came to it.

She glanced at Mia, her head full of questions about shapeshifters and other supernatural things. Mia's phone buzzed, leaving Allura frustrated with unanswered questions.

Mia answered, listened, and nodded before looking up at Allura. "Shaw wants to see you."

12

Despite every instinct screaming at her to leave the Menagerie and search for Jenna, Allura walked with Mia to Shaw's office.

"So, tell me about this magical world I've stumbled into," Allura said.

Mia shrugged non-committally. "I have a sister. She claims she can turn into a hawk as well as a tigress."

Allura studied Mia's face, wondering if she was joking. "Really?"

Mia gave another shrug. "I've never seen her do it, and I don't know any others of our kind who shift into anything but Siberian tigers, but my sister's at least a century older than me. Maybe she's just more in tune with her body. It's possible we get could more shapes as we get older. I honestly don't know. Still, what my sister claims and what she can actually do are often very different things."

"How old are you?"

Mia gave Allura a look as if she didn't like the question, but after a moment, she spoke. "I was born early in the Ming Dynasty, about six-hundred years ago. My sister's at least a century older than me, and we're the oldest shapeshifters I know of."

"You're over six hundred years old?" Mia could have passed for a teenager.

Mia laughed. "Shaw's three thousand years old. I'm just a baby."

"Three thou..." Allura began, but trailed off, uncertain what to say as they stopped at Sunshine's desk on the sixth floor.

A woman sitting in a chair opposite Sunshine's desk stared at Allura as if she recognised her. She looked vaguely familiar.

"Catch you later," Mia said. "I've got ankle-biters to wrangle. Don's probably searching his head for hair to pull out."

Allura smirked and turned to Sunshine, Shaw's personal assistant, a stunningly beautiful woman almost Allura's own age. She carried herself with a certain grace, confidence, and poise Allura associated with experience and a fair amount of steel in her spine.

"You look gorgeous," Sunshine said with a smile. The woman's hair and makeup were perfect, as always. It was clear from Sunshine's tone she knew exactly what Allura had been through, and what had been done to save her. She was a Creature, then? Sunshine appeared to be in her late thirties, but Allura had her doubts now. She could be centuries old if everything Mia had told her was true.

It was weird seeing people she'd known for years in a completely new context. She should probably be scared, but if any of them wanted to harm her, they'd have done it long ago.

"Thanks," Allura said uncomfortably, wishing there wasn't a stranger seated across from Sunshine's desk so they could talk openly. "I'm almost healthy enough to hold up a number while walking around a boxing ring in a bikini."

Sunshine's smile touched her eyes. "Mr Shaw shouldn't be long." She pointed to the spare guest seat, a modern thing that had been upholstered in vampire red. Allura hoped it didn't bite her.

The young woman in the other chair looked vaguely familiar. Whoever she was, she stared at Allura until a smile crept across her face. "Detective Cox, how the mighty have been humiliated. I hear you're a bar wench these days."

"It's Forsayeth now," Allura said. "Not Cox. I changed my name after I left the force." The insult might have meant more to Allura if she could remember who the woman was. It took a long moment to dredge up the memory.

"Sara?" Allura asked uncertainly. Sara was a heroin addict, or had been half a decade ago. Allura had arrested her a few months before quitting the force. Sara had put up a fight too, giving Allura a swollen lip. She looked like she was still spoiling for a fight. "You look well. I'm glad you've got things sorted."

Sara had been so gaunt the last time they'd met, she'd looked like she needed to be hospitalised and force-fed. Most likely, she'd been one hit away from overdosing. Now she was healthy to the point Allura almost didn't recognise her. She wore dark blue slacks, a matching jacket, and new black shoes with short heels and pointed toes. Business attire.

Sara frowned as she was forced into politeness. "You were kind to me," she admitted grudgingly. "Kinder than most cops would have been."

Allura sat beside the young woman and took a risk. "Are you a Creature now?" she asked. "You look great."

Sara rolled her eyes, snark clearly wanting to surface.

Civility forced it down. "I'm human," she muttered, but it confirmed Sara knew about Creatures. "But Tammy says that needs to change before we become co-dependent."

"What does that mean?" Allura asked.

Sara looked away. "Never mind. So, what's your story? Why are you rocking a casino job instead of arresting people?"

Someone in Shaw's office screamed. Allura stood on a rush of adrenalin and instinct, ready to rush in, but Sunshine stood too. "Sit down, Allura."

"But—"

"Sit down." Sunshine's expression hardened and Allura reluctantly sat down, glancing surreptitiously at the door to Shaw's office. What the hell was going on in there?

"You know about Creatures?" Sara asked Allura as if hearing screams was a normal part of her day. "Mister Shaw must have taken a shine to you."

"Hardly," Allura said, wishing she knew what was going on in Shaw's office.

Disbelief crept into Sara's expression. "Other than his adopted son, do you see any other humans in his inner circle? Even I'm not allowed in his office when my mistress comes to see him." She pointed to Sunshine. "He surrounds himself with Creatures, not humans."

Mistress? Sunshine looked up, smiled, and then went back to her computer.

Gathering her courage, Allura directed her next question to Sunshine. "And you're a... werewolf?" she guessed.

Sunshine shook her head, pursing her red-painted lips as if she'd just been accused of something insulting. "A banshee."

What the hell was a banshee? Her knowledge of mythology

sucked, yet she seemed to be surrounded by mythological beings from stories. She'd need to fix that knowledge gap.

Another pain-filled cry came from Shaw's office, and Allura found herself hard-pressed not to stand again.

Sara didn't look, instead raising her chin as if she were higher on the food chain than Allura. What kind of world had Allura stumbled into?

"I'm not entirely human either, you know," Sara said conspiratorially, leaning close. "Care for a kiss? I swear you'll enjoy it."

Allura leaned away.

Sara seemed to realise she'd made a mistake and sat up straighter. "Forget it."

Allura glanced questioningly at Sunshine. The woman, no, the banshee, gave Allura an infuriating smirk, but didn't elaborate. "So, you're almost a Creature, but not quite?" Allura pushed when she got no response from Sunshine.

Sara frowned like she'd embarrassed herself, refusing to meet Allura's eyes.

"Allura won't tell anyone, will you Allura?" Sunshine said, her voice resonating in Allura's inner ear, her bones tingling from head to toe.

She grimaced. "Not for less than a week's wages."

Sunshine's eyes widened, and she sat a little straighter. "How did you do that?" she asked.

"Do what?"

"You're human. You can't just ignore me."

"You mean that weird vibration?" Allura asked. "Is that what banshees do? You can make people do what you want?"

"One of my skills," Sunshine said, a puzzled frown dominating her expression as she stared at Allura.

"Unfortunately, it doesn't work on Creatures, even werewolves, or I could have spared the brutality going on in there." She glanced pointedly at Shaw's door.

Doesn't work on Creatures? Allura had bonded with Jenna thanks to her tiger ancestry. That must be why Sunshine's gift didn't work on her.

"Why isn't Luci in there?" Sara asked. "Vampires can mesmerise werewolves even easier than they can humans."

"She's busy."

Sara turned to Allura. "Are you a muse too? Is that why Sunshine's gifts didn't work on you?"

"What's a muse?"

Sara frowned again. The woman really wasn't good at keeping secrets. "I'm Tammy's muse," she finally admitted. "I can take lifeforce from humans and give it to Tammy. I also have claws." She held up her right hand. Claws, no, talons, grew out of her fingertips. They were about five centimetres long, curved, and needle sharp at the tips, perfect for puncturing flesh and holding on.

Allura went still, hoping Sara didn't use those claws on her. "What kind of Creature is Tammy?"

Sara's frown turned into a scowl. She closed her mouth as if she'd already said too much.

"Tammy's a succubus," Sunshine said. "Just like Shaw. I mean, he's an incubus, but they're the same thing. Gendered terms for male and female."

Allura turned to Sara. "And a muse is... half succubus?"

Sara rolled her eyes, apparently giving up on the whole secrecy thing. Her claws disappeared back into her fingertips like real-life movie magic. "I'm bound to her. It's mutual, but Tammy says it's not good for either of us, so she wants me to become a succubus like her."

"Sara has no will of her own," Sunshine added. "She does whatever Tammy tells her to, without question."

Sara gave Sunshine a scathing look as if she were wrong on a dozen levels. "I'm still me. I had to beg Tammy to make me her muse."

"I don't understand," Allura admitted, her list of questions growing as several dull thumps from Shaw's office made her look up. A man groaned.

Sara didn't acknowledge the sounds, and Sunshine didn't seem to have a problem with it either. "Tammy's not old enough to make Creatures yet, but she can make a muse. It's half the reason she's here."

What was the other half? Torture? Allura glanced at Shaw's closed door, wanting to be anywhere else. She really had stepped into a new world.

A tall woman with well-rounded hips approached from the same direction Allura had come from, killing the conversation. She stopped before Allura, beaming, her dark brown eyes sharing her pleasure. "Allura?"

It took Allura a moment to place the woman. They'd never met, but she'd seen her around the Menagerie. "Pam?" Allura asked. She'd only joined the staff a few months ago.

Pam held out her hands. Allura reluctantly grasped them, and Pam drew her to her feet. She was a big woman, at least fifteen centimetres taller than Allura and about double her weight.

"I was told you were here. Mister Shaw has approved your transfer."

"Huh?"

"You did request to be transferred out of bar work, correct?"

"Oh, yeah." She'd entirely forgotten.

Pam smiled in relief. "Good. From tomorrow, you'll be working for Mia in the Cancan Coffee Bar."

"Coffee Bar?" Allura echoed, horrified. "Like, as in, mornings?"

Pam nodded. "Five-am start every day."

That was not what Allura had intended when she'd asked for a transfer.

"Still a bar wench then?" Sara asked with a straight face.

13

F ive minutes later, and after considerably more discomforting noises from Shaw's office, Sunshine waved for Allura's attention. "You can go in now," Sunshine said as she touched an earpiece hidden by her hair. Sara began to stand, but Sunshine shook her head. "Allura only."

Sara gave Allura a jealous look and sat, crossing her arms.

Allura had never actually been in Shaw's office. She did her best to keep blossoming anxiety out of her expression as she entered. Hopefully, he'd have some good news about Jenna.

Shaw's old-style mahogany desk stood opposite the door, the wall behind it full of bookshelves. There was no spare space on it. She recognised a collection of Shakespeare's works and a few other classics.

A man knelt in the middle of the room, his arms bound behind his back and his straggly hair well past his shoulders. He wore a torn t-shirt and faded jeans, the fabric dirty and bloody. He glanced over his shoulder at Allura, revealing bruised and bloody features, his left eye badly swollen. His stare chilled her. She had the feeling he'd murder her if he could. Allura swallowed.

Beyond, floor-to-ceiling windows offered stunning views across Lake Burley Griffin. A leather lounge and a coffee table had been placed there so Shaw could relax and entertain while taking in the views.

The wall to her right featured dozens of sketches in shades of charcoal, all of women's faces. They seemed vaguely familiar, like they were part of a collection Allura felt she should recognise. If Shaw was the artist, he was bloody good. Allura wanted to focus on them so she could pretend there wasn't a bound man in the room.

A woman with olive skin and straight dark hair stood near the window, close to Shaw. Tammy. Had to be. Like Sara, she wore business clothes and was beautiful enough to turn anyone's head.

"You look upset," Shaw said.

Allura jumped at his voice. "No," she lied.

"Would it help if I told you he's one of the werewolves who kept Jenna caged?" Shaw added.

Anger, perhaps hatred, flared in place of empathy.

"Allura?"

Allura took a breath, pushing down her murderous feelings. "I'm fine," she lied again. She forced a smile, focusing on Shaw's friend.

The woman smiled. "I'm Tammy," she said with a distinctly English accent, though she looked more Italian than English. Tammy appeared human, but so did every other Creature Allura had met. She approached Allura like a femme fatale, her lips painted red, and held out a hand.

Allura shook, a little surprised at the warmth. She didn't know why, but she'd expected Tammy's skin to be cold.

Luci's skin was a little cool, after all. "Allura," she responded with a glance at Shaw.

Shaw's eyes turned to the man on his knees. Whoever he was, he focused intently on the carpet before him now. "He's here for information. To provide it, at least."

"He knows where Jenna is?" Allura asked, surprising herself with how desperate she sounded.

"No," Tammy responded, walking over to the man as if she wished to rip his head off. "But he did tell us about two men he knows who are involved in a local human trafficking racket. Luci's on it. If he's not lying and we can find them, we may get a lead on Noah and whoever he works for. Noah's the bastard who nearly killed you, in case you don't remember."

Allura remembered all right. "Big guy? Pleasant smile? Sadistic streak?" She glanced from the man to Shaw and back. "Are you going to kill him?" she asked, concerned that murder might be on the agenda.

Shaw met her eyes. "Nobody will stop you, if that's what you want." He moved behind his desk, opened a draw, and withdrew a silver knife. He placed it on the desk with a heavy thunk, the invitation clear.

"No, thank you." Allura backed a step.

"It's not like you haven't murdered anyone before," Tammy said.

Allura glanced up sharply, a shock of fear drawing the blood from her face. She must have gone three shades paler. "I don't know what you're talking about," Allura said as her stomach twisted, the pitch of her voice rising as she spoke.

Tammy gave Allura a half smile. "Who do you think Quicksilver called to clean up your mess when you murdered Piper's kidnappers?"

Allura felt the rest of the blood drain from her face. It was all she could do to stop her legs giving way.

"Quicksilver pulled in quite a few favours to cover for you. Bodies requiring quiet disposal always come to me in this city. Most human bodies go to the ghouls, while Creatures are disposed of at my crematorium."

Allura glanced at Shaw. His expression implied he knew what had happened all those years ago. Her stomach rolled, and she felt an urgent need to vomit. Shaw knew all her secrets then, and yet, here she was. He'd said nothing since she'd come to him for money. Instead, he'd sheltered her. Why?

And now, Slade wanted her to betray Shaw. Beating the crap out of someone for information was exactly the sort of information Slade wanted. She couldn't do it, though. Not now. Not ever. If she betrayed Shaw, he could use what he knew against her. She might as well find a bridge and jump off it.

Shaw turned his head and tapped an earpiece. "Sunshine, would you escort our guest downstairs? He'll be staying while we verify his claims. Be nice-ish to him."

Sunshine entered a moment later and walked over to the man. She said something which made Allura's bones resonate in a very unpleasant way. The man almost jerked to his feet as if hauled up by an invisible string. Sunshine escorted him out, closing the door behind her.

"I thought that didn't work on Creatures?" Allura said.

"It was more like a jump-start," Shaw said before turning to Tammy. "You sure you want to do this?" he asked the succubus.

A rush of anxiety swept through Allura. "Do what?" Blackmail her into doing something she'd regret?

Tammy nodded. "It's the only way to protect her."

"Protect me? What?" Allura backed a step toward the door. They ignored her.

"Do you need anything else from me?" Shaw asked.

"No, thank you. I'll tell Sara to come in when Allura leaves."

Tammy left the room, leaving Allura alone with Shaw. That was about Sara? Thank God. Was he going to bite her and turn her into a succubus? Is that how it worked?

Shaw picked up a polished mahogany box from his desk. It was square, as wide and long as her forearm, and a little thicker than a hefty book.

"This should provide you with some protection."

"Protection from what? Or who?" Allura asked.

He placed the box on his desk and opened it. Inside was a necklace of twisted gold wire, a twin to the one Luci wore, the gleaming gold reflecting the down lights embedded in the roof. Where Luci's choker had a big ruby, this one had a large emerald instead. The elegant box included matching earrings.

Shaw pointed to the necklace. "I don't want anyone thinking you're fair game. This tells people you're mine and I'm willing to fight for you. Or seek revenge." He added the last part as if an afterthought.

"I'm no one's property," Allura said. The necklace rested on red silk and had to be worth considerably more than her annual salary. "You know, you've never told me why you've helped me all these years or why you're helping me now. You even kept my secrets without so much as a hint you knew them."

He smiled at the words, though it was a smile tinged with regret or sadness. "Try the necklace on, please."

The unanswered question irked her, but she desperately

needed his help to find Jenna and didn't have the courage to push him on it.

She looked the necklace over. The matching studs had to be worth thousands of dollars on their own. "I couldn't wear that choker to anything but a ball for the rich and infamous." The emerald alone had to be worth more than her debt to him, not that she had any real idea what an emerald was worth. It was big, though. "And I'm not going to mark myself as your property, no matter what help you offer." Maybe. She'd do it for Jenna, but not otherwise.

Shaw's expression turned inward. "You're welcome to leave the Menagerie whenever you choose." He met her eyes, and there was absolutely no compromise in them. "But while you're here, you'll wear the necklace. Until now I've asked absolutely nothing of you Allura, so either put the necklace on and keep it on, or leave."

Allura swallowed, realising just how much she owed him. "I," Allura began, but couldn't say the ungrateful words she wanted to speak. Instead, she nodded. "I'll wear it, but you don't own me. We clear?" It was all the defiance she could manage.

"You've made that very clear over the centuries."

"What?"

Rather than answer, Shaw picked up the necklace, his size imposing and more than a little intimidating. Allura struggled not to give into impulse and back away.

"I need you to understand that this necklace also comes with authority. It marks you just as Luci's ruby necklace marks her. It shows everyone here that I value you, just as I do Luci. Understand?"

Allura nodded.

"Don't abuse the privilege or you'll be answering to me."

"I don't want authority. I Just want to find Jenna, and I can't with that thing drawing attention."

He sighed. "It also means people will help you, or at least leave you alone if they're not friendly. You'll wear it constantly from now on, and you won't leave the Menagerie without it, or an escort. Please respect me on this." His expression showed no more room for argument than he'd given the werewolf Sunshine had escorted out.

If she didn't need his help so badly... "Fine, I'll wear it, and I won't leave without an escort," she said reluctantly, lifting her hair to let him put it around her neck. "If you help me find Jenna, I'll do whatever you ask of me."

Shaw clipped the choker into place and eyed it critically, adjusting the emerald at the hollow of her throat. A feeling of déjà vu hit her, the situation so oddly familiar she could have sworn they'd done this before.

What had he said? That she'd made her intentions clear over the centuries? A chill went through her.

Allura let her loose hair drop back over her shoulders, the odd feeling of déjà vu slow to leave her.

"Earrings," he said as he returned to his desk and collected them. "Emeralds are my signature."

"Marking me as your property is likely to get me killed. You realise that, don't you?"

He gave her a long, measuring look. "You're under my protection, not my property. The necklace delivers that message," Shaw said.

"I feel like a showpiece."

"I have a lot of friends, Allura, and more than a few enemies. Wear the earrings, please."

She reluctantly removed her cheap sleepers and put the emerald studs in, half wishing she had a mirror to check herself out. She glanced at her reflection in the distant window, but she wasn't close enough to see much. Her reflection changed.

Kill him, or get out before he tries to kill you.

Anxiety coursed through Allura at Sparrow's words, but she couldn't react. Shaw would think she was insane.

The earrings were heavier than her sleepers, and the necklace was distinctly weighty as well. It felt awkward, like it was choking her, though it wasn't overly tight. Just close. She could easily get a couple of fingers between it and her neck.

Shaw followed her gaze to the window, examining her reflection with a critical eye. The emerald sat heavily in the hollow of her throat, uncomfortable and awkward.

"Why not just put me in a showgirl outfit?" she muttered.

He smirked. "Oh, that'll happen tomorrow, when you start in the Cancan Coffee Bar. You'll love it."

She wanted to die.

14

Hoping he wasn't serious, Allura turned away from Shaw and examined the framed sketches on the wall opposite his desk. Ten sketches across, five down. Forty-nine in all, with a space in the middle for one more.

All were head and shoulders portraits of women, none alike beyond a certain similarity to their expressions, if not features. Disdain perhaps, as if they were forever beyond mortal reach. Goddesses.

Most seemed to be northern European. A few were Asian and African, while a handful were probably from the Middle East or of mixed blood.

A cold shiver ran through Allura again. She knew those women. She stepped back as the feeling intensified. She'd never seen any of them as far as she could remember, but she recognised them all.

"Who are they?" Allura asked, her voice strangely soft and uncertain. "You knew them, didn't you?"

When Shaw didn't speak, she turned to find him watching her. "Yes. They're all women I met long before you were born," he said. "Mia explained about Creatures, I take it? Except for werewolves, we're all immortal."

"Something like that." She turned back to the portraits. "How do I know them?" she whispered, moving to the image at the top left. She reached out, but found herself reluctant to touch it.

The portrait captured the woman in her youth, someone of northern European heritage. She could have been from Finland or Norway or Sweden for all Allura knew. Another cold shiver ran through her.

"Who is she?" Allura asked, her hand trembling as she found the courage to touch the glass, leaving a single fingerprint on its surface.

The woman wasn't beautiful, but she had intense eyes and an expression somewhere between delight, sorrow, and strength. For that reason alone, she stood out amongst the others.

A name teased Allura's thoughts, tickling the edges of her consciousness. "Lumi," she whispered, turning back to Shaw. "Her name was Lumi, wasn't it? How do I know that?"

Shaw stared at her as if she'd found the password to all his bank accounts, and emptied them. "I..." he began, the word catching. He cleared his throat. "You need to leave."

Something on the shelves behind his desk caught her eye, a frame like those on the wall, tucked between two books. She walked to the shelves and pulled it free.

"Please don't," Shaw whispered, though he didn't try to stop her.

It was a hand-drawn image of herself, sketched in charcoal in the same style as those on the wall. "I..." she whispered. "Why me? Is this why... you've helped me all these years? Am I a project? Were they?" she asked, feeling anger rise. "Is that what they were to you as well? Are we all women you've tried to save?"

Shaw crossed the room and gently took the frame from her hand. "Leave. Please." The words had an edge of pain to them.

Allura stared up at him. "Who are they?" She knew, though, deep inside, the same way she'd known Lumi's name.

He clenched his free fist. "Please, Allura—"

"Why am I among them?" Allura asked, a hint of desperation in her anger.

He looked up and glared at her. "They're you!" he said with surprising heat. "They're all you!"

Allura backed a step. "I don't understand."

"Leave. Please."

TREMBLING with a feeling she couldn't quite name, Allura made her way down to the Atrium Bar and the press of people there. A cheer went up from one of the demonstration tables around the walls. Blackjack.

In the centre of the room behind the bar, the colourful butterflies circled in their floor to ceiling circular netting. Allura walked behind the bar and grabbed a bottle of vodka before pouring herself a double-shot. She knocked it down in a gulp and poured another, wishing her hands would stop trembling.

Why wouldn't he tell her? She'd recognised those women, even recalled Lumi's name.

She held her hand up, staring at her healed fingers. She began trembling again as the vodka turned sour in her stomach and a sickly feeling overwhelmed her. She put a hand over her mouth and ran to the bathroom, barely making it into a toilet cubicle before being violently sick.

Flushed and sweating, she spat the taste from her mouth, breathing hard, her left arm trembling where she held herself upright via the cubicle wall.

They were all her, somehow, every sketch had been of her. Is that what Sparrow kept hinting at? Was Allura really a Creature of some kind, destined to be reborn over and over with no memories of her past lives?

"Keep it together," Allura told herself. When she was certain she was done being sick, she flushed the toilet and left the cubicle. Sparrow stared back at her from the mirror above the washbasins.

"What the hell are you?" Allura asked Sparrow.

Sparrow smiled, madness there.

I'm you. I'm every incarnation rolled into one and given a persona, so you can be a coward and never have to face yourself. I'm every bitter ounce of anger and disgust and self-loathing you've ever had. I'm your hatred for the people who made us this way.

Allura pressed her sweaty palm against the mirror, covering Sparrow's face. "You're not me," she whispered, her voice rough with emotion.

Sparrow laughed.

No, I'm just I'm forty-nine incarnations of you. You're merely the latest.

"Incarnations?" she asked. When she removed her hand, Sparrow was gone. "Asshole," she muttered.

Allura washed her mouth out at the sink, facing herself in the mirror again. Her reflection was her own for only a heartbeat, but then it morphed back into Sparrow's snarky expression. This time, he was wearing a French beret and a cravat, both red.

So now you know what we are.

"Bullshit."

Would you have believed me if I'd told you a week ago? A month? A year?

"You're not me," she said bitterly. "I'd have told me, or tried to, at least."

Oh, I've tried hundreds of times, believe me.

A woman walked out of a nearby stall, giving Allura a wary glance.

With a final glare at Sparow, Allura left the bathroom, returning to the Atrium and giving the bar a wide berth. Even at a distance, the smell of alcohol turned her stomach.

She was almost at the casino's reception when someone put their hand out before her face, catching her attention. "Excuse me, but I'm looking for Allura Forsayeth."

Allura recognised the voice. "Quicksilver?" She looked up. Hell, it was Quicksilver.

He looked her over as if he didn't have a clue who she was. He wasn't exactly focusing on her, though. "Yes. I'm looking for Allura. Do you know where she is? She hasn't been answering her phone."

She stared at him as if he were an idiot. "It's me, dumbass."

He dropped his gaze to her. Frown lines creased his forehead until his eyes finally widened in recognition. "Allura? You look... different. Did you get Botox or something?"

"Thanks for the backhanded bitch-slap," she said. "No. I did not get Botox or something."

He opened his mouth, but cleared his throat instead of speaking. "The choker and earrings?" he asked with a questioning tone in his voice. "Maybe that's what's different?"

Allura raised an eyebrow. She didn't look that different, did she? She thought back to seeing her reflection in the mirror, all the hard living wiped from her features. Maybe she did.

"Um, can you please come down to the station? There's something we need to discuss."

Allura grasped the offer. If it meant getting out of the Menagerie, she'd go almost anywhere. "Sure. Where's your car?"

Quicksilver seemed a little surprised at her quick agreement. "In the big carpark near the markets. Street parking was full and I don't like using the basement here."

"Let's go." She'd promised Shaw she wouldn't leave the Menagerie without an escort, but Quicksilver covered that base even if Shaw had meant one of his own people.

"The bling's a bit tacky," he said as they started walking, grimacing at her twisted-gold necklace and earrings. "What's the deal? You don't normally wear junk jewellery. Any jewellery."

Yep, the choker and earrings probably did look tacky. "They sell them in the merch store," she muttered.

Sparrow, his beret now a dashing shade of blue, looked on from the glass doors as they left, a sneer in his expression. As she approached, his features morphed into a composite of all the lives she'd apparently lived over centuries, her own pain and hurt reflected back at her. She finally understood Sparrow now, or a part of him, at least.

"Go screw yourself," she muttered as she passed the glass doors.

"What's this about?" Allura asked as they were walking along the waterfront. Restaurants faced the water, their alfresco areas full of guests involved in alcohol-induced loud conversations. It was a warm evening, though the breeze coming off the water gave her a chill.

Quicksilver paused, his face illuminated by the lights from a nearby Italian restaurant. "An opportunity. Maybe." He clearly wanted to say more, but continued walking instead. Cutting between buildings, they crossed the road between the waterfront shops and the Old Bus Depot Markets. His car was in the open car park between them.

"So?" Allura asked once they were driving. "We're about as private as it'll get."

He glanced at her, looking her up and down, clearly having trouble reconciling the healthy woman beside him with the wreck of a woman he'd known for two decades. "I said I'd say nothing until you heard them out."

"Hear what?" She didn't like where this was going.

"Just remember, none of this was my idea." The drive to the station was quiet, Quicksilver refusing to elaborate, though Sparrow had plenty of snark working overtime. Allura stared through the windows in the desperate hope she might see Jenna. It was a short drive, far too short.

It felt awkward walking into the police station. The look and smell of the place brought back good memories, though. It was quiet, but Shaw's necklace drew plenty of looks.

Quicksilver led her into a small conference room, with four people waiting for her. Her heart-rate spiked when she saw Slade Mills, his expression neutral. His threats at the Menagerie returned, almost as sharp as the memory of Noah twisting the knife in her guts. Allura forced herself to take a deep, calming breath.

Of the other three, she only knew Lieutenant Larry Dayle Roy Jr. Two women in business suits were also there, but Allura had no idea how they were involved.

Larry was a good man, at least, but she hadn't seen him since quitting the force. He'd aged quite a bit. He didn't seem to notice she looked fresher, but Slade's eyes widened. He glanced from her face to Quicksilver's, a question there. Quicksilver shrugged and sat next to Larry, all of them now facing her.

It felt like an interrogation, not a chat.

"Take a seat please, Allura," Larry said. "This is Kelley and Sherinda from one of our special investigation units."

"Investigating what?" Allura asked as she sat, glad for the table and a couple of metres between herself and everyone else. The distance felt like a chasm, but one that wasn't nearly wide enough.

"The Menagerie," Kelley said. She was about fifty, hair dyed red but grey at the roots. Her olive complexion didn't fit well with the red hair.

"The Menagerie?" Allura pointed. "It's that way. Entry is free."

Kelley frowned, as did her companion. Slade narrowed his eyes, clearly not happy with her tone. At least he didn't say anything.

Sherinda was a little younger than Kelley, but she had the same hard look. Allura got the feeling the woman would happily bury her own children if it meant a promotion.

"Your employer, Lawrence Shaw, is under investigation for the murder of Jingyi Lee outside the Menagerie. There was also a recent incident in Fyshwick, which I'm sure you're aware of. A building was set on fire and several people murdered. We were hoping you might be able to provide some insight."

Allura did her best to keep her expression neutral, though the mention of Fyshwick dredged up the terror of being tortured by Noah, as well as her fears for Jenna's wellbeing. "I work in the bar, and I don't sleep with my boss. All I've got are the same rumours you're probably aware of, and they're hardly admissible in court."

Slade Mills leaned forward, his elbows on the table. "Allura," he began, but Larry held up a hand.

"Allura, would you like your old job back? Would you like to be a detective again? We're always short staffed, and you were a good cop."

Allura went still. How many times had she wished she'd never quit? "Who would I have to screw to make that happen?" she asked. "I mean, who would I have to screw over?"

She wouldn't betray Shaw, especially as vampires and werewolves were real. God knows what they'd do to her if she betrayed Shaw. Even Slade's earlier threat of prison couldn't compare to that.

"We just want to know if we're chasing the right man," Sherinda said.

Chasing? A sense of foreboding shadowed Allura's thoughts. "I highly doubt he's involved, if you really want my opinion. I think the body was a setup."

Kelley raised a doubtful eyebrow. "We're simply hoping you can provide some further insight into the issue," she added.

"Insight?" Allura asked, leaning forward with her elbows on the table between them. "How's this for insight? Search for a little thing called evidence," Allura said.

Slade narrowed his eyes, his expression threatening. His eyes went from her face to her necklace and back, as if he had some insight into the significance. Screw him. She should be looking for Jenna, not going halves in a conversation about betraying Shaw.

"We're sure the evidence is out there," Kelley said. "We just need your help in finding it."

Allura sat back again. "And I'm sure there's a tree out there trying very hard to supply your brain with oxygen. It's nowhere near this witch-hunt, though."

Quicksilver snorted a laugh, and even Larry seemed amused.

Slade pursed his lips. "Enough rubbish, Allura," Slade said, no more amused than Kelley and Sherinda. "What do you know?"

There was an 'or else' attached to that question. "I know you're asking me to stick a knife in Shaw's back and twist it until he screams out a fake confession."

Slade glanced at his colleagues. "May I have a word alone with Allura?" he asked. "Just a couple of minutes?"

Allura swallowed, her bravado vaporising into fear

which seemed to be pushing her stomach into her lungs. At least she'd already thrown up.

Kelley and Sherinda met each other's eyes, Sherinda finally nodding. They stood together. Quicksilver sighed, but stood as well.

Larry held out. He'd always had her back when she'd been a cop, and she was grateful for it. However, she didn't want him further involved in this. "I'll be fine," she told him, though she doubted she would be. Slade wanted Shaw's head, and she suspected he'd take hers if she couldn't find a way to give him what he really wanted. It was probably better than being torn apart by a werewolf, though.

Larry eventually nodded and stood as well. The four of them left, leaving Allura alone with Slade. Was this what it was like for a lion tamer to stick their head into a lion's jaws?

Allura wasn't a fan of the silence that followed. Slade finally pushed his chair back, stood, and carried it around the table to put it next to Allura's before sitting, his back to the observation window.

He kept his voice low. "The cameras and microphones in this room have been turned off, understand?"

"Comforting," Allura said nervously.

He smiled. "Then I'm certain this news will be even less so. I have CCTV footage of you chasing a girl through the rear yard of a business in Fyshwick last night, and more of what appears to be you riding a child's push-bike through the area."

Allura's stomach turned. "It wasn't me," she lied.

Slade took a deep breath and let it out slowly. "We've identified the girl as Jenna McLeod, a runaway girl missing for almost two years now. She's still missing. The only reason you're not getting arrested and questioned just now is because Larry, Quicksilver, and I vouched for you." He stared straight at Allura. "And now you have the hide to turn up here wearing a necklace worth more than the average suburban home while lying to my face. It doesn't take much to assume you're being paid to keep your mouth shut."

Allura resisted the urge to touch the necklace. To remove it. "Your beef's with Shaw, not me," Allura whispered. "And I didn't want the necklace. He made me take it. For protection, supposedly."

Slade sighed. "How about you stop playing dumb and tell me what you know? Nobody wants to see the big stick. We clear?"

Allura closed her eyes. "Clear."

"Then tell me what you know. I've been investigating human trafficking for nearly twenty years Allura, and I've met all sorts of nasty people I'm not fond of, Shaw amongst them." He pointed at her face. "What I've discovered is that people who suddenly look different aren't human anymore."

At her surprised look, he cocked his head.

"I'm human," she said, not exactly confirming she knew there were Creatures out there, but not denying it either."

"And I've got a gun loaded with silver bullets. Understand? I know about Creatures, and you're looking like a prime candidate right now."

She glanced down and realised he had his hand on the weapon at his hip. "I'm not a Creature," she repeated. She had no doubt he'd shoot her if she made a move.

"You've thrown in with Shaw, so forgive me if I take precautions."

"I got hurt. Bad. They gave me something to heal me. The necklace is to warn people that Shaw will come after them if they hurt me again. That's it."

"You got hurt? In Fyshwick?" Slade asked.

Allura nodded. "Near the wetlands." How much could

she get away with before being forced to tell him everything?

"What did they use to heal you?" he asked, sounding both intrigued and doubtful.

She could spill that much, at least. "They called it nectar."

He sat up straighter. "Nectar? That's rare, and very expensive. I've never seen it myself."

Allura grimaced. "That's what they told me. I was unconscious, though."

"I hear people pay millions for it," Slade said under his breath, seeming to consider the implications. "Do you know who supplies it?"

Allura shook her head. She wasn't going to mention Luci.

"Do you know how it's made, I mean?" he asked.

She shook her head again.

Slade leaned in closer, his voice soft. "Dryads drain humans of lifeforce and distil it into nectar. Nectar's made with murder."

"But..." she began, though she'd already been told much the same thing.

"If everything you say is true, then someone was murdered to make the nectar that healed you. It could have been a child or one of the girls from the massage parlour. Do you understand me? You consumed someone's lifeforce, and they died to give it to you. That's what Shaw does."

Allura swallowed in a dry throat. She felt nauseous. It was a good thing she'd only recently vomited.

"I suggest you think very hard about what you're going to say when everyone comes back in." He stood. "Help us please, Allura. We need you. Tell us about the raid and Shaw's involvement in Jingyi Lee's murder."

16

After the interview, Allura sat in Quicksilver's car, staring at the electronic bugs in the clear zip-lock bag in her hand. Her stomach churned as she tried to think of a way out of her agreement to plant them where Shaw did most of his business.

"You okay?" Quicksilver asked.

She looked up, feeling disembodied. "No."

She'd been part of the crew that had raided the brothel. She was okay with that, or at least the intention. What she was conflicted about was the possibility she may have helped sacrifice young women to dryads to make nectar. Nectar worth millions. She didn't know who'd told her the truth.

Why would Shaw waste it on you?

She glanced at the window, Sparrow staring back with one eyebrow raised. She could only think of one answer, represented by fifty faces on the wall of his office.

He wants to possess you. How's the choker fit? Feels like a collar to me.

Allura tried to ignore Sparrow, but she was thinking the same thing. Why would Shaw waste nectar worth millions on her?

She focused on the bugs. So small and easy to hide, and their batteries would last weeks. Rather than dwell on the question, she slipped the pack inside her bra. Nobody was likely to go looking for them there, unfortunately.

"You're doing a good thing, Allura. Shaw's a criminal."

"He is," she agreed, wishing she wasn't so torn. Why did she feel such a strong obligation towards him? Because he'd helped her, that's why. He'd given her money and a job, protected her secrets, and didn't interfere in her life. He'd saved her life, and not just with the nectar. In return, he'd asked nothing of her other than to wear a necklace.

"If we can put him behind bars, you'll be free," Quicksilver said. "No more debt. You could be a cop again."

"No more debt," Allura repeated, wishing that was enough. She owed Shaw, and now she was betraying him. Could she? Would she? She touched her necklace, tracing the edges of the emerald with her fingertips. She owed Shaw everything.

He deserves what you're doing. He murdered some of our incarnations.

Allura glanced at the window, frowning at Sparrow's reflection. It was dusk now, and she could barely see his reflection. Sparrow almost sounded triumphant, like her actions were a done deal and the outcome assured.

"Incarnations," she repeated. The reality was sinking in. She was more involved in this world than she knew.

"Why don't I take you home?" Quicksilver suggested.

It took her a moment to realise he was talking about her apartment, not the Menagerie. Her apartment had never felt like home, not the way the Menagerie did.

"No. If I'm going to plant these bugs, it has to be tonight, or I'll lose my nerve. Take me to the Menagerie." She suspected she'd already lost her nerve. She'd give the bugs to Shaw the moment she saw him. If she had to pick a side, it was going to be his.

"Okay," he said uncertainly.

"Can we drive around a bit first?" Allura asked. Maybe she'd spot Jenna. "I don't want to go back yet, and I don't want to go home. I need a bit of time to think things through."

Quicksilver gave her a glance. "I don't mind if you back out. This is bloody dangerous, and if I'd known what they were going to ask, I'd have... well, I wouldn't have offered to pick you up, at least."

"Thanks." She meant it.

"You understand Shaw might have you killed if you're caught?"

Allura glanced at Sparrow. He just raised an eyebrow. "Better than you know," she said.

SHIVERING, cold, and wet, Jenna crept into some bushes to keep hidden. She had no money and smelled of lake water, the latter a good disguise from werewolves, at least in a city full of thousands of different smells.

Even if she wanted to leave the city, there weren't many options to get out of town other than stealing a car, but she didn't know how to drive. That left public transport or hitching a ride.

Noah's people might be watching the bus station, and she was too afraid to hitchhike in case she got into a car with one of Noah's wolves. They'd be watching the roads leaving the city.

She could walk until she dropped, though. How far could she walk each day? How long would it take her to get to Sydney? Why would she even try when her mother was still here, looking for her?

Hopefully.

They'd bonded, but Jenna didn't know the woman. She knew how she felt, though, and she knew it was mutual.

She had to find her mother. Nothing else mattered.

Tonight she'd lie low and rest. Tomorrow she'd be strong again. Tomorrow after sunrise, Noah's wolves would fear her, not she them.

"So, are you going to tell me about that necklace?" Quicksilver asked.

Sparrow snickered, clearly enjoying her discomfort.

"No."

"No?" Quicksilver replied, annoyance and disbelief in his tone. "I'm your best friend."

She owed him that, at least. "It was a gift," she said, hoping that would do. "Protection. A signal to... never mind." She was stressed enough about Jenna without having to worry about Quicksilver's feelings, or nectar, or the fact Slade could crucify her via the legal system if he wanted to.

Tell him you're Shaw's pet.

"I'm no-one's pet."

Quicksilver gave her a sideways glance. "I was watching Slade's face. He couldn't take his eyes off the necklace."

"Like I said. A gift." Her tone was a little harsh, but it wasn't a question she knew how to answer.

You've been collared.

She shuddered at the thought. If Sparrow kept this up, she'd wind the window down.

"Explain 'gift'. That thing's worth more than I'd make in years."

"You can have it." She unclipped the heavy choker and held it out to him, emerald dangling. "Seriously, take it. I didn't ask for it and I don't want it. Consider it re-gifted."

"Yeah, and Shaw wouldn't send his goons after me and my family to get it back," he said sarcastically. "Put it back on."

Allura considered stuffing the choker into Quicksilver's pocket, but reluctantly clipped it back around her neck. If she was going to return to the Menagerie, she'd have to be wearing it, she supposed.

Shaw wanted her safe, and staying safe was the best thing she could do for Jenna. Jenna, a girl she didn't know, yet wanted to know intimately. Her daughter. It still sounded ridiculous when she thought about it, but understanding the situation didn't change how she felt.

She knew the agony of losing someone she'd bonded with, and she wouldn't put Jenna through that. How long before Noah's wolves found Jenna? She needed to do more, like turn the city upside down and shake it until Jenna fell out.

"Would you prefer a cafe or bar rather than driving around a bit?" Quicksilver asked.

Allura shuddered at the thought of a bar. "I think I've developed an allergy to alcohol, and it's too late for a coffee. Besides, I don't want to be around strangers."

Where was Jenna? Alone and hunted, she must be sick with fear. Allura could imagine the girl's terror as an echo of sickness in her own stomach.

"Sure. While we cruise, how about we talk about how you can safely plant those bugs? Or you could just get out of town."

If she planted those bugs, she might as well use Shaw's necklace to choke herself to death and be done with it. Whatever had happened between herself and Shaw in the past no longer mattered. She wasn't any of those women, even if she might have been them.

"Would you mind cruising around the university? It's been a long time since I studied there and I'm feeling a little nostalgic."

Nostalgic my ass. Why not just tell him you're an incubus's bitch on the hunt for a shapeshifter who vanished near the lake, and the university's close to the lake?

Allura scratched her temple with her middle finger aimed at Sparrow.

Oh, I'm hurt. I may never recover.

An hour of driving around the campus and some of the places did leave Allura with a little nostalgia, but she was no less fearful for Jenna. She saw several people on foot who didn't seem to fit in the area, though. One of them sniffed the air before wrinkling her nose and sneezing like she'd just inhaled a bug.

Friend or foe? The woman could have just as easily been one of Kyle's people as Noah's or Teddy Bear's. At least Allura would recognise the Menagerie's werewolves, not that she'd seen any in this area. Where were they? Watching the shelters? Searching the other town centres?

Quicksilver eventually turned back toward the Menagerie, leaving Allura frustrated. She wanted to keep searching.

"Are you working tonight?" he asked. "I'm assuming you're not on dawn patrol. Are you hoping to get drunk?"

"No," she replied a little distractedly, as she scanned the streets. "I've got bugs to plant, remember?"

"Just making conversation. You haven't said much more than boo in the last hour."

She sighed. Conversation was something that normally required alcohol. "How's Wendy and the kids?"

He snorted, clearly not liking her choice of topic. "Wendy wants me to quit the force. Says it's too dangerous and the hours suck."

"She's not wrong," Allura replied as they crossed King's Avenue Bridge. The National Carillon was lit up to their right, and the Parliament House loomed directly ahead. Once over the bridge, Quicksilver veered left toward the Kingston Foreshores and the Menagerie.

"You can drop me at the entrance. No need to come in."

"I wasn't planning on coming in."

The car's tire blew, sending a thrill of fear through Allura.

The wheel spun from Quicksilver's grip and the car lurched. He swore and over-corrected.

Allura grabbed the Jesus Bar above the door as Quicksilver fought the wheel, jerked it back straight and over-corrected again. They smashed over the gutter, another tire blowing, and bounced hard before slamming into a tree.

Allura's airbag smashed into her face, nearly breaking her nose. She moaned, raising her head and blinking, her chest aching where the seatbelt had saved her from launching through the window. The car's front had crumbled in toward her. Quicksilver moaned, a gash sending blood down his face. He didn't move.

Allura tried to speak and failed. She'd split her lip and her front teeth ached. As she turned her head, the world spun, and she struggled not to pass out. Fumbling to undo her seatbelt, she managed to get it loose after several tries, but before she could gather herself, the door opened and big meaty hands dragged her from the wreck.

She tried to cry out, but someone stuffed a cloth into her mouth and gagged her before shoving her head into a sack.

17

With the sun finally warming the bushes screening Jenna's bed of leaves and mulch, she cautiously moved branches aside, squinting into the morning light. She hadn't slept much, being too afraid a werewolf might sneak up on her, while heroin withdrawal made her muscles ache and her body restless.

She relaxed a bit when she couldn't see anyone about, and couldn't hear anything but birds and insects.

After a minute, she found the courage to struggle out from her hiding place, scratching herself on twigs before brushing dirt and leaves from her clothes and hair. Crossing her arms and hunching in on herself as if it would make her smaller, she grimaced at the bright morning light and began walking, making sure to move close to any garbage bins to help hide her scent.

As she passed a park bench with three young men sitting and eating breakfast, one spoke. "Big night too?" he asked.

Jenna jumped. They were probably about five years older than her, all three watching her pass. One was finishing the last few mouthfuls of kebab while the other two sipped coffee with toasties in their laps.

Hoping to look normal, Jenna forced a smile to disguise a growing headache, fever, and chills. "I'm fine," she said, her voice a little rough from disuse.

"You sure?" one of the coffee drinkers asked, possibly suspecting she was more than just a little hungover. He was the biggest of the three, and he put his toasty aside as he stood up with genuine concern. "Did someone hurt you? Do you need help?"

Jenna shook her head, not giving him an opening to approach as she walked away. He looked like a nice guy, but he'd only get hurt if Noah's people found her.

After crossing the campus, she reached the edge of the city centre and cut through a multi-story carpark. Thousands of people parked there every week, layering the concrete with car fumes, spilled drinks, and dropped food, as well as their body odours. It should be enough to disguise anyone's scent from a werewolf.

Beyond the carpark, she moved between tall office buildings, avoided alleyways, and kept to high-traffic areas where werewolves couldn't snatch her. Although being in the city was a risk, she tried to hide in plain sight where they'd least expect her.

Hoping against all logic she might stumble across her mother and having no idea what else to do, Jenna passed a cafe catering to people grabbing their breakfast and coffee before work. She was certain she'd know her mother when she saw her, but the risk of being seen by one of Noah's wolves stopped her from lingering and checking out everyone. She didn't want to be remembered either, just in case the wolves were asking.

Instead, she watched groups from across streets while

partially hidden by cars and evenly spaced trees, moved among people waiting for busses, and generally tried not to attract any attention. She lowered her face when she couldn't observe people discretely and walked on before anyone had a chance to notice her.

It was a fool's mission made worse by a heroin comedown, but what choice did she have? Leave town? Where would she go?

Growing tense with chills and fever, she kept walking despite the desire to crawl into a dark place and never wake up again.

If only she knew something about her mother. That she was still alive was all their bond told her. She felt no pull in any direction or had any sense of distance, just comfort in knowing someone cared and wanted to find Jenna as much as Jenna wanted to find them.

Raiding a bin a couple of hours into her wonderings, she found a threadbare denim jacket with patches on the chest and back. She put it on as much for the smell of someone else clinging to it as the fact it disguised her filthy top. It also helped hide her shivering, the morning's growing heat making her appeared fevered.

By midmorning, she was struggling with a filthy headache and cramping muscles, but tried to stay alert as the day grew hotter. She found a tap and filled her empty stomach with water, though she drank so fast it made her feel sick.

When her stomach settled down, she cupped both hands and washed her face so she didn't look too bad. She needed a brush to do her dirty hair but found a lost scrunchie, which she used to tie it into a ponytail. Hopefully, it would make her less memorable. Shoes would help, though being summer, she wasn't the only person with bare feet.

Far too soon, hunger and exhaustion caught up with her. She needed to find somewhere safe to rest and regain her strength.

Even a werewolf as big as Noah wouldn't take her on alone until nightfall, but if a group of them found her, she'd have little chance as weak as she was. Come nighttime, she'd be just as vulnerable as any human.

She had to find her mother before then, but all she knew was that she was a blonde woman a little shorter than Jenna, and at least twice Jenna's age. She'd seen a dozen women who matched that description already.

When several people at a cafe started watching her pass, Jenna decided it was time to leave the city and find somewhere safe to rest for a while.

Trembling with fatigue and muscle aches, she kept going until she found a block of flats a kilometre or two north-east of the city centre. It was around midday, the sun high and hot, but the two-story buildings were built around central carparks that offered shade and privacy.

Jenna collapsed against a wall beside someone's rusting car, hidden from sight. There were cobwebs on the rear-view mirror, so she doubted anyone would approach. It was as safe as anywhere she was likely to find. She drew her legs to her chest and rested her forehead on her knees, quickly falling into an exhausted sleep.

She didn't know how long she slept, but the sun was low in the sky when someone prodded her shoulder. "You okay?"

Jenna started in fear, but was so exhausted she was slow to open her eyes. A woman crouched beside her. She was gaunt and had a missing front tooth, lined cheeks, and grey-streaked hair. The fresh tracks up her arms were a testament to her life story. She looked better than Jenna felt, though.

Beside the woman's feet rested two shopping bags, one bulging with soft drinks and packets of chips, the other with a six-pack of beer and a large pack of home-brand peanuts.

She held one hand out, her skin stretched over too-thin arms, thin blue veins and sunspots standing out. "You look like you could use a place to rest and maybe a little pick-me-up. I got friends. Come on."

18

Allura opened her eyes to a dim room, a pounding headache, and aching shoulders. She vaguely remembered fighting back when they'd forced her into a car, but someone had clubbed her into submission and hogtied her.

She tried moving, only to discover her arms were still bound tightly behind her back and her ankles tied to them. Everything hurt, though at least they'd put her on a mattress.

She took a breath, braced herself against the pain in her shoulders, and struggled against the ropes until they cut into her flesh, causing more pain. "Shit, shit, shit," she whispered, adrenalin rising on growing fear. At least the gag and hood had been removed.

Lifting her face as best she could, she looked for a knife or something sharp, but the small room was empty except for the mattress and some disused shelves directly in front of her. A small light illuminated the space from above. It was probably a disused storeroom.

She couldn't see Quicksilver, and that scared her more

than her own situation. What had they done to him? Hopefully, he'd gotten away. Hopefully.

Her face and nose still ached from the explosive force of the airbag, but at least it had saved her from smashing her face on the dashboard. Her chest hurt from the seatbelt, though.

She swore again. Sparrow would have said something more appropriate, and scathing, if he'd been visible. Well, she deserved it. Shaw had told her not to leave without an escort and she got around it on a technicality, even if it was official police business.

The door opened, shedding bright light into the small room. Allura squinted and cringed as three people entered. Her bowels almost loosened when she realised one was Noah, and another the woman who'd gone after Jenna. Like going into labour a second time, the memories of Noah's torture came back full force.

She didn't recognise the third person, a man with a mullet and the sides of his head shaved. He was gaunt and skinny, with narrow shoulders, despite being nearly as tall as Noah. When he saw Allura, he smiled like he wanted to skin her alive. She shivered. She'd met her fair share of sadists, and this guy looked like he could teach them all a few tricks.

"I told you," the man said to Noah, his voice pitched a little too high for such a tall man. "They did something to her. She's totally healed." The smile he gave Allura suggested he'd have done much worse than gut her. "She's still human too. I can smell it."

Allura stared at the floor in front of her, shuddering at the prospect of what that man might do if allowed. Far worse than Noah, she suspected.

"What do you smell, Penelope?" Noah asked.

Penelope crouched beside Allura, taking a deep breath. She crinkled her nose and grimaced. "Fear and... tainted lifeforce?" She looked over her shoulder, frowning. "She's still human, though. I don't get it."

"Nectar," Noah said. "I thought it was a myth. It didn't just heal her. She looks younger by a year or two."

Noah went to one knee beside Penelope. Penelope stood and backed away, her expression hinting she wanted to spit bile after smelling Allura.

Noah drew a long hunting knife from a sheath at his hip. A rush of fear coursed through Allura as he touched her choker with the knife's tip. She leaned away as far as she could, which wasn't much, and tried not to look shit scared.

Epic fail.

"Touch her while she's wearing Shaw's trinket and he'll have his pack hunt us until we're all dead," Penelope said.

Noah's eyes widened with anticipation. "Bring it on," he said. "I'm spoiling to match it up to Teddy Bear. Besides, the boss will sort out Shaw soon enough. After that, I'll take Teddy Bear's pack and Shaw's territory. About time we had our own turf."

"Noah—"

"Keep your mouth shut and your legs open, got it, Penelope?"

Penelope dropped her eyes. "Yes, Noah." It was hard to tell with her dark skin, but Allura thought the woman flushed with shame. Maybe anger. Probably both. It was something Allura might be able to exploit if she got the opportunity.

Noah touched the tip of his knife to Allura's lips. If she could have moved back any further, she would have. Instead, she forced herself to give him a defiant glare, which seemed to amuse him.

"Let's see if nectar can regrow body parts, shall we?"

Considering what he'd done to her before, she was fully prepared to take him at his word. "It won't. It's all gone."

Noah grinned. "In that case, we'll send Shaw just enough of you, so there's no doubt we have his little bitch. You'd better hope he's willing to trade what's left for our tiger cub." He tapped Allura's necklace with the knife again. "And if that fails, we'll send him your choker with it still around your neck, minus the lower half of your body."

Allura spoke with a trembling voice. "He doesn't have her."

"I've seen his wolves out looking for Jenna," Penelope confirmed.

"Where's Quicksilver?" Allura asked.

Noah cocked his head as he studied her, perhaps assessing how many scars he could put on her face without killing her. "Shaw doesn't have our cub now, but that could change. I'm betting he'd trade our cub for his bitch." He slid the knife along Allura's choker, the sound of metal scraping metal too close to the artery in her neck for comfort. "Oh, Quicksilver's dead," he added helpfully. "It happens when you drive a car into a tree. Consider him lucky, and yourself less lucky."

Grief hit her like a slap. "No," she whispered, blinking tears.

She wanted to fake confidence, nonchalance, but all she felt was grief. Facing the man who'd slowly pushed a knife into her stomach left her nauseous with fear, but she did her best to glare despite the tears running down her cheeks. "Shaw won't trade me for Jenna, so why not just slit my throat now?"

Noah actually smiled. "Hell bitch, if I knew you had this much spunk, I might have recruited you myself." He turned to Penelope. "What do you say? Need a little more female company in the pack? Shall I give her a love bite?"

Penelope shook her head. "I doubt she'll make a loyal pack member, considering you tortured her." Her tone was respectful, but the words were laced with truth.

Noah grinned. "Oh, but it'd be so much fun breaking her, wouldn't it?" Rather than wait for a response, Noah gripped Allura's ponytail in one hand and sliced it off. Her remaining hair spilled about her cheeks.

"Asshole," she swore, bucking against the ropes. She wasn't sure whether to be relieved or not. Hair grew back. Body parts didn't. If that was all he was going to send to Shaw, she considered herself lucky.

Noah threw the ponytail to Penelope, the hair still bound together. "What shall we send with it? Her tongue? One of her eyes?"

Fear crashed into Allura head-on, cutting through her grief and making sweat break out all over. He'd do it. She knew he would. "Please don—"

Noah forced the tip of the knife into her mouth, slicing her lip open. Allura cried out, the cool metal hard against her tongue. Unable to speak, Allura met his eyes with a glare she hoped might murder him, but fear betrayed her true emotions

His grin broadened. "You really do have spunk. Wanna be one of us? You could take Penelope's place as alpha bitch if you prove worthy."

She would have replied, but the knife in her mouth threatened to slice her tongue open if she tried.

The way Noah watched her suggested he got off on her defiance. He shifted the knife, forcing her to raise her head to better meet his eyes. "I heard you were a worthless alcoholic on a fast track to liver rot, but you're a fighter, aren't you? No wonder Shaw keeps you around. What do you do for him? You sell the drunken act well, but that's a ruse, isn't it? Does it help you go unnoticed? What's he promised you? What do you get out of it?"

Unable to talk without cutting her tongue, Allura kept her defiant glare as best she could. Pathetically.

"Ryker, what shall we send with the hair? I'm thinking her tongue, but tongues are messy. I can be talked into something else. Maybe a couple of toes?"

"Her ear. Let me do it, please boss. I never get any of the fun jobs," Ryker said with an intensity that scared Allura. He watched her like he was salivating.

Noah must have seen the fear on Allura's face. He smiled. "Her ear? I think Allura would appreciate that more than her tongue. What do you say, Allura? Ear, tongue, or toes?"

If it wasn't for Noah's knife in her mouth, she'd have begged.

Noah glanced at the middle of her back. "Let's send a thumb. That purple nail polish is quite distinctive. After that, we'll send Shaw a new body part every day until we get our cub back."

Ryker smiled as if all his birthday presents had come at once. "Can I do it? Can I hurt her a little bit too? Just a little?"

Allura broke out in a sweat. "Please," she garbled the whisper around Noah's knife. Noah might be a sadist, but this Ryker looked like a true psychopath.

Noah slipped the knife from Allura's mouth and stood, somehow not cutting her. "Sure, but no exposed marks in case we have to trade her face-to-face." He slapped the knife's handle into Ryker's palm.

Allura struggled against the ropes as dread gripped her.

"Make sure she pisses her pants the next time she lays eyes on you. Got it?"

Ryker nodded, his intense stare never leaving Allura. "She'll do more than piss herself."

19

Ryker pressed his knee hard into Allura's back between her shoulder-blades, pinning her to the mattress. He leaned in. "We're going to have so much fun," he said.

She grunted, gritting her teeth in pain as his knee dug in hard enough to bruise her. "Get off me," she hissed, doing her best to pull her hands free from the ropes, but only causing more pain.

Ryker grabbed a handful of her remaining hair and hacked it off close to her scalp, some of it coming out by the roots. Allura bucked, but couldn't dislodge him.

The bastard sprinkled her hair on the floor where she could see. "Oops," he said. "Some of your hair fell out."

Allura bucked again, desperate to dislodge him, but he forced his knee harder into her back. She whimpered. Not easing up at all, he hacked another tuft of hair away.

"You shit-stinking wet fart," she hissed. "I'm going to shove all that hair so far up your ass you'll be flossing your teeth with it."

He hacked off more hair, humming as he went, and

stuffed a tuft in her mouth as if to spite her. She spat it out, but it didn't stop him hacking more and throwing it around the room like confetti. He kept going until there was nothing left to grab, her hair lost in a third-rate buzz cut.

Allura was almost crying by the time he lifted his knee off her. "I'm going to kill you," she whispered.

He stood beside the mattress, looking down at her like he'd only just began his games. "I heard you were a cop. Murder sounds a bit unreasonable for a cop."

"Untie me and we'll see just how far I'll go," Allura swore, her anger a front for her fear and grief.

He cocked his head, turning half towards the door and listening. Allura followed his gaze but couldn't see or hear anything.

He took two strides to the door and ripped it open. A big man fell through, crashing to the ground as if he'd been leaning on the door. Another man stood behind the first, fear on his face. He backed a couple of steps.

Ryker grabbed the fallen man by his hair, hauled him to his feet, and drove the blade into his stomach, then again, and again. The man made a pathetic sound as his knees buckled, but Ryker kept him upright by his hair.

"If you want to cream yourself over my work, how about you do it in person?"

He pulled the knife free and drove it in again, and then once more. He hauled the man back to the door on useless legs and shoved him into his friend's arms, pulling the blade free at the same time. "Go find your own bitch to torture," he said, and then slammed the door closed.

Allura stared at Ryker in abject fear now, all her sass fleeing. She knew what a knife to the stomach felt like and broke out in a cold sweat as the blade dripped blood to the floor. Ryker smiled as he turned and slammed the bloody blade through the door as if a message to the men who'd been there a moment ago. A tiny trickle of blood ran a few centimetres down the dirty white door.

"Please..." Allura began with a shaking voice. Please what? Please don't hurt me? Please let me go? Please leave me alone? She already knew the answers.

Ryker returned and lowered himself to the mattress, both knees pushing it down beside her. "Time for a little pain," he said. "You like pain, don't you?"

He caught her left hand where it was bound behind her back, took a hold of her thumb and bent it inwards on itself until Allura screamed.

"Once more?" he asked, as if they were doing something pleasant. He put pressure on her thumb again and she failed to stifle another scream. Fresh tears ran down her cheeks.

He released her hand and stood, silently padding to the door and putting his ear against it, listening.

Her sweat reeked of her fear and she couldn't stop trembling. Ryker really was insane. Actually insane. No wonder Noah kept him around. Allura almost wished Noah were torturing her instead.

When Ryker turned, he raised a finger to his lips and met Allura's eyes. All that insanity and sadism she'd seen before vanished.

She stared, wondering what new torture he was planning now. Was he going to pretend to be her friend before slitting her throat?

Ryker began untying her hands. "Don't speak," he whispered. "Understand?"

Uncertain how to respond, Allura just nodded. When he finished untying her, he helped ease her arms out from behind her back. Her shoulders ached, and she whimpered pathetically as blood returned to her hands.

He put a finger to his lips again and leaned in close to whisper. "Don't speak, just listen. I'm trying to get you out of here, but if they don't hear screaming, they'll know something's up and we'll both be killed. I'm really sorry."

"Uh," she began, but couldn't think of anything more to say.

"You haven't seen half of what Noah's capable of. I'm going to help you, but I have one condition—Shaw and his cronies don't come after me or Penelope, got it? Not now. Not ever. That's the condition."

Allura rolled to her side and edged away until her back pressed against the wall. Her legs were still tied, but having her arms free felt like a victory. Unfortunately, she was as far from Ryker as she could manage. She cradled her aching thumb. "I'm not stupid."

He stared at her hand. "Your thumb's not damaged and your hair will grow back," he whispered. "Can you... trust me for a second?"

Allura glanced at the door. Stabbing the man hadn't seemed like much of a means of getting on her good side. "Yeah, sure. Bestest buddies in all the world?"

He narrowed his eyes. "This place is full of werewolves and they've got very good hearing. If you want to speak, for God's sake, whisper."

That, at least, she believed. "What do you want from me?" Allura whispered, hoping to string this out for as long as possible. She'd had enough torture for one lifetime. "Besides asking Shaw not to murder you to death?"

He raised an eyebrow. "Murder me to death?"

"Whatever."

Frustration flirted with a solid attempt not to murder her as far as Allura could tell. At least, if he lost his temper and did kill her, it'd be quick.

"Noah's working for someone. I don't know who, but they promised him free run of the city if he helps screw Shaw over. And hurt you, for some reason. I don't know what game they're playing with the tiger girl, but this isn't Noah's game. Whoever Noah works for has a grudge."

"And I'm a bargaining chip?"

"You want out of here or not?"

"I want Jenna safe," Allura said before she realised she'd just shown her hand. She cursed inwardly. She wasn't this stupid unless she was drunk.

He frowned, clearly considering her words. "What's the tiger cub to you?"

"I used to be a cop. We help people."

Ryker's frown remained as he studied her face, clearly not buying it, but then shrugged. "Keep your secrets," he said. "You can't help her if you're here. You want out, or are we going to debate choices?"

"I want out," Allura said cautiously, hoping that maybe, just maybe, this conversation might be genuine.

"If I help get you out, you need to keep me and Penelope out of Shaw's hands when this is done. Agreed?"

"Deal," she said. If this was even half legit, she'd wouldn't trust him until she was back at the Menagerie, but she'd keep her word if it was true.

"Make it a promise. Promise me you'll do whatever it takes to keep me and Penelope safe."

It seemed like a pretty good bargain. "Get me out of here and I promise to help keep you and Penelope safe from Shaw." She shivered.

"Give me your hand." When she hesitated, he reached out and caught her wrist, his size and strength far too much for her to fight off. He applied the same thumb lock to her, like before.

Allura screamed until he released her. "Fucking bastard! Go shove that silver tongue up your ass!" She clutched her aching thumb to her chest.

Ryker pulled a foil-wrapped object from his back pocket and placed it on the mattress between them. Undoing it, he revealed Allura's phone. "I had to wrap it so Shaw couldn't trace its location."

Allura reached for it, but he gripped her hand and squeezed until she screamed again. When he released her, she snatched her hand back, holding it to her chest. It ached.

"If you don't scream regularly, someone might come to check." Ryker held a finger to his lips as he nodded towards the door. "Will that magic nectar stuff grow back an amputated thumb?"

A shiver of fear ran through Allura. She glanced from the phone to Ryker, wondering if she could get it and make a call before he killed her. "Please..."

He caught her by the neck and squeezed. "It's going to take Shaw a couple of hours to get organised and mount a rescue, even if you call him now. We've got maybe five minutes before Noah starts asking why I haven't brought him your thumb. Understand?"

Allura didn't bother trying to pry his hand from her neck. If she passed out, it'd be a blessing. He released her and drew another knife from behind his back where his belt was. It wasn't as big as Noah's, but it was big enough to do plenty of damage.

"We have to buy Shaw enough time to get here with force, and that's not going to happen in the next ten minutes. You know of a better way than to give Noah what he wants?"

"Go drink horse piss."

He released a frustrated sigh. "I can't keep playing the part of Noah's psychopathic offsider. He's already killed three of my best friends, and Penelope's the only person I still care about. If I take your thumb, do we still have a deal?"

Allura stared at the phone for long seconds. "Yes."

He snatched at her left hand, and after a brief struggle, he hauled her half off the mattress by the wrist. Pressing her palm to the floorboards, and pinned her wrist under his knee.

Allura screamed as her bones came close to fracturing under his knee. Almost hyperventilating, she tried to twist away, only to cry out once more.

"I know you're not a Creature, but you still promised. You better keep your promise."

"Screw you!"

She watched in helpless horror as he pried her left thumb away from her fingers, and then she screamed in agony as he cut it free.

S haw stopped a hundred metres down the street from the abandoned suburban shops, pinching his temples with thumb and middle finger. He thought about the *gifts* he'd received shortly after Allura had called to give him her address.

Suburban streetlights shed small pools of visibility up and down the road, as did some of the homes with gaps in curtains and blinds. They didn't shed much light on the fenced-off buildings.

"You smell her too?" Teddy Bear asked.

Shaw shook his head, tension rising at the risks he was taking in coming here. "No. I was thinking about Allura's thumb and hair, and how I want to murder the bastard who removed them from her. I have lots of regrets, Ted. Lifetimes worth of them. Let's not let this get any worse than it is. Your pack in position yet?"

Shaw wore black clothes and a black beanie despite the warmth, and a neck gaiter could be pulled up to cover his face below his eyes. Everyone else wore the same. Even disguised, it was still a risk being here.

Teddy Bear took a deep breath and held it. They were downwind from the derelict shops and kept at bay by the chain-link fence surrounding the old buildings. There was a sign out front calling for community consultation on a proposed site redevelopment, making it a perfect place for a feral pack of werewolves to hole up while bureaucracy kept the buildings unused.

"I recognise a few scents," Teddy Bear said as he released his breath. "Noah's. Penelope's. A couple of others. But not Allura's. Not from here, at least. If she's inside, they haven't allowed her out. I can smell about a dozen wolves all up, but I've got no idea how many are inside at the moment."

"Take no risks you don't have to," Shaw said. "We go in and out without disturbing the neighbours. Knives only. No guns."

It wouldn't take much noise for someone to call the police, and that would complicate everything. There were suburban homes across the street and a small car park out front of the derelict shops, but it was quiet otherwise.

Shaw had eight wolves with him, including Teddy Bear. Luci was in position across the street to the rear of the building. "I want prisoners if you can manage it," he said. "We need to know who Noah's working for. This won't end until we figure that out."

"And Ryker? We just let him go?"

Shaw nodded. "That was the agreement." It galled him to lose someone with so much insight into Noah's intentions, but he'd agreed. "Him and Penelope, assuming they're inside. If what Allura said is true, there's only four other werewolves, and one of them was injured."

"Or it's a trap and we're being played," Teddy Bear said.

Shaw studied the buildings. "There's no obvious surveillance, and no vehicles nearby to indicate the place is being used." The windows had black plastic sheeting preventing any light from escaping, but that was it. "They're keeping their presence quiet here, like they're hiding out. Give the word to go in."

Teddy Bear touched his earpiece. "Go."

Seven werewolves sprinted toward the fence, slipping through a vertically-cut section behind some bushes. Shaw pulled his gaiter up and ran after Teddy Bear, looking for signs of an ambush.

By the time he reached the fence, Teddy Bear and the other wolves were already at the rear doors. There were four shops in the one building, and four rear doors. He had no idea if any internal doors joined up the premises on the inside. He hated splitting his people up, but there weren't many other options.

Teddy Bear smashed through the first door and Shaw followed him in. It was dark inside, the place reeking of dry mould and stale air but not people.

A window smashed in another building, followed by a lot of swearing. By the time he got there, the raid was over, the werewolves holed up within having changed form and run off like scared rabbits.

He swore. He wanted to question them.

"I found her!" someone called from another shop.

Allura was lying on a mattress on the floor of a disused storeroom. Her head had been shaved, her left hand poorly bandaged, and the smell of her blood remained in the musty air. Relief broke some of Shaw's tension when he saw her alive and breathing, though she appeared to be unconscious.

As he approached, he noticed a couple of bloody nicks on her scalp had crusted with blood. Allura looked up at him before closing her eyes with a relieved sigh. By the time he got to her, she was unconscious.

What the hell was he going to do with her? She'd become a significant liability, the necklace still around her neck doing nothing to protect her.

He lifted her into his arms and stood, surprised at how little she weighed. "You've got two minutes," he told Teddy Bear. "Find anything you can and then get out. I'll meet you back at the Menagerie."

SHAW WATCHED ALLURA, the lines of her face softer in sleep. Other than to send her away until the issue with Jenna was resolved, and maybe longer, he didn't have a clue what to do with her.

Luci, as silent as ever, approached and put a hand on his shoulder. "I can watch her for a bit. You need rest."

He grimaced. He needed more than sleep. He needed to know why Allura continued to appear in his life, incarnation after incarnation. He'd tried everything he could to resolve things between them, but she kept coming back, their fates intertwined.

Allura moaned in her sleep and he almost stood. She took a deep shuddering breath, holding on as if in pain. He didn't relax again until she released her breath. "Fifty incarnations and I still can't accept her mortality," he said softly. "I've even made her a Creature three times."

Luci's hand squeezed, the taint of her vampiric lifeforce seeping through his jacket. "She was killed?"

"Twice. The other time she did it herself."

Luci's hand vanished. "She needs nectar," she said,

pulling a small vial from a pocket. "Even then, it may take time for her thumb to grow back."

"Is that all you have?"

She smiled grimly. "There's a few potential victims I'd be happy to trade to the dryads for more."

"Be careful. I've never met a dryad I trusted."

"They're like everyone else. Some are trustworthy. Some aren't." Luci put the small vial on the bedside table. "It's not urgent this time. Give it to her when she wakes."

Allura's roughly hacked off hair and patchy scalp made her look like another person entirely. In some places it had been cut so close her head might have been shaved professionally, while in others it stuck out in small tufts.

"If you're still intending to send her away, she'll need to change her identity to stay hidden. Want me to organise it?"

"Not now." He stared at Allura, a grimace of pain momentarily contorting her features. "I've watched her die so many times, often violently, you'd think I'd be numb to seeing her hurt and in trouble."

"That necklace did nothing to protect her. Most of the Creatures here believe she betrayed us."

Shaw almost wished Allura had died so she could be reborn into a fresh life. It would probably be better for her that way. "Do you believe she intended to?" he asked.

Luci shrugged. "Piper's death broke her. If they promised her Jenna's return, I believe she would have, without question."

"Any idea who Quicksilver took her to meet at the police station?"

"I've asked a few friends to look into it."

"Cops," he muttered. It didn't necessarily point to anything, but someone had the power to pull strings. It was a lead, at least. Shaw grasped Luci's hand, the direct taint of her vampiric lifeforce almost making him pull back. After a moment he released it, the touch uncomfortable. "Any news about Jenna?"

Luci shook her head. "Not even unverified sightings. Noah's wolves are looking too, so we're confident he doesn't have her yet. Noah's not smart enough to play the misdirection game. If he had her, his wolves would have gone to ground."

"Keep searching."

"What are you going to do with Allura? Everyone's pissed with her."

His eyes went to the listening devices on the bedside table. "The Menagerie isn't safe for her anymore. Neither's this city."

Mary, Mia and Charlotte had found the listening devices on Allura when cleaning her up. The word had quickly spread.

"Go help Teddy Bear look for Jenna," Shaw said. "Please."

Luci gave a slightly frustrated sigh, but didn't argue as she left. His apartment door closed with a gentle click.

A while later, Allura stiffened and winced, the movement accompanied by a whimper. She opened her eyes, becoming perfectly still when she didn't recognise where she was.

"You're safe," Shaw said.

If anything, Allura's stillness deepened. She swallowed, but didn't look his way. "Where am I?"

"My apartment. How are you feeling?"

She began to shove the covers back, but gasped in pain, her jaw clenching. With nearly morbid fascination, she drew her hands out from under the covers. Mary had bandaged her hand. Packed with gauze, it was clear her left thumb was missing.

Allura's face crumbled, and she began to tremble. "It was real," she whispered.

"I'm sorry," Shaw said, meaning it.

She glanced at him, back to her bandaged left hand, and then away as if looking at bedsheets would make it less real. She drew her hands to her chest.

"Where's the bathroom?" she finally asked.

"That way," Shaw said, pointing to the open ensuite door to the right of the bed, the same side Allura had been sleeping on. His side.

She carefully pushed the covers back and sat up, failing to notice she was wearing silk pyjamas, or at least ignoring the implications.

She stood, taking a moment to recover before moving, her feet scuffing. Not picking up her feet was a trait she often brought into a new life. It was funny how some things seemed to follow a soul, but not others.

Although her appearance was always different, she managed to find the same expressions and mannerisms. The way she smiled, though rare in this incarnation, always felt reminiscent of Lumi's smile, as did the wary way she watched people.

Shaw frowned when he realised her footsteps had stopped too soon. She'd only have gotten to the hand-basins and mirror, but no further.

Allura said something he couldn't quite catch and then moved on. It sounded like swearing. He tried to tune out as she used the facilities.

Allura returned and sat on the edge of the bed, keeping her eyes on her bandaged hand. "Sucks to be me, huh?"

"How's Sparrow?" he asked.

She stiffened but kept her face blank. "Who?"

He held quiet for a long time, waiting until she looked up. "Is he still telling you to kill me?"

She looked away. "I don't know what you're talking about."

"I see. Maybe it's time you left the Menagerie, Allura."

Her head whipped around as if her neck was spring loaded, fear and panic on her face. "What? I need your help to find Jenna. Please."

"Things have changed here. I doubt you'll be safe if you stay." He tried not to let her see how those words hurt him.

"Because I wouldn't tell you about my psychotic imaginary friend? Are you serious?"

"If you stay, someone might decide to deal with the problem you represent."

Allura snorted, though her eyes returned to her damaged hand. "I'm not a problem. Do you know where Jenna is? Is she okay?" The need, desperation, and fear in her voice almost made him change his mind.

"Jenna's still missing. I'll let you know when we find her. For now, I'll organise some clean clothes and a car to take you back to your apartment. Pack light for travel. I'll have everything else shipped."

"What about Jenna?" By her expression, the tiger cub was her biggest concern, not her own life.

"We might have found her already if I hadn't been forced to pull Teddy Bear and his pack off the search."

Allura flushed.

"You haven't asked about Quicksilver," he said, curious about why.

Allura closed her eyes. "What's to ask about? His funeral arrangements?"

"That's what they told you?"

She frowned, looking up with a hint of hope in her eyes. "Yeah."

"He's in hospital. Very alive, if somewhat banged up."

Relief crossed her features. "Thank you. Is he going to be okay? Can I see him?"

"I don't think that would be a good idea." He pointed to the side table.

Allura glanced at it, all movement stopping dead when she saw the bugs. "Oh shit. I wasn't going to use them."

"Of course not."

All the blood drained from her face at his tone. "I really wasn't."

"What happened?" Shaw asked in as neutral a tone as he could manage. "Why'd they give you bugs to plant?"

She swallowed, taking a long moment to consider her response. Her shoulders slumped slightly. "The police have footage of me in Fyshwick the night Jenna escaped. They can tie me to the scene. What was I supposed to say?"

"The Creatures here know about the devices."

"I don't understand."

"I think you do," he replied.

Slowly, she nodded. "Yeah, I do. It's not in my best interests to stay in a place full of Creatures who feel betrayed, right?"

Shaw nodded. "I'll bring Jenna to you when we find her."

"I wasn't going to use them," she whispered.

"As you say."

She cleared her throat. "How's Quicksilver? Any long-term damage?"

Shaw stood. "He'll be fine. I'll call one of the tigers to help you dress."

"I can't go without Jenna," Allura said in a whisper. "I've

stopped drinking, and I helped rescue Noah's captives. That says something, doesn't it?"

He considered it, but shook his head. "I suggest you figure out where you want to go. Halfway across the world would be best, but I'll leave the choice to you." He pointed to the bedside table. "Drink the nectar before you go. It's enough to grow your thumb back and fix any other damage. Goodbye, Allura."

"Wait?" She held up her left hand. "It'll really grow back my thumb?"

His eyes flicked to the vial. "As long as the wound hasn't healed properly, yes, but the longer you leave it, the greater the risk it won't work."

When he returned to his apartment an hour later, the nectar remained on the bedside table with the necklace, earrings and bugs. He released a long breath. Lumi would have taken the nectar. Allura wasn't Lumi though. Not anymore. Not for three thousand years.

Then again, he was hardly the same man he'd been when he'd murdered her.

Shortly after sunrise, Allura and Mary climbed the stairs and opened the door to her tiny apartment.

Mary sniffed, grimaced and backed away. "Um, I think I'll wait downstairs. Or maybe in the next suburb."

"Sure," Allura said with a healthy dose of sympathy.

The dirty dishes piled high on the sink were wafting an unpleasant aroma, compounded by the apartment's closed-in musty smell. Her mattress's scrunched-up sheets vaguely resembled what passed for an unmade bed, which added an additional hint of stale sweat.

How the hell had she lived like this? She supposed that being drunk most of the time, she hadn't cared. She cared now.

Avoiding looking at reflections to prevent a comment from Sparrow, she opened the kitchen window with her good hand and then the living room window. Allura frowned as the hot, still air outside refused to gust in and clear out the smell.

"Fair enough," she muttered. She didn't want to be in

here either, although that was as much to do with disgust at herself for living like this as it was her need to find Jenna.

She put some fresh cat food on the metal plate for whatever stray wanted it and looked around.

A shower would have been nice, but she didn't dare go into the bathroom in case she caught Sparrow's reflection in the mirror. He'd have plenty to say, and Allura had no desire to hear it. She didn't want to get her wound wet, either.

Despite Shaw's insistence, Allura wouldn't leave town, not without Jenna. She had no doubt Noah and his sadistic werewolf pack would kill Jenna rather than risk losing her, and Allura needed to make sure that never happened. Somehow.

Werewolves, vampires and incubi. Who'd have believed it?

Rather than dwell on things she couldn't control, she entered her so-called office and began writing down what she knew. The list was short. Jenna was about fifteen or sixteen, a little taller than average, with dark brown hair. Allura had last seen her running on the cycle path around Lake Burley Griffin. Later, apparently, she'd waded into the water to escape Noah and Penelope. There'd been no sightings of her since.

Either Jenna was a good swimmer, or she'd drowned. Allura frowned. Would drowning kill Jenna or just leave her floating near the bottom of the lake? How could she find out? The thought made Allura sick. Drowning had been one of her own worst childhood fears.

Allura stared at the mostly blank piece of paper, willing more information to appear. She could make a few guesses. Jenna was probably a local girl, possibly once in foster care or a runaway street kid, and would have disappeared a couple of years ago. Quicksilver could probably dig up more info.

She groaned and covered her face with her hands, careful to avoid bumping the stump where her thumb had been.

Quicksilver wouldn't be on duty for a while, and she didn't dare risk going to anyone else. She also needed to visit him in hospital at some point. Maybe she should take a present, perhaps a bottle of something the nurses would disapprove of.

A fist thumped into her apartment door and Allura jumped in surprise. Curious, she left her office. Her stomach curdled at the sight of Slade with Quicksilver's partner, Graham.

"Is Quicksilver okay?" Allura asked before either could speak, though she was more interested in heading off awkward questions.

Slade nodded. "Quicksilver's fine."

"May we come in?" Graham asked.

Allura pointed at Slade. "He can, but this is a zealot-free zone."

Graham scowled at her. "I'm part of this investigation," he said.

"What investigation?" Allura asked, assuming it was something to do with the bugs they'd given her. "Nothing illegal I hope, like blackmail?"

Slade narrowed his eyes.

"Just a few questions," Graham said.

"Bonus," Allura replied sarcastically. "Because I've heard enough preaching from you about my godless ways to last me three lifetimes. How about instead of hanging around, you go find a bible group to annoy?"

Graham began to reply, but Slade put a hand on his

shoulder. "It's fine, Graham. I can take this one. Why don't you head back to the car? This won't take long."

Graham seemed to want to argue, but pivoted and walked away, heading down the corridor towards the stairs.

"Thanks for bringing Captain Religious," Allura said. She moved aside, allowing Slade to enter. "The guy's a good cop, but I banished him from my presence when he started preaching at me. He thinks I'm going to Hell."

"He could be right," Slade said with a shrug.

Allura tried not to snort. She'd been in hell for a while already. "Why are you here? More blackmail? If so, I've been kicked out of the Menagerie, so good luck with that."

Slade glanced at her hand. "Shaw do that?"

Allura shook her head. "An asshole called Ryker. He works for a bigger asshole called Noah. Don't worry, it's not the first time I've been tortured. It's almost fun now."

Slade took a long breath and released it slowly. "Quicksilver said a tire blew and his car hit a tree. After that, you vanished. How is it you've managed to turn up at your apartment with a bandaged hand and no other injuries?"

"I'll tell you what happened," she said sharply. "I got kidnapped, tortured, rescued by Shaw, and to top it all off, Shaw found your bugs on me. All things considered, I'm lucky I'm not dead multiple times."

He raised an eyebrow, as if doubting most of what she'd said. "Then you need to find a way back into the Menagerie. We had a deal, Allura." His flat tone offered no compromise.

Allura glared. "I just told you I just got kidnapped and tortured, you asshole. I've also lost my thumb, and all you care about is the deal we *had*?" Allura asked. "You really are a shitstick. How about you act like a cop and open an investigation into my kidnapping? That tire didn't blow by accident."

He sighed as if this were an old argument, not a new one. "I can't see evidence of you being kidnapped."

The muscles in her jaw attempted to shatter her teeth as she held up her bandaged hand as proof. "Go screw yourself. Somewhere else, of course. I don't want to watch."

Slade's expression hardened as he stepped closer. "Let me be clear, Allura. I own you. Unless you want to spend the rest of your life in prison, you'd better find your way back into the Menagerie."

Allura backed a step. It was a small room, and he was a big man, if not overly broad like Teddy Bear. Still, she had nowhere to go. "I'd rather go to prison than face Lawrence Shaw again. He thinks I've betrayed him. What did he do anyway? Steal your dog? Swindle you? Screw your girlfriend in your bed like you did to me?"

He stiffened when she mentioned *girlfriend*. "Don't," he warned.

Several pieces of the puzzle came together. "Shaw stole your girl? Is that what this is all about? Considering I caught you in bed with another woman when we were dating, your hypocrisy is epic."

He took another step forward, fists clenched, and face flushed. "Lumi," he began, not seeming to recognise the significance of the name.

"You're a Creature," Allura accused as she felt the blood draining from her face. "How else could you know that name?" she asked in a whisper.

Slade froze, all the answer she needed. He was definitely a Creature.

If Slade knew Lumi, then this whole thing had to be a love triangle. Shaw must have won Lumi's heart, and to get his revenge, Slade was punishing Allura lifetime after lifetime.

"I mean Allura..." Slade began, backpedalling.

He had to be thousands of years old to have known Lumi. Allura backed a step, and then another. "Did you and Shaw fight over Lumi?" She saw the confirmation on his face. "And she died..." Allura concluded as the pieces came together. Lumi had come between Slade and Shaw, and Slade had never got over it.

Slade looked away, clearly cursing his own stupidity. When he raised his face again, his expression was full of hatred.

The rest of it came together. "You killed Jingyi Lee to get at Shaw, didn't you?" she asked, guessing, but it made sense. "You're an incubus too."

She took another step back, meeting the wall. "Lumi chose him over you, back in the day, didn't she? It's been three thousand years, you asswipe. Get over it."

"Allura," someone said urgently from the door. Mary stood at the entrance to the apartment, hands pressed against an invisible barrier. She glanced at Slade, and then Allura. "Invite me in," she hissed.

Before Allura could speak, Slade stepped forward and gripped her mouth. She struggled and tried to pry his hand away, but he slammed her into the wall next to the bathroom door.

She gouged at his eye, but he caught her wrist and pinned her right arm against the wall.

Mary pushed hard against nothing, still held back. "Invite me in!"

Slade leaned in close, his face beside Allura's. "It's not just Shaw I hate," he whispered. "It's you, Lumi. It's always been you. It doesn't matter how many lifetimes you live or how we start out, you always scorn me in the end. I've made it my mission to make you suffer."

Allura made a garbled noise and struggled but couldn't break free.

"Oh, how I laughed when you got yourself pregnant on the rebound. I laughed again when you became a full-blown alcoholic following Piper's death, and I laughed even more when you took up with the one man you once hated even more than me. Shaw."

Oh God. Slade was insane. How had she never seen it?

"I'll admit your ruthlessness surprised me when you married that sap Greg to keep your career. I thought I'd broken you then, but no. I had to organise to have Piper kidnapped for that to happen. Yes. I had her kidnapped, and I killed her."

Allura stared, shocked. Slade murdered Piper?

He released his grip on her mouth, but Allura couldn't speak. She couldn't breathe.

"You've got no idea how I enjoyed watching grief tear you apart," he said. "I savoured every night you drank yourself into oblivion to drown out the pain. Watching you spiral has been one of the greatest pleasures of my life."

"I'm not Lumi," Allura finally said. "Lumi's dead. Whatever she did to you, that wasn't me."

"Oh, but it was you. Her soul, reborn into a new body. I'm not going to kill you, Allura. I've seen you die so often that killing you has no appeal anymore. In fact, I hope you live for a very long time, because I want you to suffer through every moment of it."

"You're psychotic."

He smiled, and it was the smile of a sadist. "Guess who I'm going after next?"

Allura paled even further. Jenna. "No."

"Yes, that sweet little tiger cub everyone's keen to catch. She's had such a hard life already, but I'll make sure she suffers for centuries just for the pleasure of seeing you with the knowledge."

"Please. She's innocent."

His smile widened, and she realised he'd traded in his soul for emptiness. "I'll send you photos on your birthday, and hers."

Allura turned her face away.

"They'll be delightful photos, too. I'm sure you can already imagine her in the worst shit-holes around the world, in the worst circumstances I can make possible."

Something finally reached through the fog in Allura's mind. A voice. Allura glanced at the door to find Mary desperately trying to force her way through a barrier Allura couldn't see.

"Come in," Allura whispered hoarsely.

Mary almost fell through the door. Heat washed through the room as Mary's clothes explosively shredded, and then a massive Siberian tigress stood in her place.

Slade swore and backed into a defensive stance as the tiger leapt at him, taking him full on. They crashed through Allura's office door, the top hinge ripping away from the frame.

Allura pressed herself against the wall as the tiger snarled. Something smashed and furniture broke, probably her desk. The next snarl turned into a roar of pain as bodies and furniture crashed to the floor.

Silence.

Allura hesitated a heartbeat, and then another, before finding the courage to approach her office. Her desk wash shattered, filing cabinet knocked over, and bookshelf broken.

Gasping near the far window, Mary lay beside Slade Mills. His left arm was bloody, but it was the knife protruding from Mary's chest that turned Allura's stomach.

"No," Allura whispered, too shocked to move.

Slade forced himself to his knees, ripped the knife free from Mary's chest, and stabbed her again.

"Stop!"

Mary made a surprisingly soft whimper, her teeth pulling back in pain, a massive paw rising as if to beg.

Allura screamed in rage and ran at Slade. In the same motion he pulled the knife free, he backhanded her, knocking her onto her back as light exploded before her eyes. Momentary darkness offered oblivion.

Allura moaned in pain, her nose throbbing and blood running over her lip. She could taste her own blood.

"This is what you get for defiance," Slade said as he stabbed Mary again.

"Stop it!" Allura whispered. With a fresh rush of adrenaline, she rolled to her side and pushed herself to her knees, but couldn't make it any further. "You're killing her!" Mary was gasping, blood coating her teeth and dribbling from her mouth.

Slade got to his feet, still holding the bloody knife.

Allura cringed back as he took a step towards her. She blinked away tears she hadn't realised were there until now. A drop of blood slid off Slade's knife to the floor.

"This is your fault, Allura. Yours. She'd have been fine if you'd never let her in."

Allura met his eyes, wishing she could murder him with a glare. "What did Lumi do to you? I don't remember any of it!"

"Oh, I'm sure you remember everything somewhere inside that self-absorbed little soul of yours." Slade caught Allura by her shirt and dragged her to Mary's side. He took

Allura's right hand, pried her fingers open, and forced her to hold the knife.

She went cold at the realisation of what he was about to do. "Please don't," she whispered, her tone pitched too high as his hand closed around hers, his grip hurting and preventing her from releasing the knife. She tried to pull away, but he shifted her hand, forcing the tip of the blade toward Mary's exposed neck.

"No. Please," Allura whispered.

Mary's body abruptly rippled and shrank back to a woman a fraction of the tiger's size. "Please," she said, eyes wide with fear as she coughed blood.

"When you're reborn, remember that it was Allura who killed you." Slade drove the blade into Mary's neck. She stiffened, mouth wide as if gasping for air one last time, and then her body went limp and the life faded from her eyes.

Allura could barely see through her tears.

Slade released Allura's hand and stood, staring down at her with the coldest expression she'd ever seen. "Your fault," he repeated, and then left the apartment.

Allura, on her hands and knees, ripped the knife from Mary's throat and slipped her arms under Mary's neck, pulling her bloody body close. The woman's eyes were open, but she saw nothing. "Mary? Mary? No, no, no, no."

She didn't know how long it took to stop crying and gather herself. When she finally lay Mary's body on the blood-soaked carpet, Allura went back into her living room, almost offended by how normal it looked compared to her study.

Mary's clothes were shredded and thrown in all directions. She needed to tell Shaw. He could help. Maybe Mary wasn't dead. Just... asleep, or whatever immortal Creatures did to regenerate.

She found the remnants of Mary's top, but the woman's phone wasn't in the pocket. She found the phone with Mary's purse in her handbag near the doorway, the strap broken, but the rest of the bag intact.

She had no idea what Mary's passcode was. Returning to the office, Allura held the camera to Mary's face with trembling hands, and thankfully it unlocked. She opened Mary's contacts and scanned through them until she found Shaw's number, but hesitated. She searched for Mia's number instead and called. It took several long seconds for the familiar voice to answer.

"Mary?"

Allura tried speaking, but the words wouldn't come out properly, or fast enough.

"I don't understand what you're saying," Mia said. "Take a moment and start again."

Allura took a deep breath. "Mary's dead. Slade killed her."

The line went silent. Allura stared at the phone, uncomprehending for several long seconds. When she put the phone back to her ear, she could hear Mia on the other end, her words muffled.

"Where are you?" Mia asked a moment later.

Trying not to sob, Allura took a breath. "My apartment."

The phone went dead. Allura stared at it before accepting that Mia had hung up on her. She returned to Mary.

Teddy Bear found her holding the dead tigress about fifteen minutes later, cradling Mary's bloody body to her chest like a long-lost child.

2 2

Allura's shock eventually lifted, only to be replaced with a murderous rage. "I'm going to kill him," Allura said to Charlotte, who stood between Allura and the door, her arms crossed. "And if you don't get out of my way, I'll murder you on the way out."

Charlotte raised both eyebrows. She lifted her right ankle and pulled a silver knife from her boot, the blade about as long as Allura's palm.

"What are you doing with that?" Allura asked, wanting to step back, but not willing to show fear.

Charlotte flipped the knife and held it out hilt first, thumb and forefinger just above the blade, to avoid touching the silver. "If you really want to murder me, go for it."

The memory of Slade's much larger blade in her hand made the blood drain from Allura's face. She stepped back, hands trembling so hard she had to cross her arms to stop from revealing it. "Please put it away," she whispered hoarsely. "I'm sorry. I didn't mean it."

"Are you really sorry?"

Why Slade Mills hadn't called the police, had Allura arrested and charged with Mary's murder, she couldn't say. It would have been an easy solution for him.

Instead, Teddy Bear had brought Mary's body back while others cleaned Allura's apartment. At the Menagerie, Charlotte had cleaned Allura up, even helping her remove her blood-soaked clothes and getting her into a shower.

Allura dropped her eyes. "Yes. I'm sorry. I really am." She glanced at the room's door. "But please let me leave. I'm not going to do anything stupid like go after Slade. I need to find Jenna. Please let me go out and look."

"How about you sit down? We've got two packs of werewolves out looking for Jenna. You can't help." Charlotte remained resolutely in Allura's path.

Sit down? Impossible.

Charlotte's phone buzzed, and she pulled it from her jeans pocket, putting it to her ear. "Yes?" she asked. She listened for a moment and sighed. "I'll be there in a minute." She put the phone away.

"Jenna," Allura asked hopefully.

Charlotte shook her head. "Mia's as murderous as you, only she's talking about killing you first and Slade second. I doubt she's serious about killing you, but you may not want to invite her over for tea and scones. Can I trust you not to leave this room?"

Allura stared regretfully at the door. "Yes. Go help Mia."

Charlotte gave her a wary look. "That was hardly a promise."

"I'm hardly a Creature, so what difference does it make?"

Charlotte gave her a long look before conceding the point. She left, the door closing heavily.

Allura gave it a full minute before opening the door and glancing up and down the corridor. Relief helped her relax slightly when she discovered nobody had been sent to watch her.

Rather than take the lifts, she made her way to the fire stairs. Fifteen floors, even downstairs, were a lot for someone out of condition. At the bottom, she pushed open the door to the outside of the building, no doubt tripping an alarm somewhere in the security room. She didn't care. Fresh air gave her energy and hope.

Squinting in the bright sunshine and with the afternoon sun belting down on her, Allura ran across the road to the footpath and turned left toward the foreshore. When she got to the boardwalk, she checked behind her, but couldn't see anyone after her.

That might be her only break, though. She was now alone, with no money, no identification, and no phone. All she had was determination.

It would have to do.

LUCI TOUCHED HER EARPIECE, grimacing in the bright sunlight despite her sunglasses and broad-brimmed hat. She was old enough that sunlight wouldn't hurt her, but it was still bloody uncomfortable.

"Allura ran, as predicted. She walked past the restaurants fronting the boardwalk, probably heading for Civic. It'll take her about an hour to get there on foot."

Shaw's voice came back to her over the phone. "She can't do worse than the werewolves. Let her go. We know Slade's not going to kill her."

"Noah would. You want me to follow her?" Luci asked, regretting the impulsive offer, considering how sunny it was.

"Yes, please."

She sighed. "It's been three thousand years, Lawrence. You're no longer responsible for what happens to her."

"If that were true, she wouldn't keep being reborn into my life. Something needs to change between us. Maybe it's Jenna."

Luci didn't know why he didn't kill Allura every time he encountered her reborn soul. It'd have to be easier. "Fine. But if this goes badly, don't expect me to stick around when she's reborn again. Three times is enough for me."

Silence.

"You know I'm only doing this for you, right?" Luci asked.

"Luci," he began, sounding tired and not in the mood for another argument about Allura.

"Forget it." She broke the connection.

23

Stones crunched as Noah parked his van among the eucalyptus trees near the scenic lookout, misting rain obscuring the cliff some ten metres ahead. The rain had ensured nobody was about, while the trees hid the van from the main road. The weather had saved him another half hour of driving to a more remote spot.

Noah and Penelope got out and opened the van's rear doors, the internal light coming on.

Inside, Ryker struggled against the wire binding his arms and legs to a black tubular-steel chair.

"Hello Ryker. Fancy meeting you in a van like this," Noah said.

Ryker yelled abuse into a gag, his face red with rage as the wire cut into his flesh, leaving trails of blood down his arms.

"Did you really think we couldn't hear what you said to Allura? Traitor."

Ryker tried to yell more abuse through the cloth stuffed in his mouth, duct tape wrapped several times around his head to hold it in place. He glanced at Penelope, eyes begging, but she looked away.

"Help me get him out," Noah said to Penelope. Between them, they hauled Ryker from the van and carried him and his chair through trees and across dead grass to the cliff's edge, avoiding the tourist lookout about twenty metres away.

Water gently lapped against rock about twenty metres down, the view slightly obscured by drizzle, which hid everything beyond a few hundred metres as well. Perfect.

Noah pulled out his phone and turned on video recording, handing the phone to Penelope. Her hands shook slightly as she took it, but she held it steadily enough. If he thought she'd known Ryker was sweet on her and knew about his plan, she'd be in her own chair. As it was, this was a test for her. One hint of hesitation and he'd break her neck and dump her with Ryker.

He grinned, looking around. Trees, hills, and misty drizzle screened any chance of being seen except by a fishing boat on the water, and that was unlikely.

"Recording," Penelope said, her voice shaky as she aimed the phone at Ryker. That was good. She didn't need to like this. She just needed to prove her loyalty. Fearing him was good.

Noah drew a knife and cut the tape holding Ryker's gag in place, slashing open the man's cheek at the same time. He ripped the tape from Ryker's mouth before pulling the rag out, the tape still stuck to the back of Ryker's head.

"Noah, please don't do this. I'll disappear. You'll never have to see me again," Ryker said. "Please."

Noah crouched, eying Ryker. "A life on the run? That doesn't sound like fun. Oh wow, I'm a poet," he said.

"Noah, please—"

"Why don't you scream, Ryker? Cry for help? There's got to be someone camping out here within hearing distance. We could have even more fun if they turn up."

Ryker glanced at the trees as if considering it. "Please let me go. I won't say anything, I swear—"

Noah held his knife up. "That's the rub, isn't it? I trusted you. I made you my second-in-command. I let you run with me. I even called you brother. You've repaid me by trying to cut a deal with Shaw's human slut. Very poor form."

Ryker strained at the wire holding him in place, wincing as fresh blood seeped from the cuts. "It's not like—"

Noah held up a hand and glanced pointedly at Penelope before returning his attention to the man in the chair. "Ryker, you may want to reconsider whatever you were about to say."

Ryker closed his mouth.

Noah smiled sadistically. "See, I always knew you were smart. Too smart, perhaps." He sighed. "Do you have any idea how rare feline shapeshifters are, Ryker? How valuable? Allura is our key to getting the cub back, and you tried to blow that for us. The entire pack could retire on what we'd make from her, and you made that so much harder. If we don't get her back, whose balls do you think Slade will cut off first? I like my balls, Ryker. I like them a lot."

"We could all clear out," Ryker said. "The whole pack. Disappear into the interior. Go north to Townsville. Even overseas."

Noah shook his head. "Why do that when there's still so much money to be made from our little cub? Slade's connections are the key to international customers willing to pay millions to make their own snuff film dreams come true. Jenna could keep the pack in coin for generations.

Tigers are immortal, after all. You wanted to screw that up for us with your stupid little deal."

Noah turned the knife to catch the light, glancing up at Penelope. "You want to say anything in his defence?" It was a dare, and she knew it.

Penelope swallowed and shook her head slightly, too scared to speak.

"Good bitch." Noah returned his gaze to the knife. Long and single-edged, it was the kind of knife a hunter used to skin an animal. The blade was silver, too.

Ryker stared at it, begging with his eyes. "Noah—"

"Why did you betray me?"

Ryker shook his head. "You know why."

Noah tightened his grip on the knife. "I could have crushed your nuts in a vice before throwing you into the lake, you know? Fortunately for you, I like you, so consider this a favour." Noah stabbed the knife into Ryker's thigh, twisting the blade. Ryker made a strangled cry, leaning forward as far as he could as he bit through his own lip. Noah twisted the blade again and Ryker thrashed against the wire holding him to the chair.

Noah crinkled his nose at the smell of silver cauterising flesh. He pulled the blade free, waiting until Ryker lifted his head, pain still in his expression.

"You bastard," Ryker slurred, blood dribbling down his chin.

"I know who my father is," Noah said as he stabbed the blade into Ryker's other thigh, twisting once more. Ryker made an agonised noise before passing out, chin slumping to his chest as the silver blistered his flesh.

Several slaps brought him around. Ryker slowly lifted his head, blood dripping onto his white t-shirt.

"If you apologise," Noah began, holding the blade up

between them. "Maybe I'll forgive you." The blood on the knife was already blackened from the silver. "You really were a good second. I want you to apologise. Say the words, Ryker."

Ryker, clearly delirious with pain, raised his face and gave Noah a single finger salute instead, though his arms were still bound to the chair. "You're going to kill me anyway."

Noah caught the finger and bent it back until it snapped. Ryker made a whimpering sound, but didn't cry out this time.

"Yeah, fair enough. An apology wouldn't have saved you, and you're smart enough to know it. I just wanted to hear you say it."

Ryker spat at Noah, but most of it dribbled down his chin.

Noah stabbed the blade into Ryker's shoulder.

Ryker cried out, leaning away as much as the wire would allow, head back and veins in his neck standing out. His upper body rocked. He slumped when Noah pulled the knife free.

"Silver's a real double whammy, isn't it? I'm told it disrupts a Creature's lifeforce, not that I believe in all that magical bullshit the vampires keep talking about."

"You missed my neck," Ryker whispered.

"Oh, you'd like that, wouldn't you? How about this, then? Apologise and I'll cut your throat before throwing you into the lake. Who knows how many times you'll regenerate before you stay dead, otherwise?"

Ryker just gave him a steady glare, though the effort seemed to cost him. "Never," he slurred.

"Fine." Noah stood and wiped the blade clean on Ryker's shirt before returning it to its sheath. He picked up the metal chair, muscles bulging, and threw Ryker over the edge.

"One, two—"

Splash.

Noah took his phone from Penelope's still-trembling hands, reviewed the recording, and gave her a pleased smile. His smile seemed to make her tremble more. "Let's go teach our pet cub never to run away again, shall we? After that, we'll kill Shaw's bitch and every Creature he calls a friend."

"You really want to take on Shaw?" Penelope asked, her voice weak.

He met her eyes. "Question me again and you'll wish you were in Ryker's place. Got it?"

24

Despite her nervous energy, it took Allura over an hour to get to the city centre. She entered the first cafe she saw and walked up to the counter.

An elderly woman who looked like she should have retired twenty years earlier smiled and picked up a pen to write Allura's order down, despite the tablet in front of her. "What can I get you, love?"

Allura felt guilty for not ordering. "I was hoping you might have seen my daughter. She's sixteen and about hundred and seventy centimetres tall..."

The woman looked confused. It took Allura a moment to realise her mistake. She did a quick calculation. "About five foot seven?"

The woman gave her an 'ah' expression, but only stared at Allura as if expecting more.

"She's got long, dark brown hair, most of the way down her back. Her name's Jenna, but she may not be using it."

"Why is that, dear?" There was a critical tone in her voice, implying Jenna had run away for a reason.

Allura's irritation flared at the woman's presumption.

She countered with a lie. "She got involved with an older boy and it got pretty bad. She called me this morning but didn't turn up at the meeting place." It wasn't hard to let concern colour her voice.

"Have you contacted the police?" Again, that hard edge of criticism. Allura wanted to tell the woman off.

"Yes. I used to be a detective. Now I'm a full-time mum."

The woman's expression changed dramatically then, suddenly all sympathy. "Oh, I see. Well, um, I do see a lot of young women here, but they're usually university students. If I see someone younger and matching the description, I'll be happy to call you."

Allura only knew three numbers without relying on her phone's memory. Her own, which she no longer had. Quicksilver's, but he was in hospital. And Shaw's personal number. Huh. Funny how that had stuck.

"I'd appreciate it if you could call The Menagerie Hotel and Casino. Ask for Mia. She's my friend and she's helping me look for Jenna."

Allura went through a similar routine in a dozen more shops and cafes, but nobody could confirm they'd seen Jenna.

It was late afternoon when Allura finally plonked herself down on a bench on City Walk near some small statues of running dogs, her growing despondency getting the best of her. She glared at the statues for want of a better target, figuring they were more of a trip hazard than art, particularly at night.

She put her face in her hands as people walked past, leaning forward and not sure what to do other than visit more shops or stop random people and ask them. She had no transport, no money, and no friends she could rely on, and with Noah's people probably on the lookout for Allura as much as Jenna, no options.

With time to think she could feel her missing thumb beginning to throb in the thick bandages, or rather, it only felt like it was throbbing considering it wasn't attached to her body anymore. She should have taken that nectar, dammit. Pride had always been her biggest downfall, or maybe dumping her pride in the gutter when too drunk to stand.

"You okay?"

Allura sat upright. A young woman had sat next to her. Allura hadn't heard her approach. Petite, blonde, and about twenty, she stared at Allura with the kind of confidence most people didn't acquire until they were considerably older. A large bag that looked like it was full of books sat at her feet. It looked heavy. A student, then.

Allura spoke from the script she'd been practicing all afternoon. "My daughter's missing," she began before describing Jenna, latching on to any unlikely hope this young woman might offer.

"Not much to go on. She got hangouts nearby? She a party girl? Does she have friends with cars?"

Woah, this girl should be aiming to become a detective when she finished studying. "She may have an issue with drugs," Allura said, though she couldn't be sure. It was the only lead she hadn't followed yet, and mostly because she didn't want to face it.

The young woman nodded. "I've got some friends who buy from a guy who lives in one of the flats on the other side of the city. They usually meet near Ainslie Avenue. You could start by asking around there."

Allura sighed at her own stupidity. She used to be a cop and knew the areas where drug addicts and dealers hung out. The dens had probably moved, but the locations wouldn't be much different except where some of the older flats had been knocked down.

"Thanks," she said, holding her hand out. "I'm Allura."

The girl shook. "Kim."

"Thanks, Kim." Allura stood.

Kim stood too, lifting her hefty backpack to her shoulders and shrugging it into place.

"Wait a sec," Kim said. She wriggled her bag off, unzipped the front top section and reached in, pulling out a bottle of orange juice and a chicken and avocado wrap with mayo, clearly labelled. "You look like you need some fuel." She handed them to Allura along with a muesli bar. "I had lunch with my friends and never got to this."

"Oh. Uh, thanks. But—" She struggled to hold everything without her thumb and winced as the juice put pressure on the wound in her left hand.

"They're yours," Kim said. "Go find your daughter."

"Thank you." Hungrier than she'd realised she'd been, Allura tucked the juice under her forearm, pocketed the muesli bar, and gingerly began unwrapping the rolled-up wrap as she walked away.

Perhaps Kim knew which apartments or flats to start with? She turned back. She stared around in amazement. Kim was gone. Allura did a full circle, but couldn't see the girl anywhere. A cold feeling sunk into her stomach. Kim couldn't be human to move that quickly.

She stared at the wrap in her hand, sniffing it before taking a nibble. It smelled and tasted okay.

Something sat on the bench where Kim had been. Allura examined it. A short knife and leather sheath with straps, designed to be buckled against a person's calf.

Allura looked around again with a cold shiver. Could

Charlotte have sent her? Was Kim a tigress? What other Creature could move crazy-fast in the daytime? Who else but Charlotte, or maybe Mia, would send Allura food and a weapon? Would Shaw have done it?

Allura put the wrap and juice on the seat and checked the knife. It looked like it was made of silver. Of course. Pursing her lips, she accepted the gift horse, hoping it didn't bite her later.

She struggled to strap the knife to her right leg just above her ankle though, wincing as every bump sent pain through her hand. The lack of two thumbs probably made the task almost monumentally comical to anyone who might be watching.

Eventually, she pulled her jeans down over the knife, and standing, she took a few steps to test it out. It didn't show, and it wasn't uncomfortable, though it did feel weird.

On the bench where the knife had been sat rested a small square of folded paper the size of a sticky note, with her name written on it.

Allura picked it up and unfolded the note, and a cold shiver ran through her as she recognised the name.

Save Jenna before sunset or you'll lose her forever. Kimbriel.

STANDING on City Walk a good fifty metres away, Luci did as little possible to draw attention to herself. She leaned against a tree in the blessed shade and pulled her phone out, calling Shaw. He answered on the first ring.

"Luci?" Shaw's voice was calm, but with an element of tension.

"No, the tooth fairy."

He sighed. "Mia's getting antsy, and a pregnant tigress isn't on my list of people I want to try to calm down today. She wants the cub brought in safe, and being unable to do it herself means she's in my ear every five minutes. What's Allura up to?"

"Not sure. Kimbriel's just got involved."

Shaw swore. "What the hell does Kimbriel want from all this?"

"Dunno, but she gave Allura a silver knife and some food."

There was a pause. "Did you hear anything she said?"

Luci shook her head before remembering Shaw couldn't see the gesture. "No, but Allura's hightailing it towards the mall."

"Did Kimbriel see you?"

"Are you kidding? She knows when a butterfly farts on the other side of the planet. She's not confiding in me, if that's your question."

He sighed, the sound a hiss over the phone. "Stay close and keep me informed... and let me know if Kimbriel interferes again. Have you seen any of Noah's wolves?"

"Yeah. I took care of one an hour ago when he started tailing Allura. I mesmerised the asshole and sent him to Tharwa. I doubt my influence will hold any longer than that, but it'll keep him out of the game for a while."

"Very restrained of you. Keep the rest off Allura's back if you can, and call Teddy Bear to let him know what's going on. He's in the area."

"Will do." She put her phone away, watching as Allura walked past the old merry-go-round in its prime position on City Walk. Three children and their mother were waiting for it to stop so they could get on, the kids almost bouncing with excitement.

Luci pushed herself off the tree as Allura reached the

corner, but spun as someone tapped her on the shoulder from behind.

Jumping away and ready to defend herself or run if she had to, she found a small blond woman standing there, her long sundress hanging limp from a lack of breeze. The woman was shorter than Luci, and Luci wasn't even close to average height. A sickly feeling crept through her stomach. "What do you want, Kimbriel?"

"Spying on people isn't normally your game, Luci."

Luci backed a step, not that it would have helped when facing a Demi-god, or whatever Kimbriel was. "What's Allura to you?" Luci asked.

Kimbriel smirked. "Would you like some advice, Luci?"

"Sure," she said with as much sarcasm as she could. Kimbriel had her own agenda, and that didn't always work out for other people.

Kimbriel smiled, her gaze turning inward. "You'd think foresight would be a wonderful gift, wouldn't you? It's not."

"Yeah, sounds tough," Luci replied in the same tone, now awkwardly tempted to glance over her shoulder in Allura's direction. "Not exactly advice, though."

"You've lived long enough to see people being reborn."

"Again, not advice. You want to get to the point?"

Kimbriel met Luci's eyes, and the vastness of her gaze was enough to silence any further criticism. "Strength within humans is forged across lifetimes, each rebirth like a hammer blow against the anvil of experience. You should know that billions of lives will one day depend on the steel forged within Allura's soul. You'd do well to look after her today."

Luci swallowed in a dry mouth. "How do you mean?" she asked.

Kimbriel looked in the direction Allura had gone. "You saw me give Allura the knife?"

"Yeah," Luci replied cautiously. "What of it?"

Kimbriel gave a non-committal shrug. "Let's just say there'll be a lot of misery and suffering if you don't have Allura's back today."

Luci's scalp tightened like a shiver gone wrong. She glanced along City Walk past the merry-go-round, but Allura was out of sight. When she turned back, Kimbriel was gone too.

"Shit," she muttered.

25

Allura was being followed. Trying to ignore the creeping chill running down her body, she raised her arm and coughed into her bent elbow, using the opportunity to glance backward down the footpath. From the corner of her eye, she swore someone moved behind some bushes next to the footpath to keep out of sight. Someone big. Tall, at least. Athletic.

She swore under her breath and continued walking, pretending she'd seen nothing as she crossed the double-lane road, a wide grassy island in between the four lanes. Anyone following her would have to risk being seen to keep up the pursuit.

Once across the road, Allura changed direction, heading back the way she'd come.

Whoever was pursuing her stayed out of sight. They may have even jumped the fence into someone's rear yard in one of the townhouses lining Ainslie Avenue.

Uncertain if she'd lost whoever was following her, Allura slipped into the old cluster of buildings that made up

Gorman House arts centre. She cut through the first courtyard at an angle, leaving on the other side and quickly getting to the street.

The street sign read *Batman Street*. How the hell had she never known Canberra had a Batman Street?

Rather than go back to Civic, she crossed Batman Street and turned right, following a footpath, then turned down another footpath between homes. It opened onto a leafy, tree-filled park.

Pretending to rest, she bent over and put her hands on her knees, glancing back, but couldn't see anyone following.

Keeping to side streets and footpaths, Allura made her way towards the clusters of flats where the suburbs of Ainslie, Braddon and Reid came together.

The area was a contrast of very old and expensive inner-city homes, some heritage listed, vibrant new apartments, and run-down flats that had probably been build early in Canberra's history.

The people in the area reflected that diversity too. She passed upwardly mobile singles and couples, retirees walking dogs, and long-term public housing tenants.

"Spare some money for the bus? I need to get to a job interview," a too-thin young man asked, his hair lank and his nose crooked.

"Sorry," Allura said. "All I've got is lint and a bad headache. You can have both."

The guy frowned, but kept walking towards Civic without saying anything more.

Taking a risk, Allura headed back toward Ainslie Avenue, moving further from the city centre. In twenty years, most of the flats in the area would probably end up bulldozed to make way for more apartments.

"Hey, can you spare a dollar?" asked a woman about Allura's age, though she looked like she'd had a hard life and could have been younger. "I need to catch the bus for a job interview tomorrow."

Same line? Really?

Thin to the point of being skin and bone, she was either a drug addict or a long-term alcoholic. Hell, Allura probably hadn't looked any better a week ago. All her judgement and snobbery suddenly felt hypocritical.

Ashamed, Allura checked her pockets this time. She had nothing but the muesli bar Kimbriel had given her. She held it out. "This is everything I have," Allura said. "I was saving it for my daughter, but you can have it."

The woman's expression changed. The difference wasn't exactly sympathetic, but more like a fellow traveller in need of a hand up. "Your daughter chasing the white unicorn?"

White unicorn? It took Allura a moment to remember that was slang for heroin around here. Allura nodded, unwilling to voice her fears. "I was hoping—"

The woman took the muesli bar. "Then she won't be wanting food." She pointed to the traffic lights at the far end of the street. "Cross over and go to the end of the next street. There's a block of flats there with a den on the top floor. Place reeks so it shouldn't be hard to find. If she's not there, then someone might know where to look, but watch your back. The boys who live there got themselves a harem, and they don't like their girls walking. Get me?"

Allura nodded, already imagining what she was about to walk into and wishing she had an alternative. "Yeah. Thanks."

QUICKSILVER LOOKED up as Slade and Graham walked into his hospital room, his head spinning from turning too fast. The concussion he'd received in the car accident helped his nagging headache to blaze back into full life.

He closed his eyes and took a couple of deep breaths to let the dizziness settle down.

"You ready to make a statement?" Slade asked.

Annoyance simmered to the surface. "It's nice to see you too, Slade. The flowers were a lovely touch."

Slade glanced at his hands, empty of flowers or anything else. "Allura said you two stopped for a couple of drinks, which is why you crashed."

"Why are you here, Slade? Get demoted to investigating traffic incidents?"

"How are you doing?" Graham asked.

"I'm not dead, so that's a bonus. Can't say I'm up for answering bullshit questions designed to rile me up."

"The blood test came back positive. You were almost double the legal limit," Slade said.

Quicksilver glanced at Graham, who nodded.

"Bullshit. Allura's off the grog and I rarely drink. We certainly didn't stop at the pub on the way home, so your blood test is bullshit."

"What do you remember?" Slade asked, as if the man hadn't just been insulting him.

"Allura didn't want to go back to the Menagerie straight away, so we drove around for a while." He glanced at Graham. "You said she was okay. Is she? Has something happened?"

Graham rubbed his chin with his left hand. "She was fine last time I saw her, but that was at her apartment, before the accident."

"She told me you were both drinking," Slade said a little to casually.

Slade was lying. He had to be. What did Slade really want, then? "Show me her signed statement and a copy of the blood test and we'll talk about it. Until then, I'm not buying anything."

If nothing else, Slade appeared annoyed.

"Why don't you tell us about the crash?" Graham said.

Quicksilver looked away, the memory of the crash vague, at best. "We drove over King's Avenue bridge and went left. The tyre blew, and we hit the curb. Just flashes, otherwise."

"Allura's been missing since I spoke with her over the phone, but she wasn't at the crash site when we arrived," Slade said. "When Graham and I returned to her apartment, she wasn't there. She's not at the Menagerie either. Any idea where she is?"

Quicksilver studied Slade. "You're only now telling me Allura's missing? Maybe you should have started with that when you came in."

"Do you know where she is?" Slade asked.

Quicksilver glared at the man. "She certainly hasn't been in to visit. You worried she might have told Lawrence Shaw you're trying to bug his office?"

"We're worried Shaw might have fixed the problem himself," Slade said.

Graham nodded.

That was possible. "So why are you trying to pin a bullshit drink-driving charge on me? This is all to do with Lawrence Shaw, right?"

Anger simmering, Quicksilver tried to sit up, but his head spun and the headache returned in full force. Palms pressed against his forehead, it took him a long moment to settle his dizziness. "I know you're a lying sack of shit trying to rile me up into saying something," he finally said. "Problem is, I don't know anything."

"We'll come back tomorrow," Slade said, a threat in his tone. "You might want to think about your situation, and if you remember anything."

26

Allura's stomach knotted as she stared at the long row of two-story, light brown brick buildings, any one of which might conceal her daughter.

The units took up an entire street block, making a long rectangle with parking and other facilities in between. They didn't give off inviting vibes, though that could have been due to the cars parked on the grass out front. Nine of them on this side alone, the grass mown around at least two of them. There had to be a hundred residential units or more.

She also counted three broken chairs dumped at irregular intervals, and what looked like a rusted-out barbeque that had been pushed over onto its side. Closed in stairwells gave access to the top-level homes, while driveways led to the parking areas behind the buildings.

"Crap," she whispered. It looked like it was a clannish community too, and Allura wasn't part of the clan. There was a good chance she'd encounter trouble if she started snooping around.

She cautiously made her way up the second driveway along the block, walking into the shadow between buildings to one of the parking areas and a series of carports. Nothing was amiss, yet nothing felt good either, but that could easily have been nerves.

If she wanted to buy drugs or pick a fight, this was where she'd come. If Jenna was here, she was in trouble.

Like prophecy inspired by the thought, a window on the second floor shattered and two people crashed through, still fighting in the air as if murdering each other on the way down was more important than the concrete they were about to hit.

Allura staggered backwards as they crashed to the ground a few dozen metres away in a shower of broken glass, both still struggling as if the fall was as easy as a step from a footpath to the road.

A small, white-haired woman landed on top, but the much bigger man rolled with the momentum and pinned the woman down.

"Stop!" Allura yelled as the heavy-set man put his weight behind a punch that could kill. Allura dashed forward on a surge of adrenalin, but the white-haired woman caught the man's wrist with one hand and slammed her free fist into his ribs. Something broke, and Allura wasn't sure if it was the woman's wrist or the man's ribs.

"Get away, you stupid girl!" the woman yelled at Allura as she shoved the man off with the force of a bear. He crashed to the ground three metres away and rolled to his feet as she stood.

Allura stopped so fast she almost tripped. They were Creatures. They had to be. Either of them could probably kill her with a glare.

She abandoned them to their fight and ran, only to pull up before she'd made a dozen steps.

Noah, the sadistic werewolf who'd tortured her, had

followed her into the parking area. "Oh shit," Allura hissed, a renewed surge of fear coursing through her. A cold sweat broke out all over Allura's body while her stomach threatened to create skid-marks in her underwear at the memories of him slowly pushing a knife into her guts. Strength left her, and it was all she could do to breathe and stay upright.

Noah seemed even bigger in daylight, almost as big as Teddy Bear, and looked like he'd been chewing steroids since his voice broke. He had to be more than twice her weight and there wasn't a hint of fat on him. In a straight-up brawl between the two of them, she doubted her best punch would give him a black eye, if she could even reach.

He smiled as if he knew exactly how she was feeling, sadistic hunger in his eyes.

Behind her, the two combatants crashed into a car, the window shattering. No alarm rang out, but plenty of people were watching through windows.

Allura clenched her fists to stop her hands trembling, and for an insane moment considered going for the knife strapped to her ankle.

Even if she managed to get in a slash or two, he'd still overpower her and use it on her as he'd done before. He was bigger, stronger, and had greater reach, and being a werewolf could take a wound better than she could.

She wanted to run, but her legs weren't participating despite all the training and experience she'd had as a cop.

"Move your ass, Allura," a familiar voice said from behind her.

Noah glanced past Allura, his eyes narrowing.

Forcing herself to breathe, Allura glanced over her shoulder. "Luci?"

Luci stood in the shade of the building wearing sunnies

and a broad-brimmed hat, as if to disguise herself. "Clear out," Luci said. "I'll take care of the asshole."

It was enough to get Allura moving again. Finding her legs, she backed away from Noah, who seemed hesitant to take on a vampire, even in daylight. Allura only stopped when she reached Luci. She bent and drew the silver knife, holding it out to the vampire hilt first so she didn't have to touch the silver blade. "Take it," she said. "It'll do you more good than me."

Luci accepted the knife, a look in her eyes implying she didn't rate her chances. Assuming both Luci and Noah were only stronger at night, it would be little more than a fight between two regular people, and Luci was less than half Noah's size.

Allura whispered in the hope the werewolf wouldn't hear. "I'll distract him. You go for something vital with that knife. Okay?"

Luci smiled. "No. Go find your daughter. This isn't your fight."

"But—"

"I can handle one werewolf, even a big one. Go. Jenna needs you."

At the mention of Jenna, Allura made a hasty decision and ran down the far driveway between the two buildings. She barely made it through when an arm slammed across her chest, knocking the air out of her. Dread filled her and she would have fallen, but whoever had hit her caught her and dragged her back against their body.

A hand clamped over her mouth and Allura found herself lifted off the ground. Finally remembering to struggle, she began twisting to get her arms free, but whoever had her held her tight.

"Stop struggling, you stupid woman, or you'll give us away," a woman's voice hissed in her hear.

Allura froze. Panic still ruled her emotions, but she had enough sense to take stock. The woman who held her had dark skin and lean arms, corded and hard, and had no trouble holding Allura off the ground.

Penelope? It had to be. Ryker's werewolf friend. Allura kicked back and got a grunt in response, but the woman didn't let go.

"I know where Jenna is," Penelope hissed. "Stop struggling and I'll tell you!" Penelope shook Allura, a massive feat of strength considering she was already holding her off the ground.

Against all her instincts, Allura forced herself to calm down, breathing through her nose until Penelope relaxed her hold a little. Not enough for Allura to get free, but not hurting either.

"Better," Penelope said. "I'm pretty sure Jenna's in the building at the far end of the complex, most likely on the top floor. There's a broken office chair and a couple of dead televisions near the stairs. Understand?"

Allura nodded.

"Good. Now I'm going to set you down. When I do, run, and don't look back. If you turn on me, I'll have to kill you and... that won't be good for Jenna. She's a sweet girl and I really want to see something good come into her life, but I value my own skin more than hers. We understand each other?"

Allura nodded again.

Penelope lowered Allura to the ground. "Go."

Allura took a few steps and turned. "Why stay? Why not run?"

"Because Noah'll find me and kill me. Go."

LUCI SQUINTED through her sunglasses as sunlight beat down on her, sapping her strength and speed. Daytime was a cruel mistress.

The huge werewolf watched her with unnerving attention, though he wouldn't meet her eyes even from behind her sunnies in case she mesmerised him. Mesmerising him was her only chance, though. He was twice her size and, despite being a vampire, in sunlight, she'd be dead in a minute unless she got lucky. Or maybe she'd be dead *if* she got lucky.

What she needed was for Teddy Bear to show up, but he was five minutes away still. Allura needed her now.

Noah kept his arms low and his hands curled slightly as if he couldn't wait to get them on her, his eyes on her chin as he sized her up.

Luci gripped the silver knife Allura had given her, her knuckles white. Why the hell had she listened to Kimbriel?

"Come on Noah," she said. "We're not lovers. You going to avenge Cheri, or buy me a drink?"

"Cheri was a bitch. You did me a favour. Considering that, if you put the knife down, I'll kill you quickly."

"Of course you will," she said. "Or I'll kill you instead."

Luci had lived a long life since Shaw had rescued her from her former master, and he'd treated her like an equal since. At least if she died now, she'd be doing something for him and the Menagerie. She doubted Allura was worth it, but Jenna might be, and Allura was the key to Jenna.

"In that case, I'm going to kill you slowly," Noah said, taking a step forward. "I'll use that knife to flay you."

Luci almost groaned. "You sound like a B-grade movie. Got any original threats?"

A slow smile spread to his eyes. "Fine," he said. "I'm going to rip your arms and legs off and feed them to the water rats down at the lake. The rest of you, I'll mount on a wall with your throat ripped out so you can't speak. Make you our mascot."

Luci shifted her weight into a fighting stance and lowered her knife, giving him an opening she hoped he'd try to take advantage of. She'd get at least one slash in. Hopefully, it'd be debilitating.

"Can we discuss our favourite foods while I'm there?" she asked. "Mine's human blood, though I don't mind a good merlot."

Noah narrowed his eyes and almost met hers. Almost. Damn.

"After I gouge out your eyes with that knife, I'll gift them to Shaw."

Glass shattered to her left and Luci flinched, but she didn't risk a glance. More glass broke as a body slammed into sheet metal. A car alarm went off. She'd seen two people struggling when she walked into the carpark. Good. Maybe it'd distract Noah.

"Come on Noah. Have a go. My fangs are getting itchy for some werewolf blood." She almost shuddered at the thought. She'd rather drink raw sewage.

He looked over her shoulder and smiled, obviously trying to bait her into distraction. He winked at whoever was supposed to be behind her. "Do it," he said.

"Your acting lessons were a waste of—"

Something hard slammed into the back of Luci's knees with inhuman force. Pain shot up her legs, taking her breath away as she fell backwards and hit the ground, her knife spilling from her fingers and clattering onto the asphalt.

Someone stomped a heavy boot down on her forearm

and bones fractured. Luci cried out and almost blacked out with the pain, fresh fear rising when she realised she'd lost the fight before it had started.

She'd lost her sunnies too, forcing her to squint against the sunlight's glare. God, she hated sunlight.

"Bad acting?" Noah asked as he stood over her, though he still wouldn't look her in the eye.

The boot pressed down on her broken arm again and ground her bones together. Luci screamed and everything went dark.

It was a long moment before her vision returned, the world made too bright with sunlight. She found Noah in a squat beside her, looming. He already held her knife.

He turned it tip down and positioned it over her chest.

"You should thank me," he said. "As much as I'd love to see you as our mascot, I've got other things to do today. Say hello to your ancestors."

He drove the blade into her heart.

27

The stairwell Penelope had directed her to reeked of rotting food, rat droppings, and smoke of the getting-high variety, the combination turning Allura's stomach.

Unarmed after giving Luci her knife and acutely aware how dead she'd be if she encountered a Creature, she fought her instincts not to run. She would have if not for Jenna.

How had a girl she didn't even know wrapped such unbreakable strings around her heart?

Allura carefully put her weight on the first stair, wincing as the loose concrete slab scraped against metal and echoed through the stairwell, a clear demonstration of her awesome ninja skills.

Holding her breath, she waited ten long seconds before moving again. She was probably being paranoid, but after encountering Noah and Penelope, Allura wasn't expecting luck to go her way.

She made it to the top landing without attracting attention, grimacing at the trash piled up against the walls as if the occupants couldn't even be bothered throwing it down the stairs. Fresh rodent droppings suggested the vermin appreciated it, at least. If the people here knew about werewolves, the reek alone would probably keep them away.

She decided to try the apartment to her left, considering the other door on this landing looked like someone had vomited on it.

Picking her way through the garbage, she tried the handle. It wasn't locked, but she had to lift the door thanks to a damaged hinge, or risk it scraping across the threadbare carpet. Inside, the hallway was gloomy, the reek of marijuana a barrier to anyone who didn't want to float back down the stairs.

"Oh Jenna," she whispered. "What have you gotten yourself into?"

A girl stumbled from the room to the left. For a heartbeat Allura thought it was Jenna, but the woman was in her mid-twenties, her hair lank, unwashed and almost reddish. She looked up, saw Allura, and smiled vacantly. Without apparent care, she stumbled to the next door along the hall and entered. A moment later, Allura heard a toilet seat drop loudly. A man must live here too. At least one.

She might have been able to fight her way past a couple of stoned girls without too much trouble, but it'd be a lot harder if she had to defend herself against someone bigger and stronger, even if they were as high as a satellite.

Allura released a nervous, pent-up breath, barely realising she'd been holding it. Her pulse felt like it was running above what was humanly possible. She unclenched her fists, her fingernails leaving marks on her palms, and sought courage. There wasn't much of it, but she grasped what she could.

She cautiously took a couple of steps into the hallway and paused when a bottle clanked in the far room, though the door at the end of the hallway was mostly closed. She took a deep breath to calm herself and nearly gagged on the smoky air.

Not wanting to risk looking through the doorway at the end of the hallway unless she had to, Allura crept to the first room where the girl had stumbled out of, leaning around the doorframe to look in. What little light there was in the hallway barely illuminated two mattresses and three girls, all unconscious or at least not moving. Two girls to a mattress then, counting the one who'd gone to the bathroom.

"Jenna?" Allura whispered.

One of the girls stirred, pushing long dark hair from her face.

Allura's heart stopped and then thudded. It was Jenna!

Her adopted daughter was laying against the far wall, barely conscious, but at least fully clothed. Half a dozen used needles lay on the carpet next to the mattress, along with a spoon and a couple of lighters.

Allura tried not to look at the paraphernalia.

As if forcing herself to full consciousness, Jenna blinked slowly, and then she smiled when she saw Allura.

Despite the horrid place they were in, the entire world brightened.

Luci gasped like a landed fish as Noah plunged the knife into her chest again. Red soaked her shirt, and she couldn't breathe, blood already clogging her ruined lungs. She couldn't even spit it out.

Noah raised the blade and stabbed her a third time, and she did her best to raise her hand, but didn't have the strength. Fresh agony erupted as the knife cut through her ribs. The pain was almost welcome because it meant she was still alive, if not for long. Her head lolled to the side.

Noah said something. Luci recognised the warning tone in his voice, but not the words.

The knife suddenly jerked to the side, sending a renewed wave of pain through Luci, and then Noah's weight vanished. Luci blinked, struggling to turn her head enough to follow the commotion. A small white-haired woman was laying into Noah, fists pounding into him like he was a rag doll.

Luci heard something break, and then he sprawled. The white-haired woman picked up the bloody knife, examined it, and then tossed it aside. "Get him out of here," she said to someone. "If I see either of you again, I'll kill you both. Got it?"

She moved closer until she stood over Luci.

"Crap, you're a mess. Idiot probably thought the knife was silver. The little crosspiece was, enough to make it smell like silver, at least."

She grabbed Luci by the arm.

Pain shot through Luci's chest and body as the woman dragged her across the car park and into some cool shade, propping her up against a wall and crouching before her. The movement hurt more than the stabbings.

She caught Luci by the jaw and turned her face back and forth, examining her. "You'll live."

Luci doubted it, though now she had time to reflect, she hadn't felt the knife burning her, just pain from being stabbed.

"My name's Ellie, by the way." Ellie rooted through Luci's pockets until she found her phone, unlocked it using facial recognition, and scanned through her contacts. "Only one favourite, huh? He looks special." She winked.

Luci tried to speak, but her ruined lungs wouldn't allow it. She successfully dribbled her own blood down her chin, however.

The woman made a call. "This Lawrence Shaw? Good. There's a featherweight Creature here in pretty bad shape. Asian appearance. Has your number in her phone." She leaned away from the speaker for a moment as Shaw's voice blasted out, but Luci couldn't understand the words.

The woman put the phone back to her ear. "Yell at me again and I'll leave your friend to fend for herself, got it? Good. I'm guessing she's a vampire by her aura, but a fairly young one. If you're her friend, I suggest you come and get her. I'll text you the address."

Ellie hung up and examined Luci again. "He didn't sound very happy." After she'd finished texting, she dropped Luci's phone back in her lap. "I don't suppose you saw the lamia run off, did you? Or where it went?"

A stab of pain seared through Luci's upper body when she tried to speak. All she could do was shake her head slightly and almost blacked out from that.

"Fair enough." Ellie stood and looked around. "I'll wait until your friends arrive just to make sure those wolves don't come back. Not much I can do to help you, though. You certainly don't want any of my blood."

GOD, Jenna was heavy. There was nothing to her, but she had to weigh a good ten or fifteen kilos more than Allura. Just getting her to stand was an effort, and now Jenna was up, Allura couldn't get her to move.

Jenna put her head on Allura's shoulder, slumping and forcing Allura to grip her more tightly or let her fall. "I love you Mum," Jenna whispered. "Can I sleep now?"

"Not yet," Allura said with a grunt. Despite the thrill of being called Mum, she gritted her teeth as she tried to support Jenna's weight. "You need to stand, Jenna. Help me please, or I'm going to drop you."

Jenna sighed like a child half her age and shifted her weight, reluctantly lifting her head from Allura's shoulder. She still leaned heavily on Allura, as if she'd fall if she didn't have support.

"We have to go now," Allura said softly, though it was unlikely she'd wake the other two women here. What the hell would become of them? She couldn't save everyone, but wished she could.

"Hey!"

Allura looked up to find the girl who'd gone to the toilet now standing in the doorway.

She gave Allura an incredulous look. "Bevan!" she yelled. "Some bitch is stealing your new girl!"

"Move!" Allura hissed. She dragged Jenna to the bedroom door and shoved the woman aside with her free hand. It wasn't a hard shove, but the woman stumbled back, hit the opposite wall, and slumped to the ground with a comically surprised expression.

As Allura helped Jenna through the doorway, the woman tried to trip Allura with her feet.

"Piss off," Allura swore. She kicked free before steering Jenna to the front door.

They'd almost got there when someone grabbed Allura by the neck and hauled her back. She stumbled and tripped, sprawling on the filthy carpet at the far end of the hallway.

Allura scrambled to her feet and braced for a blow that

didn't come. A red-headed man pointed at her, though he was a little unsteady on his feet. "Nobody steals my bitches."

Allura would have backed away if there'd been room, but the door behind her was closed. The man, maybe in his early forties with sun-damaged skin and plenty of padding around the middle, began moving toward Allura after stepping casually over the half-prone woman.

Allura braced herself and prepared to fight.

She swung and landed a punch to the side of his head, but he only grimaced and slammed an open palm into her face. She staggered back, pain registering after she hit the door and slumped. Her nose felt broken. Blood ran over her lips.

"Get her, Bevan!" the prone woman in the hall called helpfully.

Before Allura could recover, Bevan caught her by the neck, lifting her off the ground with both hands. He might have been soft around the middle, but he was still bloody strong. Growing panic and flashbacks to Noah's abuse helped her struggle and kick, but he squeezed hard, cutting off her air.

Allura gasped and grabbed at his fingers, trying to pry them away and maybe break one, but just as she almost succeeded, he slammed her against the wall, knocking half the fight out of her. His breath reeked of the last kebab he'd eaten, mostly onion and garlic sauce.

She felt giddy as she clawed at his eyes, but the world shifted crazily as he dropped her. Her legs hit the ground and gave way.

Bevan reached for her, but she still had enough presence of mind to bite. "Bitch!" he yelled and ripped his hand free, almost ripping out a couple of Allura's teeth.

The bastard grimaced as he raised his bleeding fist to hit

her again, but a small pale hand caught his wrist and jerked him backwards. His eyes widened and his feet kicked out as he tried to keep his balance, but he sprawled anyway.

Bevan got to his feet fast, only to draw up. Jenna now stood between him and Allura, swaying a little, but entirely focused on the much bigger man. "You hurt my mum," she said dangerously.

"Get back to your room, Jenna," Bevan said as he stood and approached again. He reached for her shoulder, but Jenna caught his wrist and shoved him at the far door. The man smashed through it as he knocked it off its hinges, crashing into the solid railing above the stairs. He didn't move.

Jenna turned to Allura again. She smiled, but then the smile faded as she saw the damage done to Allura's nose. Still a little unsteady, she crouched before Allura, gently brushing her hair aside. "Can we go home now?" Jenna asked softly. "I'm tired."

Allura nodded.

It took a while to navigate the stairs without stumbling, but they emerged into the late afternoon sunlight without further mishap. Allura kept her right arm behind Jenna's back, keeping her close and never intending to let her go, but it was a margin call as to who was supporting who.

"Which way to home?" Jenna asked, a slur in her voice.

It took Allura a good thirty seconds to figure out where she was in relation to her cruddy apartment, but she eventually pointed. It would take them at least an hour to get there. "That way," she said hoarsely, her voice affected by the swelling in her nose and making her sound like she had the flu.

Jenna's arm tightened behind Allura's back, and she squeezed her closer. Together, they made for the road. They were almost there when a large black four-wheel-drive pulled up before them and the door opened.

Anxiety gripped Allura. She couldn't run and wasn't up for any kind of fight, but didn't know what else to do.

"Allura? God, you're a mess."

She almost passed out with relief when Teddy Bear got out. Jenna fearfully backed a step, drawing Allura with her.

"It's okay," Allura whispered. "He's a friend."

28

Teddy Bear approached, blood to his elbows and all over his tight t-shirt. "You okay?" he asked, reaching out to examine Allura's face.

She flinched at the drying blood on his hands.

"Sorry," he said, before backing a step under Jenna's murderous glare. He put his hands up, palms out, though he seemed more amused than concerned. "I wasn't going to hurt your mum," he assured the young tigress before returning his focus to Allura. "How about you put Jenna in the front seat and hop in the back with me and Luci so I can get a better look at the damage? Okay?"

Allura held back a tired smirk. Teddy Bear only wanted Jenna in the front, so she had less of a chance of ripping his head off if Allura winced when he checked her out. "Okay," she responded, which was about all the words she could manage.

Visible through the car's open side, Allura could just see Luci slumped against the far door, unconscious and covered in blood. Shit. She owed Luci big time. She didn't look like she was breathing either, but Allura wasn't sure if that mattered to a vampire.

"This is Teddy Bear," Allura said to Jenna, her broken nose making her sound funny. "Hop in the front seat," Allura added, but Jenna's grip on her waist tightened. "Please Jenna. We have to get Luci home. She's hurt."

Jenna didn't let go of Allura until Teddy Bear opened the front door for her, and she reluctantly got in. When Allura and Teddy Bear got into the back, Austyn, the driver, hit the accelerator and the huge vehicle leapt forward like a sports car.

"Is Luci going to be okay?" Allura asked.

Teddy Bear gave her a sidelong look. "Yeah. She's taken a lot of damage though, even for a Creature. The physical damage will heal fairly fast, but it'll be a while before she gets her full strength back. She'll need a lot of blood."

"I'll happily donate."

Jenna glanced over her shoulder at Luci, frowning, but not surprised or otherwise turned off by the bloody sight. "I've had worse," she said matter-of-factly.

Those words almost broke Allura, and she had to look away. "Please don't look, honey," Allura said, accidentally using the pet name she'd given to Piper. It sent a shock of emotional pain through her. "Please."

Jenna shifted her weight before turning back to face the front. Austyn hit a pothole and Allura winced as she jolted, her nose and face throbbing.

"Anything hurt other than your nose?" Teddy Bear asked as he examined her without touching.

"Not now Jenna's here." Allura tried not to stare at the back of Jenna's head simply for the reassurance she was in the same car with her. Jenna's indifferent reaction to Luci's condition concerned her. She'd have to be gentle if she was going to help her.

The drive to the Menagerie seemed to take forever, yet it was over before Teddy Bear could give her a proper look over and assess the damage. "Your nose is definitely broken. How do you feel?"

Allura shrugged. "I'm good."

Teddy Bear glanced at Jenna. "I suspect your euphoria will dry up soon. I'm surprised you haven't passed out already."

Pass out? She wasn't going to miss a moment with Jenna.

"How long have you been wearing that collar, Jenna?" Teddy Bear asked.

The girl glanced back over the seat at Allura, apparently questioning if it was safe to speak with Teddy Bear. Allura nodded.

"Since I was fourteen. I'm sixteen now."

"You haven't shifted form in all that time?"

Jenna didn't speak, just glanced enquiringly at Allura again.

"You can tell him."

Jenna shook her head. Teddy Bear cursed under his breath.

After they drove into the Menagerie's basement carpark, getting out of the car proved difficult. Fortunately, Charlotte was waiting for them.

After Teddy Bear got out, Allura followed him and opened Jenna's door. "Honey?" Allura said.

Jenna looked like she wanted to sleep, but smiled when she saw Allura. "Mum," she whispered as if the word were a miracle. Perhaps it was.

Allura felt herself growing warm on the inside, all the

pain in her body momentarily vanishing. She took Jenna's hand and helped her out.

Jenna abruptly stopped, staring at Charlotte. "You're like me," she whispered. She glanced at Allura as if seeking confirmation.

"Yeah, she's like you."

"Twinsies," Charlotte said, though her eyes seemed a little haunted. "Except I'm a head shorter and technically a Malaysian-born Chinese girl now calling Australia home, but yeah, we're the same. I'm a tigress, too."

Jenna blinked as if trying to make sense of that.

Allura stared at Charlotte, trying to figure out what the problem was, and then it came to her. She was still mourning Mary, and now a new tigress had turned up in their lives. Bitter and sweet.

Allura noticed scarring around Jenna's right ankle, red and harsh. She'd been chained with silver then, probably recently. No. Much worse. Chained, and drugged to keep her compliant, and... Allura didn't want to think about it.

Jenna tried to take a step and failed, leaning on the car, her arm trembling.

"You okay?" Allura asked, hesitant to take the girl's weight. She could barely stand herself.

Jenna gave a slight shrug, the movement hiding a deepening tremble. "I got weak and..." She glanced at her left arm, though Allura couldn't see a track mark. "I..." she closed her eyes. "I got weak and said yes. I know I should be stronger, but I couldn't help it." She sounded like she wanted to cry.

Charlotte stepped up beside Allura. "How about I see if I can find you somewhere to stay for a few hours, at least until we can get you checked—"

Jenna reached out and gripped Allura's hand with fear-fuelled strength.

Trying not to wince, Allura squeezed back, meeting the young girl's eyes. "I won't let anything bad happen to you. Not today. Not ever. Okay? I swear it Jenna."

Tears filled Jenna's eyes, and she threw her arms around Allura. "Thank you, thank you, thank you," she whispered over and over again, her trust complete and unwavering. "Thank you for saving me."

Despite the girl's filth and stench, Allura wrapped her arms around Jenna, squeezing her thin frame with what strength she dared. "You're safe now. You really are." She meant it, too.

"She needs help," Charlotte said. "Treatment for heroin withdrawal, and we have to get rid of the collar."

"Mia's on her way to help," Teddy Bear said. "She just needs five minutes to duct tape her kids together so they can't move."

Allura smiled, slipped an arm around Jenna as Charlotte took the other side, and together they helped the girl to the lift while Teddy Bear carried Luci.

Allura couldn't hide her relief when she found Mia already in the lift, but the moment the door opened, Jenna's grip tightened on Allura.

"She's another friend," Allura said. "Another tigress. She's here to help."

Mia's eyes widened when she saw the collar. "May I approach?" Mia asked Jenna, the same haunted look in her eyes as Charlotte had.

Jenna leaned into Allura.

"She's my friend, like Charlotte. She can be your friend, too. I promise she won't hurt you."

Reluctantly, Jenna nodded, watching Mia fearfully. Mia,

a little awkward thanks to her pregnancy, approached cautiously. "I knew it," Mia whispered with a wondrous smile, the grief momentarily vanishing from her face.

"Knew what?" Allura asked. Was there something wrong with Jenna?

"Do you know how long we've been looking for you? You're Jenna, right?" Mia said. "Do you mind if I look you over when we get you to an apartment? We need to get that collar off so you can start healing properly."

"The collar hurts and makes it hard to sleep."

Mia carefully reached out, wincing as her fingertips touched the silver. Even so, she gently turned it around until she found the lock, examining it. Her fingertips were red and scalded when she withdrew them.

"The keyhole's been filled with solder. We'll have to cut the collar off. Let's get her inside first."

29

Partially supporting Jenna, Allura and Charlotte guided the girl into the elevator and up to the seventeenth floor.

"Apartment twelve," Mia said, leading the way and opening the door.

"Wow," Allura said as they walked into the richly appointed private apartment. It looked like it had been renovated and decorated in preparation for a private sale.

"The bathroom," Mia said, guiding them in. "Allura, stay with Jenna and get her cleaned up. Charlotte, help her, please. Shaw is helping Teddy Bear with Luci just now. I'll call Don." She pulled her phone out and dialled, leaving the bathroom.

Allura helped Jenna to strip off her filthy clothes before turning the shower on for her, wincing in pain every time she tried to use her amputated thumb.

"Don't go!" Jenna said in near panic.

"I was only getting you a clean towel. I won't leave. Okay?" She glanced at Charlotte. "Can you grab a towel, please?"

Jenna still seemed to be on the edge of panic, though.

"I won't leave your sight. Hop into the water now, honey," Allura coaxed, squeezing the girl's hand with her good one. With a little more reassurance, Jenna moved into the water even as she kept her eyes on Allura.

The poor girl was so skinny her ribs were showing, but at least she didn't have any obvious injuries. She stood under the warm water, not moving, as if she hadn't had a shower in years and had forgotten what to do.

"Why don't you put some bodywash on the washcloth and give yourself a scrub?"

Jenna's eyes found the small tube of body wash, but she didn't pick it up. She took a deep shuddering breath, her expression breaking as she began to cry. Allura swore and got in the shower with the girl, putting her arms around her and holding her tight.

"It's okay," she said soothingly. "It's okay. You're safe."

They must have stood there like that for at least ten minutes before Allura took the washcloth and doused it with a ridiculous amount of body wash and began scrubbing Jenna clean.

Careful of her damaged hand and missing thumb, she shampooed Jenna's hair next, washing it three times. By the time Allura turned the water off, they were both as crinkled as prunes, but at least Jenna smelled like a person now.

Jenna stood with a towel around her shoulders while Allura stripped off her wet clothes and dried herself before slipping into a bathrobe. Everything was ten times more difficult without a second thumb, but she managed.

Afterward, she helped Jenna do the same. The girl was trembling, but whether from exhaustion or heroin withdrawal, Allura couldn't tell. Leaving the bathroom, Allura almost squealed in fright when she saw Don waiting in the living room along with Mia, Teddy Bear, Austyn, and Tony, another security guard and most likely a werewolf, given he was there.

Teddy Bear was no longer covered in Luci's blood, at least.

"How's Luci?" Allura asked.

Teddy Bear gave a non-committal shrug. "She'll be okay. Bit of a shame, considering she's a vampire." Austyn and Tony both laughed as if that was supposed to be funny.

Allura frowned at them.

Tony picked up a battery-powered angle grinder.

"Bring Jenna over here," Mia said, pointing to the spot they'd cleared of furniture where a large canvas drop cloth had been spread out on the floor.

Jenna didn't move, staring fearfully at Tony.

"Werewolf," she said.

God, Allura's world was getting weird considering that statement seemed normal. She'd known Tony for years though, but never associated with him. "He's a good guy," Allura said reassuringly. "He's here to cut the collar off. I won't leave your side. I promise."

"Swear it," Jenna said, her skinny body trembling in Allura's arms.

"I wouldn't let them near you if I thought they were going to hurt you."

Jenna reluctantly let Allura lead her to the drop cloth where Allura helped her lie down on her right side. She pulled Jenna's hair out of the way, Jenna clinging painfully to Allura's bandaged hand the whole time.

"Hey little tigress," said Teddy Bear, kneeling beside Allura. "Allura's worked here for a long time. That makes her part of my pack, so you're family now too. Understand?"

To Allura's surprise, Jenna nodded.

"Good. I need to explain what we're going to do and what you need to do to help. Is that okay?"

Jenna looked to Allura for assurance. Allura nodded.

"Okay," Jenna agreed.

Teddy Bear smiled. For such a big scary-looking man, he seemed to have a way with kids. "We're going to tuck some leather under your collar, above and below to catch the sparks so they don't hurt you." He held out a couple of ear plugs to Jenna. "You'll need to put these in your ears, too. It's going to be loud."

Jenna stared suspiciously at them.

"They won't hurt," Allura said.

"I'll help you with them in a minute," Teddy Bear added. "All of us creatures will need to wear masks too, as the grinder will put a lot of the silver in the air for a bit. It's not a lot of fun to breathe for us. There's one more thing you need to know. When the collar comes off, you're going to want to change. In fact, I doubt you're going to be able to stop changing. Understand?"

Jenna nodded.

"It's going to feel good, but you could hurt someone, particularly if you're scared. I need you to not be scared. This is very important. If you're scared you might lash out, and Allura's not a Creature, okay? If you hurt her, you could kill her."

Jenna pulled back as if she'd just been threatened with murder, but Allura squeezed her hand. "I'm not scared. You won't hurt me. I know you won't."

Jenna shook her head. "Leave the collar on."

Mia crouched awkwardly beside Jenna, moving slowly to accommodate her growing stomach. "Charlotte's here, Jenna. She's a tiger like me. She can change and stop you doing anything you don't want to. I'm strong too, even if I can't change right now. That good enough? We'll make sure you don't hurt your mother."

"I trust them," Allura said encouragingly.

It took a long moment, but Jenna nodded a little uncertainly. At least she agreed.

"Okay, let's start with the earplugs, then the leather to protect you," Teddy Bear said.

Allura held Jenna's hand as they prepared to cut the collar off, and then Teddy Bear handed Allura some earplugs as well.

"Thank you for this," she said.

"Here, let me help you with those. I've got more thumbs than you, after all. It's a werewolf thing."

Allura couldn't help a smile at that.

He squeezed and rolled each earplug between his thumb and forefinger before working them into Allura's ears. It tickled and made her shiver, but he was careful not to touch her nose. The moment she thought of her nose, it started to ache again. She must look terrible.

Jenna watched the whole time as if prepared to jump up and protect Allura if she had to.

Allura gave the girl's hand a squeeze of assurance, struggling not to pull out the earplugs. "They feel weird." She could hear, but everything was muffled. Teddy Bear gave Allura protective glasses, and by the time everyone was kitted up, Tony was ready to cut.

"Don, you better clear out," Mia said through her mask. "Thanks for bringing all the gear." She gave him a hug. Her husband squeezed her back and left the room. She backed away herself as she glanced at Allura, but seemed to realise that getting Allura to leave was going to be a losing fight.

"Ready," Allura said.

"Remember Jenna, when the collar comes off and you

change, don't panic. Just lay still. We'll be here, okay?" Teddy Bear said.

"Just keep looking at me," Allura said.

"Okay," Jenna said, her face and shoulders now protected with leather, and her own mask muffling her voice and protecting her face from any silver sparks.

Tony turned the angle-grinder on, the noise loud enough to make both Allura and Jenna jump despite the earplugs. Mia stood behind Allura while Charlotte gripped Jenna's ankles.

"It's okay," Allura yelled over the noise.

Tony carefully lowered the angle grinder toward Jenna's neck. The girl's grip tightened painfully on Allura's hand, but she lay there without moving, even if her wide eyes suggested she was close to panic. "It's okay," Allura said, mouthing the words, the only person in the room without a mask.

Jenna jumped again as the grinding wheel touched the collar and orange sparks flew. Tony pulled back for a moment and then lowered the angle grinder again while Teddy Bear braced the collar with gloved hands. Sparks flew again, but this time, they didn't stop. Jenna's hand didn't relax, but she didn't fight it either, her fear-filled eyes not leaving Allura's.

Allura smiled in reassurance as the collar screamed and the room began stinking of burning metal. It didn't take long, though it seemed like it did, and then Tony lifted the grinder away. Teddy Bear gripped the collar, keeping it in place.

"You okay?" Allura asked Jenna.

Jenna nodded but didn't speak, her grip still tight enough to make Allura's hand ache. Mia removed Jenna's earplugs and then Allura's for her, Jenna's mask remaining.

Mia glanced up. "Charlotte, can you grab an ice cube or a glass of water? That metal's going to be hot. Allura, you need to move back now."

Jenna's eyes widened in panic.

"No," Allura said. "I'm staying."

"Allura—"

"No!" There's was no way she'd leave Jenna's side.

Mia muttered something under her breath. When Tony was clear, Teddy Bear nodded. "Okay, let's do this."

Charlotte trickled water over the metal, and it hissed briefly. She moved away and then Teddy Bear bent the two halves open. Jenna lay still as he drew the collar from under her neck. Her eyes widened, and Allura swore she felt the girl's adulation.

In a heartbeat, Jenna's eyes went from dark brown to tiger yellow, and then her body rippled. With a flash of heat, she changed into a huge, if skinny, tigress, tearing away the bathrobe and mask she was wearing.

Jenna shook as if struggling to stay calm, her massive claws biting painfully into Allura's wrist, but Allura kept her eyes on Jenna's. "It's okay," she whispered. "I'm here." Jenna was beautiful. Incredible.

Jenna panted as if she'd been running, possibly from the silver in the air.

"See, you're fine. Everything's okay."

Allura noticed Mia's look of horror, and glanced down to see one of Jenna's claws had punched clean through her wrist, the tip of the bloody claw protruding from the other side. Allura gasped, the pain finally registering.

Jenna, apparently sensing something wrong, tried to move, her claw cutting through Allura's flesh. Allura cried out and Jenna began to panic as Mia ripped Jenna's claw free of Allura's wrist, producing a spray of blood.

"Get back!" Teddy Bear yelled as Charlotte transformed and jumped on Jenna, pinning her to the floor.

Someone, Mia most likely though Allura couldn't see behind her, pulled Allura away, blood gushing from her wrist. Tony got to Allura, his back to Jenna and Charlotte as he gripped Allura's wrist hard enough to cut off the blood flow.

Allura tried to fight them off. She had to get to Jenna. The girl needed her. "Let me go!" she screamed, but Teddy Bear put her in a choke hold and everything quickly went dark.

30

Allura woke, a massive black and orange furry face so close she felt the tickle of warm breath on her nose. She smiled. "You're safe now," Allura told Jenna.

Her nose no longer hurt, and neither did anything else. She examined herself. The bandage was gone from her hand, and her thumb had regrown, the skin baby soft. Youthful.

"Holy shit," she said in awe. Someone must have given her more nectar. If it had saved her hand and kept her fit enough to look after Jenna, it was worth the cost. Maybe.

Jenna, still sleeping, didn't react. The huge Siberian tigress breathed deeply, her body barely fitting on the king-sized bed.

One of Jenna's huge paws was folded up between them, the other draped across Allura's ribs. It was heavy, but Jenna's nearness soothed her like a balm.

Allura touched the tigress's face. One yellow eye opened to regard her, and Allura smiled. "You're beautiful," she said softly. "So beautiful."

She ran her fingers through the fur of Jenna's neck

before tracing the patterns on her face with her fingertips, and marvelling at the thickness of her fur. Jenna gave Allura's nose a raspy lick.

Jenna's ear turned at a noise. When Allura raised her head, she found Mia watching with a gentle expression from the bedroom door.

"I thought Jenna was going to take Teddy Bear's head off when he choked you out. It took the rest of us to keep her pinned down. You nearly bled to death."

Allura began to sit up, but Jenna's paw got heavier, holding her to the bed. "I have to pee," she told the tigress, but Jenna wouldn't lift the massive paw. "Please," she said. Jenna stared, clearly reluctant to let her go. "I really need to go." Jenna finally withdrew her paw, watching closely as Allura got up and left the bedroom.

"Thank you for everything," Allura said as she walked through the luxuriously appointed two-bedroom apartment. "Who owns this place?"

"I had it renovated in the hope we'd find Jenna. It was going to be a home for her. We've been looking for her for two years now. Go do your business. We'll talk when you're done."

In the bathroom, Allura examined her nose in the mirror. It looked like it had never been broken. No bruising or damage, and as straight as she could ever remember it. Unfortunately, her hair hadn't grown back. It was still just as patchy as before.

There was a sense of youth about her features, though. The lines at the corners of her eyes and mouth were so fine now they were almost gone, and her skin no longer showed the effects of sun and hard living. She didn't exactly look younger, but more as if she'd been taking care of herself better.

"Wow." She tried not to think of the cost someone had paid for her appearance.

Her reflection abruptly reformed into Sparrow's face.

Yeah, it's like you don't have to pay for your own excesses anymore. Lesson failed, I see. What next? I hear cocaine's a blast, and it fits nicely in social settings.

Allura gave Sparrow the finger and ignored the comment.

After freshening up, Allura found Mia waiting on the sofa. The woman patted the seat beside her, and although Allura felt a strong urge to return to Jenna, she accepted the invitation.

Mia put an arm around Allura's shoulders and drew her close. "You know my children are human, right?" Mia asked, putting her feet up on the coffee table with a sigh, her free hand on her belly.

"You've mentioned it," Allura said cautiously.

"If they get together with another tiger's human children, there's a good chance some of my grandchildren could be born Creatures like me. Alternatively, my children could become tigers or tigresses themselves with the right stress at the right time. I think Jenna's like my children. Stress or trauma changed her as she was going through puberty. We don't know much else about her yet. Her records were wiped from the system."

"Slade?"

Mia nodded. "Probably. I'm guessing Noah works for him, too."

"I really need to go back to her." Allura began to stand, but Mia's hand tightened on her shoulder.

"Hear me out. Please?"

Despite her growing tension at being away from Jenna,

Allura reclined back into the seat and accepted Mia's hug. It was surprisingly comforting.

"To bond with Jenna, you have to have a common ancestor, and it can't go back more than a few generations or the genetic variations dilute it down to nothing. What can you tell me about your grandparents?"

Allura shook her head slowly, staring into nothing as she thought. "Not much."

"You'd die for Jenna though, wouldn't you?" Mia asked.

"Of course." It seemed like it had always been true.

"From the moment you turned up, myself, Charlotte, and Mary..." she hesitated when speaking Mary's name, and had to take a deep breath to continue. "We all felt protective of you. In hindsight, that tells me we must have sensed you had some tiger ancestry."

Allura scratched her head as she considered it. "Mum emigrated from northern Europe as a child after her parents died. She stayed with an uncle and aunt here, but I never knew them or what family remained in Europe."

"And your father's side?"

"Dad's parents broke up when he was a baby. Grandpa got custody when Grandma left. I remember Grandpa a little, but he died when I was about five. About Grandma..." she shrugged. "No idea. I've got one grainy old photo of her, but that's it. She was short, maybe your height, but the photo's pretty old and she's standing a fair way away from the camera. The only thing I could say for sure is that she had dark hair like you."

"You and Jenna may share a grandmother, then."

"A mystery for another day," Allura said, not really caring how it happened, only that it had.

Mia removed her arm from Allura's shoulders and stood. "Allura?"

Allura didn't like the tone. "What?"

"Something's going on, though Shaw's trying to head it off. I don't know the details yet, but I think there's a fight coming our way. We need to get Jenna out of the Menagerie as soon as she's recovered."

ALLURA LAY face to face on her bed with Jenna, human to tigress. Jenna's body weighed the mattress down so much Allura had to balance herself to avoid rolling Jenna's way. Being close to her daughter had a calming effect on the recovering girl, though, and Allura was unwilling to leave. Even Jenna's breathing seemed to get easier when Allura moved close.

She ran her fingers through the tiger's thick fur as Jenna shuddered and stiffened. Heroin withdrawal. Allura continued caressing her face until ever so slowly Jenna relaxed again. Hopefully she'd recover faster than a human, but it wouldn't be fast enough for Allura.

"I can't imagine what you've been through," she whispered, but that was a lie. She could imagine very well and only wished she couldn't. She'd been a cop working in the field of human trafficking for long enough to know enough of the things Jenna must have endured. It would take years of therapy to sort it out, if that were even possible.

Allura traced her fingertips over the girl's forehead, just as she'd done with her biological children when they were babies. Hurt welled up at the thought, a pain so deep she couldn't stave it off before her vision blurred. Perhaps she needed help, too. God, she'd been an atrocious mother after Piper's death. She had a lot of making up to do.

Despite the grief, Allura eventually dozed, only to wake

when the doorbell chimed, panicking when the lingering dream made her think someone had kidnapped Jenna while she slept. It took long seconds and touching Jenna to calm herself. Jenna's ear turned, her soft breathing changing tone.

Allura listened, but Mia didn't answer the door, which implied she'd left. Feeling vulnerable without Mia there to back her up, Allura reluctantly got up and answered the door.

"Luci?" she asked, a little apprehensively. She seemed so... human. "You didn't look quite so sprightly the last time I saw you."

Luci smiled wanly. "Took a transfusion or two, I'll admit."

"Transfusion. Right," Allura said, hoping Luci hadn't killed anyone. "Do people turn into vampires when you bite them?

Luci frowned, as if insulted. "Of course not. May I come in?" she asked as she glanced a little apprehensively toward the bedroom Allura currently shared with Jenna. The folding doors were open, revealing Jenna sprawled on the bed and far too big for it.

"Of course," Allura said, making way. Luci had saved her life, after all. "Come in."

Luci kept an eye on the bedroom as she stepped across the threshold.

"She's harmless," Allura said.

Luci snorted. "She almost ripped your hand off last night. You would have bled out in a minute without Teddy Bear's help."

"It was an accident."

"Accidentally killing someone has the same results as killing them with intent. It'll only take moment of teenage angst, and you could find yourself disembowelled or worse, so treat her with respect and be extra mindful while she's recovering."

"That's..." She was going to say it couldn't happen, but perhaps Luci was right. Jenna was big enough in animal form to kill Allura just by sitting on her.

"May I?" Luci asked, pointing at Allura's wrist.

Allura held her hand out, hoping Luci wasn't planning another blood transfusion with herself as the donor. Ew.

Luci probed the wrist with her fingers. It was a little tender, but that was it. "Perfectly healed, along with your nose. Your hand and forearm were a mess last night. Amputation zone. I'm glad the nectar went to a good cause."

"Am I the good cause, or Jenna?"

A half-smile crossed Luci's lips. "You, of course."

Allura replied with a smirk of her own. "How are you feeling?"

"Alive, but weaker than a butterfly. I'll be okay in a week or two," Luci said. "I'm not here to check your wrist, though. We have a problem."

"Mia mentioned something."

"Slade's trying to get a search warrant. He knows Jenna's here, and if he gets a warrant, he'll find her. She'll disappear into the system and we'll never find her after that."

Allura felt as if she'd been punched in the solar plexus. "What if I called Quicksilver? He could help."

Luci shook her head. "Quicksilver's just been released from hospital and won't be back on duty for a while. He can't help."

"What if Jenna stays in animal form? They can search this place and never find her that way."

"It's not exactly legal to keep tigresses in apartments. Besides, Slade doesn't care about Jenna. This is about you and Shaw."

That made all kinds of weird sense to Allura. "Slade called me Lumi the day he killed Mary." She met Luci's eyes and saw the truth there. "I'm Lumi, right?"

Luci looked away. "Yes and no."

"What happened between him and Lumi?" She thought she knew, but it would be good to get some confirmation.

The vampire sighed. "Lumi chose Shaw over Slade, millennia ago. They fought over her and Lumi died as a consequence. Slade's never let it go. He blames Lumi for not choosing him, and Shaw for Lumi's death."

"That's some psychotic-level hate. He even dated me when I was younger, just so he could break my heart. What's wrong with him? I'm not Lumi. Not in this lifetime."

Luci shrugged. "As far as I can tell, Slade wants you both to suffer as much as possible. My guess is that he intends to use Jenna to pin a child prostitution charge on Shaw and take Jenna away from you. Two-for-one special."

"Oh, shit."

Luci watched Allura as if trying to figure something out. "Shaw will protect Jenna if he can, but he won't do it at the cost of everyone else here. You and Jenna will have to run as soon as she's recovered enough. We're making preparations."

"We'll be gone in half an hour."

Luci held up a hand to prevent Allura from going for the bedroom. "Slade knows what Jenna is and what to look for. The Menagerie's already being watched. Even if you get away, you won't be able to protect Jenna outside of the Menagerie without help, and Jenna's going to need a lot of care until she recovers."

Allura ran through the options. There weren't many. She couldn't run, and she couldn't stay here. "Is there somewhere in the basement we can hide until we figure something out?" Time was the key, then.

Luci shook her head. "Werewolves would sniff her out. At night their senses will be extra keen while Jenna would be at her weakest. Shaw is trying to buy us a day or two so we can figure out a plan to get you both away safely. Kyle and Zannah and their allies are helping, but things could change very quickly."

Allura felt useless. "So, there's nothing I can do?"

Luci met Allura's eyes. "How far are you prepared to take this, Allura?"

The tone more than the words caught her attention. "What do you mean?"

Luci studied Allura's features. "I'm saying that if things go far enough, cops might die. Good cops. Are you okay with that? Some of them could be your friends."

Allura wanted to say no, but there was only one answer to the question now Jenna was involved. Whatever this bond had done to her, she couldn't live without Jenna. "Whatever it takes." She wouldn't let Slade get Jenna, not while she lived.

Luci nodded. "We protect our own. When the dust settles, remember what you just said. If we survive."

Someone knocked at the door and Allura reluctantly opened it. Mia and Don stood there, both holding fresh clothes and boots for Allura and Jenna. "We need to be prepared," Mia said.

31

Allura paced at the end of the bed, watching Jenna sleep. The sick and exhausted tiger had barely stirred all afternoon, and the closer it got to evening, the more Allura worried for her safety. When she transformed back into human form at dusk, they wouldn't be able to hide Jenna from Slade, and Allura had no idea how many police officers might be Creatures with grudges against Shaw.

Allura glanced out the window, only to see her reflection turn into Sparrow's form.

We're going to die if you stay here. Run. Now. Leave the girl.

Anxiety and anger flared afresh, but Sparrow faded away before she could respond, leaving her staring at her own reflection and her too-short hair. Outside, the sun was still above the horizon, if barely.

"It's going to be okay," Mia said.

Allura jumped. She hadn't heard the woman enter the bedroom.

"I should call Quicksilver," Allura replied. "He's not on duty, but he might know what's happening. Maybe he can give us a heads up?"

Mia put a hand on Allura's forearm. "Would you trust him with Jenna's life, considering everything else that's gone on? Slade may have got to him. He could be blackmailing him or threatening his family."

Allura began to reply, but hesitated, surprised by her own doubt. "Maybe. But..." She left the bedroom to give Jenna some quiet. "He's one of the good guys, and I have to do something."

Mia followed her out. "You're looking after your daughter. That's enough."

Daughter. The word didn't feel familiar yet, but it still sent a thrill through her. "This affects everyone, Mia. Even without Creature involvement, the media attention and public allegations of human trafficking will ruin this place. Everyone's going to be affected."

Mia's phone chimed with a text message. She glanced at it, frowning as she met Allura's eyes. She made a call and Allura recognised Don's muted voice as Mia moved away. When Mia ended the call and came back, her expression said enough.

"They're here, aren't they?" Chills ran through Allura.

"With warrants to search the entire hotel, including private apartments like this one."

Allura closed her eyes, fighting for calm.

"Slade knows there are tigers here, so he might suspect Charlotte or I bonded with Jenna. Maybe that's the point - provoke us into fighting for her. The only thing he couldn't have counted on was you bonding with her, but I don't know if that's a good thing. You can't protect her like a Creature can."

Allura began to disagree, but Mia was right. She had nothing but her wits and swearing ability to fight with. "I don't suppose you've got a suit of armour made of silver?"

Mia gripped Allura's hands. "We have to play along for now, but that doesn't mean we'll give up. Shaw is already preparing media releases, misinformation campaigns, and official statements. For now, we'll play the victim and use the public to ensure Slade won't be able to shanghai Jenna, at least not immediately. She won't disappear yet."

"Yet," Allura said, though she wasn't even sure of that. Despite playing dozens of scenarios through her head, Allura hadn't come up with a viable option, but that didn't mean there wasn't one. "I can't risk letting them get her. If she goes into the system, I'll never see her again."

Mia's hands tightened on Allura's. "Don said the police have the entrances and exits covered, both on foot and by car."

Allura tried to think calmly, but it was a struggle. If Jenna ran in tiger form, she'd end up shot or caged, and it was so close to nightfall that she'd soon be human again anyway. "Zannah and Kyle? Can they help? Or Shaw's succubus friend, Tammy?"

Mia seemed doubtful. "They might be able to do something, but not before nightfall." Still, she made a call, explaining Allura's request to Don. "No, Don, get whoever's available here now. Just having more bodies here can help, and that's good enough for me." She hung up.

It was a nervous wait, but Kyle and Zannah arrived within ten minutes, along with Don, Luci and Charlotte.

"I couldn't get a hold of Tammy," Don said as Mia let him into the room. "It's too late now, anyway. The cops are in the building. Dad's holding them off."

Kyle and Zannah waited outside. "May we come in?" Zannah asked.

Mia turned to Allura. "You need to invite them in."

"What? Why? This is your place, not mine," Allura said.

"I had it transferred to you this afternoon. You had to invite me and Luci in earlier, remember? Jenna's been inside the whole time, though."

That was almost too much to take in and process. "Come in, please," Allura said after some hesitation.

"Thanks," Zannah said as she entered, Kyle, Luci and Charlotte following. "Kyle and I can help, but we can't do anything until after sunset." Zannah glanced at the window, though by the size of her ripe stomach it was unlikely she'd be doing anything herself.

"Help? How?"

Allura took Zannah's hand and half dragged her to the bedroom. Allura pointed at Jenna. Although painfully skinny for such a huge cat, she still had to be over two hundred kilos. Ironically, she'd still outweigh a regular Siberian. Mary had looked half again Jenna's weight, too.

Jenna raised her head, gave a half-hearted snarl, then put her head back down as if even snarling were too much effort.

"I need to get her out of here, Zannah. The police have all the exits covered and Creatures have infiltrated the police. If they catch her, she'll end up in another silver collar, probably in an illegal brothel halfway around the world. Please help us. What can you do?"

Zannah seemed hesitant to approach the tiger. "We can't carry her like that," Zannah said. "She's too big. Will she change at dusk?"

"Yes," Allura said.

"Okay, this is breaking some rules, but we need to get her to the roof. Kyle can get her to safety."

"Why the roof?" Allura gave Zannah a pleading look. "What are you going to do?"

"We can fly," Zannah said with a wicked grin. "Oh God, I've been busting to tell someone that forever."

Considering all the things Allura had seen in the last week or two, that seemed like one of the most mundane things she might have expected. "Good enough for me," she said. "You tell the others. I'll get Jenna up."

Allura crawled onto the bed and took Jenna's huge furry face in her hands. Jenna didn't even stir enough to look at Allura.

"Hey honey, you have to get up."

Allura gave Jenna's fur a vigorous rub until Jenna gave her a reproachful glare.

"Get up please," Allura said, slipping one hand between Jenna's head and the pillow and lifting, or trying to. "God, you're heavy." She glanced through the bedroom doorway. "Mia, can you help, please?"

Mia hurried to Jenna, grabbed the tiger by the scruff of the neck, and dragged her off the bed to the floor without showing any regard for her comfort or condition.

"Hey!" Allura cried.

Jenna's eyes went wide for the briefest moment, and she snarled as she hit the ground.

"Be gentle!" Allura protested.

Mia backed away.

By the time Jenna got to her paws, Allura was by her side. "Jenna? Can you change back now? Please, Jenna." Allura pointed at Mia, then herself, making walking movements with two fingers. She pointed at Jenna then, hoping she got the message. "Change."

Jenna glanced at the people watching, snarling with teeth that could bite through a person's arm with little effort.

"Can you give her some privacy?" she asked the

assembled group through the open bedroom doors before closing them. As she turned back Allura felt a rush of heat and Jenna was human again, the girl laying on her side. Pitifully skinny with her ribs cutting into tight skin, Jenna got to one knee and used the bed to climb to her feet. Allura grabbed a robe and rushed to help Jenna into it. "Come on, we have to get to the roof," she told Jenna.

"Why?"

"Bad people are coming. If we can get you to the roof, you'll be safe." Hopefully.

Hugging herself, Jenna began shuffling toward the bedroom doors, bare feet brushing the carpet. Mia opened them just as the room's doorbell chimed.

Allura's stomach did a sickly roll and a fear-fuelled sweat broke out all over her skin. She looked up as Don opened the door and... "Oh shit," Allura whispered. Two large police officers she didn't recognise stood in the corridor outside the apartment. One held out a warrant to Don. The other pushed past.

Luci got in the way. "Back off," she said.

The huge man averted his gaze as if he knew exactly what Luci was, while more police officers entered the room to back him up. Five of them, Noah included, dressed in a police uniform that seemed far too tight for him.

Oh God, not Noah. The sickly feeling in her stomach intensified, particularly where he'd stabbed her.

"You're not a cop," Luci said to Noah. "Get out." In her weakened condition, her bravado was impressive.

He grinned at her. "And you're tougher than you look. Round two?"

"They're all werewolves," Mia whispered as she moved close to Jenna. Charlotte got between Jenna and the werewolves while Zannah crossed to Allura's side.

"Get to the window," Zannah hissed. "There's no time for the roof."

Although the windows didn't open, they could smash one. Allura began steering Jenna that way, but the werewolves spread out, cutting her off.

Allura swore under her breath. Where did these guys come from? They weren't cops. Not all of them, at least.

Kyle moved closer to his heavily pregnant wife, but he'd be hard pressed to defend her if it came to it. All the cops had guns, anyway. A commotion near the door caught her attention.

Shaw stood there. "Mind if I come in?" he asked.

Mia nudged Allura. "Say yes."

"Yes," Allura said automatically.

Shaw entered, followed by Slade Mills, or at least Slade tried to enter. He bounced back as if he'd ran into a force field.

Slade forced a smile and stared at Allura as if they were still lovers. "May I come in please Allura?"

Mia leaned close and whispered in her hear. "He can't come in unless you give him permission. Don't allow it."

Hell, she was going to use that for all it was worth. "No fucking way, Slade." Slade's career choice made so much sense now. The guy in charge of investigating human trafficking was best placed to protect his own enterprise.

"Come now, Allura. It's only personal." He glanced at Shaw. "And I take every chance I get to piss my old friend and partner off."

"Partner?" Allura asked, meeting Shaw's eyes.

"You've been setting this up for years," Shaw said to Slade.

"I've been putting pieces in play for well over a decade," Slade agreed. "Not that I had any idea how it would play out.

I was just putting myself into position to take advantage of an opportunity, and it was worth it." He winked at Allura.

"Screw yourself."

Slade ignored her, focusing on Shaw instead. "Who are you getting nectar from? I've been looking into it, and dryads don't trade with just anyone."

"They don't like assholes," Allura said as if she had any idea what she was talking about. Jenna was leaning more heavily on her now, already exhausted from standing.

Slade's grin broadened as he turned to Luci. "The real question here is, how did Shaw blackmail you into staying with him for a century and a half? You're a vampire. It's not like you two can screw without killing yourselves. Vampire lifeforce is toxic to our kind."

Allura saw Luci's fist tighten and decided it was best to prevent a brawl before Slade could provoke one, which seemed to be his intent. "What do you want, Slade?" Allura asked. "Nothing here is your concern."

He frowned at her. "I'm very disappointed in you, Allura. If you're looking for someone to blame for all this, find a mirror. You were part of the group who freed my little tiger and a bunch of my other girls, after all. You started this. I'm finishing it."

Luci backed a step toward Allura and Jenna. "Take your phony cops and leave before we make you leave."

"You're not getting Jenna," Allura added, her daughter trembling against her. She finally noticed Jenna was staring at Slade with abject fear. She knew him then.

"It's almost dusk. That makes it five werewolves against one very weak vampire and one incubus. The odds are in my favour."

"Then we do this now," Charlotte said, flexing her shoulders.

"Wait!" Allura said, hoping to avoid putting Jenna in danger. "Take me instead," she added before she could think about it. "It's me you really want anyway, isn't it? Promise you'll leave Jenna alone and I'll come. Willingly."

"No," Jenna whispered, her grip tightening on Allura's shoulders.

The room went quiet.

Slade looked around as if he just won a victory, releasing a long, slow whistle from his position outside the door. He leaned against the doorframe as he assessed the situation, turning to Shaw. "You've been chasing Allura's tail for three thousand years. You going to let her walk now she finally seems to need your company?" he asked with a smile.

"Allura," Shaw began with a warning in his tone. "Teddy Bear and his pack are outside the room. We've got the numbers."

Slade's grin broadened. "Oh, there's plenty of legitimate cops in the building too," Slade said. "Human cops. And the warrant's real. You want to turn this into a bloodbath on your own turf? I can see the headlines already. Go for it. I dare you."

Shaw clenched his jaw. "This is between you and me, Slade. How about we finish it privately? Tonight?"

Slade turned to Shaw, astonishment on his face. "It was never just us," he said with venom.

Allura tried not to think about everything Slade had said in her apartment. "I'll go with you." If it kept Jenna and everyone at the Menagerie safe, she'd do it.

"Mum, no," Jenna whispered.

Slade nodded. "I accept your offer, Allura. Come willingly and I'll make the warrant disappear. Noah and his pack will also leave peacefully. You have my promise."

"Done," Allura said before anyone could protest.

"Deal," Slade agreed with a shiver. "It's a good deal for you, Shaw. I suggest you take it, partner."

"You're still not my partner."

Allura began steering Jenna back to the bedroom.

"Allura, no," Mia said, though she didn't try to prevent Allura taking Jenna back to the bedroom.

"Well, she's clearly not your bitch," Slade said to Shaw.

Allura gave him a finger over her shoulder.

Shaw spoke. "Luci, get the werewolves out of the apartment. They can wait in the corridor with their master. Mia and Charlotte, help Luci please."

Surprisingly, Shaw helped Allura get Jenna back to bed after closing the bedroom doors to cut off everyone's view.

Allura sat beside Jenna, gripping her hand.

"Don't do this, Mum. Let him have me. I can take it. You can't."

"I'll die before I let him take you." Allura gave Jenna a kiss on the cheek. "When you get strong, you and the other tigers can come for me. Okay? You've held on for years. I can hold on long enough for you to get strong again."

She turned to find Shaw with his back to the bedroom doors like he intended to trap her in the room.

"Are you going to stop me?" Allura asked.

"He never promised he wouldn't come back for Jenna. You know that, right?"

She nodded, an idea coming to her. "So, make me a succubus."

He leaned back, clearly shocked. "I—"

"Would it help?"

He shook his head. "We don't have time. It requires sex and time to transition."

"Can you make me your muse?" she asked, thinking of

Sara and her claws. Claws would be very handy right now. "How long would it take?"

"Only a minute, but Allura, you'd be bound to me. That can't be undone, and you'll lose a part of yourself to make it happen."

She closed her eyes, not wishing to give up her independence. "Will Jenna still be my daughter if I become your muse? Will it break our bond?"

"No."

"Do it, then," she whispered, hoping she was making the right decision. Any advantage gave her a better chance, and claws would be a serious advantage if nobody knew she had them.

"You'd trust me that much?" he asked. "I'd control you. Completely."

"Of course." He'd had her back for years now. How could she not trust him? She felt something vast change between them, something monumental, like a dam shattering, freeing a murky torrent that had been trapped for generations. It felt good.

Clearly surprised, he gave a reluctant nod. "You can't let him kiss you, understand? He'll know you're my muse and there's no way he'll let you live after that."

32

Shaw drew a pocketknife, opened a blade, and used the point to prick his thumb. A small bead of blood appeared. "Stay still," he whispered.

Allura tried not to cringe as he smeared his blood on her lips. "Ew," she said when he was done.

"After everything you've been through, you're complaining about a drop of my blood?"

"As lip-gloss? Yeah, it's gross."

In the bedroom's window, her reflection morphed into Sparrow's, his stare intense. Murderous. Outside, the sun had almost set, the city covered in long shadows thrown by its own buildings.

You'll never see me again if you do this. Your bond to him will destroy me.

Her bond to Jenna would remain, though. "I'm sorry," she whispered to Sparrow, and she really was. As snarky as he was, he'd been her companion for so long she couldn't remember what it was like without him.

Shaw reached for her left hand and placed the tip of the

blade just to the outside of her palm where a cut wasn't likely to be seen. "Aren't you going to clean the blade?" She could taste his blood on her lips.

"Yes. Later."

She winced as the tip pierced her skin. "Ow! You better not have any diseases," she muttered, a bead of her blood welling as he clicked the blade closed and pocketed the knife.

Sparrow's frown deepened, his words beginning to gain weight as the reality of her situation became real.

Don't. Please.

She took a deep breath, but Shaw spoke before she could reply to Sparrow.

"If Slade asks, you nicked yourself. Now smear your blood on my lips. You have to do it willingly. Hurry, before he gets suspicious."

She caught the drop on her fingertip and smeared it across his full, soft lips. "What now?"

Now I die.

She met Sparrow's eyes. He wasn't lying. Binding herself to Shaw would end her connection to him, real or imaginary. She wished it weren't a choice between him and Jenna. "Jenna needs me more than I need you," she whispered.

Shaw cleared his voice. "You have to kiss me, Allura, not the other way around. You've got to... desire it. It won't work otherwise."

She'd sacrifice her life to save Jenna, and Shaw was giving her the chance to survive as well. That was worth anything. She stood on her toes, slipped her arms around his neck, and drew him into a kiss.

His lips were warm and soft, the kiss sweet despite the

taste of blood. Nothing happened. Oh, shit. She mustn't have wanted it enough.

As Allura began to break the kiss, something vital tore from her body. Lifeforce. It felt like a part of her very soul tearing free. Her lips burned, her face heated with a flush, and her legs gave way. Shaw caught her.

She was dying. Suffocating. Panic consumed her, and she tried to pull away as her body desperately fought to claw back the part of her spirit Shaw had taken. He held her tighter, crushing her to him, and kissing her harder.

Lifeforce flooded back into her, the same energy he'd ripped from her, but it felt different now. Changed somehow. The world shifted around her, and everything felt far too hot. She couldn't breathe.

He broke the kiss and guided her to sit on the end of the bed, all the strength gone from her body as she finally took a breath. She was trembling all over. "Oh shit," Allura whispered. "I was expecting the ultimate payoff, not the ultimate suck-face."

Pleasure spread through her at his touch, gentle and warm and suffusing her entire body. God, she craved that touch.

"I can sense you already," Shaw said. "But be careful. The further you get from me, the weaker that sense will become. Say goodbye to Jenna. We can't delay."

Jenna? Her bond with the young girl returned with a rush, stronger and more vital than before, a sense of perfection and joy as if they weren't whole without each other.

Just as Shaw said he could sense her, Allura could sense Jenna's presence much more strongly now. They were, quite literally, joined in some unexplainable way, the tiger bond preceding and altering her newer bond with Shaw.

Allura glanced at the window. Her reflection was entirely devoid of Sparrow's presence, as was the feeling in her soul. He was gone. Really gone. The loss sparked longing and pain. Almost unconsciously, Allura slipped a hand into Shaw's.

"Allura," he said. "Focus."

She did. On him. She leaned in to kiss him. She needed his touch.

He caught her jaw with his free hand. "Stop," he said, the tone a command.

She blinked, dazed. The desires fled. "But you want me," she said, confused. "I can feel it."

"You did this for Jenna, remember? Suppress everything you're feeling about me. Focus on the things you care about. I know it's overwhelming at first, but don't get lost in this."

It was as if her feelings were reaching into her mind and reordering her emotions. Her bond with Jenna flared again, vital and fresh. It anchored her.

"Thank you," she whispered.

With Shaw supporting her, Allura moved round the bed and kissed Jenna's forehead, the unexpected and strange sense of the girl's weak lifeforce reaching her through the kiss. "I'll be back for you," Allura said.

Jenna didn't speak. She just stared at Allura as if she couldn't believe what she'd seen. "I love you," was all she said.

Shaw opened the bedroom doors. Everyone silently watched as Allura walked out. They were all clearly concerned, Mia in particular.

Not just her friends. Her people. They'd come to help her. She just needed to hold on long enough to give them the chance to help her again.

She felt different as she walked, physically altered in

some fundamental way. She didn't feel any less human, but her perceptions had changed like her sense of Jenna's lifeforce as she'd kissed her. That, and colour, and... and something more. Something innate had woken within her. Feline. Predatory. Her tiger ancestry trying to surface, perhaps.

She could sense lifeforce from Don as she passed him, strong and vital and purely human. Mia and Charlotte's lifeforce felt a little off, as had Jenna's, but Don's turned her on in a very disturbing way. She tried not to let him see how much it affected her.

She couldn't sense anything from Luci though, or even Zannah and Kyle. They were voids as far as lifeforce went.

"We'll get you back," Mia said as she took a few quick steps to catch up, briefly grasping Allura's hand. Allura nodded as she squeezed back. If she spoke, she'd lose it.

Slade remained at the doorway, watching her speculatively. As she reached the corridor, the lifeforce from the werewolves behind him hit her like spoiled milk. Like her, they were still human, but not entirely.

"I smell blood," Noah said from behind Slade.

"Never had a girlfriend before?" Allura asked. "It's a monthly thing. Look it up."

"You know," Slade said as she left the safety of her apartment. "I have a feeling you might make a good toy-girl for me. Perhaps I'll chain you to my bed."

Hatred rose like bile from her core. "Three thousand years of trying and failing and you can't get yourself a willing woman, huh?" Allura asked, echoing something Sparrow had said to her a while ago.

Anger darkened Slade's expression, and he punched her in the stomach so hard Allura dropped to the ground, unable to breathe. She barely noticed someone pulling her arms behind her back and cuffing her wrists. Unable to stand, Noah hauled her upright, supporting her.

It took a long moment to suck in her first breath, shallow and gasping. When she eventually looked up, she found Shaw and the tigers at her open door, all of them glaring at Slade like they were about to rush through and attack.

"Don't," Allura gasped. "It's what he wants." If Shaw interfered, it'd give Slade an excuse to break his promise, and that was the best-case scenario. The werewolves had guns, probably loaded with silver.

Still unable to stand on her own, Noah and another werewolf supported and half-dragged her toward the elevators.

A strange sensation came over her as they waited for the elevator to rise to their level, an anticipatory tingling in her extremities before a warm flush of energy rippled through the world. It brought her senses fully awake. The feeling of tainted lifeforce from the werewolves suddenly grew stronger.

Dusk.

The sun must have set. She was probably feeling an echo of what Shaw felt.

An elevator chimed, and the doors opened, the werewolves forcing her in and turning her around. Slade entered with the rest, the group crowding the elevator as they descended.

When the doors opened again, she found the hotel lobby deserted of guests. Only half a dozen of the Menagerie's security personnel were there, werewolves all judging by her sense of their tainted lifeforce.

Teddy Bear stood closest to the exit, one finger to an

earpiece. He gave a discrete shake of his head to the others before he met Allura's eyes. He offered her a slight nod of respect before making way for her and her unwanted escort.

Like two packs of dogs hoping for an excuse to brawl, the cops and the Menagerie's security personnel eyed each other.

As Allura stepped into the evening air, Quicksilver approached, moving like he should still be in hospital. He got between her and the waiting police car, clearly surprised by her apparent arrest. God, he looked like crap, but at least he was upright.

"What the hell is this?" he asked. "Allura?"

"I'm glad you're okay, Quicksilver," she replied, hoping to protect him. His lifeforce was completely human at least, and like Don's, it felt good. She wanted to breathe it in.

The werewolves tried steering her around Quicksilver, but her ex-partner got in their way again, a little more spry than his appearance suggested. "Why are you being arrested?"

"She interfered with an ongoing investigation," Slade said from behind Allura. She'd bet money he was smiling. "Unless you want to be arrested too, get out of the way, Quicksilver."

Quicksilver seemed a little too surprised to argue. Noah forced Allura to walk around him. Another werewolf opened a police cruiser door, forcing her in. He slammed the door shut on Quicksilver's protests.

"I'll meet you at the station!"

Allura smiled, but didn't have the heart to tell him she wasn't going to the station.

A few blocks away, they transferred her to a plain white van, searching her. "Asshole," she said to Slade.

"Shut her up," Slade said.

Noah gagged and blindfolded her, and they drove off again, not that there was any call for a blindfold. She couldn't see anything from the back of the van, anyway.

It was a long drive with plenty of turns and two more vehicle transfers.

Judging by the tyre screeches, they eventually drove into what Allura suspected was a basement car park. The van pulled up, and they got out, their footsteps echoing on concrete.

Still blindfolded and cuffed, Allura stumbled when they forced her to climb stairs. She counted twelve landings with turns. Half a dozen floors, starting in a basement. Hers was the fifth floor then, or the fourth if there were two basement levels.

Pushed unexpectedly, she stumbled and fell and, without hands to protect herself, she hit the ground hard. She curled in on herself in pain, her shoulder aching, as someone caught her foot, their lifeforce reeking of a werewolf's taint.

Allura tried to fight back as they locked a heavy metal cuff around her left ankle. They released her then, the door to the room slamming shut.

Still blindfolded, cuffed, and gagged, she got to her knees and then rocked onto her feet. The cuff around her ankle dragged a heavy chain across the concrete.

Blindly, she made her way around the room, cursing through the gag when she cracked her knee on a bed against one wall. With nothing else to do, she sat on the mattress. If Jenna had endured worse than this, Allura could too.

She didn't know how long she sat blindfolded and gagged, but the door eventually opened and someone walked in. She felt no lifeforce when they got close enough. A Creature, but not a werewolf. The footsteps were solid. Heavy.

A man, probably. He removed the blindfold, and she blinked, squinting at the brightness of a single light set into the ceiling.

Slade watched her in a disturbingly interested way as he removed the gag. "Good to see you looking so... chained, Allura. Not really how I pictured you, but then I never thought you'd show any true loyalty to Shaw, either."

She glared at him. "You're supposed to be protecting kids, not trafficking them."

He gave her a look implying she was painfully naïve. "I've been trading slaves for thousands of years. People are just another commodity and always have been. All you need to ask yourself is, are you a trader or a commodity? Right now, you're looking like a commodity."

She met his eyes. "Go jerk off somewhere else. You're making the room feel dirty."

He dropped to one knee and put his right hand on her thigh. She stiffened and raised her chin in defiance, determined not to let him see her fear.

"I have a proposal for you, Allura."

She forced herself to produce a bright, happy, fake smile. "Oh goody! Do you want me to slit your throat with a silver knife? I will. Just for you."

Amusement rather than anger crossed his face. "Breaking you will be fun. I bet you were a wild kid, always in trouble."

"No throat slitting?" She sighed with overly dramatic disappointment. "I'm bored. Can I go to sleep now? I've had a big day."

His amusement grew. "See, that's why I like you. You don't take anyone's shit. It's refreshing. Lumi was like that too. Conversely, I surround myself with yes-men. They're all scared of me. You're not. I like it."

She faked a yawn.

He slapped her hard across the cheek. Allura closed her eyes until the pain eased.

His amusement seemed to have limits, it seemed. Nastiness crept into Slade's expression, as if he were determined to hurt her now. "When I first... acquired... Jenna, she spent about six months in this particular room before I sold her to Noah." He slipped his hand down Allura's leg to her ankle and the heavy cuff there. "She even wore the exact same jewellery."

Hatred so intense she couldn't control herself filled her, and Allura lost it. She head-butted Slade so hard her own vision went black. She fell back, her nose and forehead full of pain. "Oh fuck," she whispered.

Slade chuckled. "You've never been in a bar fight, have you? Did you break your nose?"

"Fuck off." She might have.

"You see something that scares you and you charge at it. Most people run. Why is that?"

She wanted to put her hands to her face, but groaned in frustration when the cuffs prevented it. "Why don't you hurry up and murder me so I can get some sleep?" Taunting him was all she had left. At least her vision was coming back, although her eyes were still filled with tears.

"By the time I'm done, you'll be begging me to kill you, unless we reach a different agreement. Care to discuss my proposal? I'm always up for a good deal. It's how I've stayed alive for thousands of years."

She forced herself to sit up, though it brought a wave of darkness and pain. "You did your deal when you brought another woman into our bed. You had me and you blew it. You could have had me still if you'd wanted it. Never again.

You're just an unwanted notch on my garter belt now. Go find someone else to propose to."

He smiled like he was actually enjoying this. "I'm offering you a job, Allura. Good pay. Great benefits. You wouldn't be forced to work on your back, either."

Was he serious? A job? "Say what?"

33

"What's this job? Chaining kidnapped girls to beds? Do I need to kidnap them myself, or will they be delivered ready for chaining?" She wished she could have physically slapped him with her sarcasm, or preferably dropped him into a vat of steaming turd soup before sealing the lid shut.

He shook his head in mock disappointment. "Assassin. Obviously."

"Assassin?" she asked, wondering if she'd heard him properly. "In what universe would I ever want to be a fucking assassin?"

"Shaw's got Luci to do his dirty work. Now I've got you." He was watching her like he knew something she didn't.

"Never. You don't own me, and you can't force me into it." She glanced at the heavy chain and cuff around her ankle and felt the whip-crack of irony across the back of her head.

"Immortality will suit you, I think. You're hard enough to take to it and it'll prevent you from being reborn into Shaw's life over and over. How's it sound so far?"

"Immortality?" She stared at him, trying to figure out the

angle. "You want to turn me into a vampire? Ew. Exsanguinating people isn't my thing. Hard pass."

He cocked his head, watching her as if he hadn't considered that. "You misunderstand. I don't get what I want by attracting attention, and exsanguinating people tends to do that. That's Shaw's stupidity. He advertises. I like subtlety. A succubus can ensure people die without a clear medical explanation. For that matter, so can a muse." He frowned as if considering something. "I've never had a muse. I hear they're pretty useful. Let's run with that, instead."

She felt herself go cold. "What's a muse?" she asked, hoping she sounded believable.

His expression became a little less congenial.

"My enterprises rely on humans. They're the first line of defence for a building like this. A human who calls a place like this their home can keep out unwanted Creatures like Shaw's tribe of misfits, excluding werewolves, of course. A muse, being mostly human, can walk into a building without being bound by Creature limitations too, just as werewolves can. Werewolves, unfortunately, tend to do a lot of damage. A muse is far more subtle."

He was serious? "You want me to keep the owners of your illegal brothels in line?" she asked. "And kill them if they play up? That's your lame plan?"

"Among other things."

She shrugged, aiming for non-committal. "If it involves killing rapists and kidnappers, I might actually consider it."

He looked her over, as if trying to determine how serious she was. "The bulk of my business is moving people around the world or keeping them in place once they arrive. The more exotic someone's looks, the better. You'll be my enforcer. I'm liking this muse plan more and more. Maybe in a few decades I'll reward you with immortality if you do a good job, but let's hold off for now, shall we?"

The thought of working for him sickened her. "And Creatures like Jenna? Why them?"

His smile grew, probably calculated to hurt her. "Creatures can take a lot of abuse, and they don't age. Tigers have the added advantage that they're mostly human at night, and they can't bite and turn anyone the way werewolves can. I wish I had more of them. I intend to breed more tigers from Jenna, eventually."

A chill slowed Allura's blood. When she spoke, she deliberately kept her voice soft. "You know I want to murder you right now, don't you?" She met his eyes, wishing her hatred could kill him right there.

He gave her an unconcerned look. "Of course. I'd rather you resent me now than later."

"Oh, there won't be a later. I'll kill you the first chance I get."

"Rather dark for an ex-cop." That thought seemed to amuse him. "I'm willing to make you a promise, Allura. Care to hear it?"

"Amuse yourself," she said coldly as she tried to wriggle her wrists from the cuffs. It was pointless, but it gave her something to focus on.

"I want to spare you a lot of pain. Real pain. Emotional pain too, of course."

"Please say you're going to kill me quickly, then."

He pursed his lips, watching her with that unfading amusement as if they were having a friendly conversation. "If you agree to do what I tell you, I'll promise not to touch your friends at the Menagerie or force you to act against them, including Jenna. Sound like a good deal so far?"

It wasn't what she'd been expecting, and it might be the

best deal she was likely to get. For them and Jenna, she actually considered it. "Killing rapists and slave traders in exchange for you not killing my friends? Sounds like a dream job."

"But only if you become my muse. Unlike becoming a succubus, that requires your willingness, I understand. Desire, even."

That wasn't possible, but she could hardly say so without dire consequences. "I've heard about muses," she admitted, hoping her voice didn't betray her. "I'd rather be a vampire, fuck you very much."

He laughed congenially. "I figured as much, but Luci killed my only vampire in the raid, and vampires aren't my people, anyway."

This conversation wasn't going anywhere. "Thanks for the job interview. If you'll just uncuff me now, I'll find my own way out."

He smiled. "How about I turn you into a succubus and force a promise from you instead? It won't work quite as well as far as entering properties goes, but we'll make do."

She went cold. "No, thank you. I'd rather be human."

He frowned. "I don't need your permission to change you, Allura. That's only for muses."

"Maybe I am a muse," she said. "That'd screw up your plans nicely, wouldn't it?"

He laughed. "Not at all. Muses, like werewolves, are still human, and can be turned into real creatures. It just requires more lifeforce to do it."

Oh shit. "How about I think on it? Six or seven decades should be enough."

He moved closer, close enough for her to headbutt him again. Her nose still hurt from the last time, though. "Do you have any idea how much pain and abuse a Creature can take without dying? I could make you suffer for centuries. Eventually, you'd promise me anything. That's the beauty of making someone immortal, Allura."

"Please don't," she whispered. "I don't want to be a succubus."

"You'll be my muse or my succubus, but either way, you'll obey me. There's a very short window of opportunity where I'm willing to keep the Menagerie and all its Creatures in the deal. Don't waste it."

"Shaw's going to kill you," she said, certain of it. "It doesn't matter what you do to me. He'll kill you. You know that, right?"

He met her eyes. "Shaw and I have been playing this game for three thousand years, Allura. I've stolen you from him half a dozen times. He doesn't care about you anymore. Not since Lumi. She was the only woman he truly loved. We both loved her. You're not her though, are you? Not anymore. You're different."

She was running out of insults. "If I'm different, what do you want from me then? You obviously don't care about the Creatures in the Menagerie if you're willing to trade them away to get what you want from me. So, what is it you really want from me?"

He stood, looking down at her. "Three thousand years ago, all three of us were human, but you chose him over me. What do you think I want?"

"You had me as your willing lover once, so it can't be as simple as sharing my bed. What's driving you, Slade?"

He closed his eyes, inhaling deep as if he could smell her anxiety. "You broke me when you chose Shaw. Breaking you, and seeing you so damaged you can't live a normal life, is perhaps the best therapy I could ever hope for. If you don't want to be my assassin, we could start with a world tour of my brothels. Natural blondes bring in a premium price in so many places."

Allura turned away.

"I'll let you think about my offer for an hour, but no longer. There's a truck scheduled to arrive at dawn. It'll be carrying a lovely shipping container with all the modern conveniences for international travel, like water jets to wash the piss and excrement out every morning. I'm sure you'll fit in with the other girls. Decide quickly." He began walking away.

"My friends will come for me," Allura said. "They will." She didn't sound nearly as confident as she'd hoped. "And when they do, I'm going to kill you."

He paused, looking back over his shoulder. "Only humans and werewolves in human form can enter this building uninvited, and I hope they try. We're waiting for them."

The thought of anyone dying on her behalf made her feel sick. "I need to use the bathroom, please." She twisted to show him her cuffed hands. "I need my hands free." It wasn't a convincing lie, but it might work.

He smiled. "Okay, let's play that game." He unlocked one wrist, pulled her hands in front and cuffed them again. "There's a bucket in the corner. Enjoy yourself."

Her hopes fell over a cliff and died.

34

Allura hunted around the room for a sliver of metal she could use to try and pick the cuffs, but the bucket didn't have a handle or anything loose, and the bed frame was made from solid metal bars. Otherwise, the room was clean.

She examined the ankle cuff and chain. There was a keyhole, the lock accessible from the underside, but nothing like a padlock she might be able to break with enough leverage. The chain led to an o-ring bolted into the floor, the four large bolts rounded off so they couldn't be undone.

She gripped the chain in both hands and pulled, but it did nothing. Much stronger people had probably tried.

Fighting off fear and stress, she figured if she was going to get out of this, she would need to steal the key or wait until Slade unlocked her to transport her. She might find an opportunity then. Unlikely, but it would still give her a chance and she needed to figure out how to take advantage of it.

Allura checked the frosted glass window opposite the door. It was a single panel that didn't open, though it was big enough to get through if she could get past the bars on the outside and slip her ankle cuff and chain. The five-storey fall didn't appeal much, but it might be better than Slade's alternatives.

Squinting to see through a chip in the window's bottom corner, she saw a dark, disused car park and a boarded-up building that looked like a storage shed. A burned-out car offered testament to the chances of anyone being around at night, or even during the day. Where was she? Everything beyond the storage shed looked like scrubland, suggesting she was on the edge of an industrial estate.

Even if she broke the window and screamed until she was hoarse, no one would hear her. Slade had clearly picked this building for a reason.

Broken glass, however, was a weapon. It wouldn't kill a creature, but a shard buried in a werewolf's stomach might help her get the keys. She could do it. She'd have to.

She pulled her t-shirt over her head, wrapping the cloth protectively around her right hand so she'd be ready to pick up a shard, and lifted the bucket to smash the window. It was better than nothing, and they'd come running as soon as the window smashed.

The door rattled. Her hopes did a slow revolution around the toilet bowl and disappeared as Slade pushed the door open and entered. The incubus glanced at the window, one eyebrow raised. "Go for it. I'll wait."

Allura raised the bucket. She had nothing to lose.

Noah walked into the room behind Slade, dragging a young woman by the arm. She had a sweet, heart-shaped face, but was clearly terrified and too cowed to fight back.

"I've moved up the schedule," Slade said. "I need a decision now."

Trying not to let her hatred show, Allura reluctantly put

the bucket down and unwound her t-shirt from her hand before pulling it back on, catching Noah checking her out as she did.

"Excellent decision," Slade said, pretending to give her a clap.

"Sit on your middle finger and spin," Allura said, demonstrating which finger he should use.

His smirk grew. "Care to be my muse, or do I need to work a little harder to persuade you?"

"Why don't you—"

Slade nodded to Noah. He drew a knife and slit the girl's throat, the violence and speed catching Allura by surprise.

Blood sprayed across the room and the girl fell to her knees and then face forward, her hands to her throat as she tried to prevent herself from bleeding out.

Allura screamed and launched herself at the werewolf, chain clinking behind her, but Noah casually backhanded her. She didn't even realise she'd hit the ground until she found cold concrete pressed against her aching cheek. Her head felt like a church bell.

She moaned as she rolled to her side, the room spinning. "I'm going to kill you both," she said in a tiny, unconvincing voice. "Maybe tomorrow."

Noah snickered. He stepped over the girl's body and hauled Allura to her feet, giving her cheek a pat, which hurt enough to make her knees give.

She'd failed to notice another cop had entered the room behind the other two, a short, weedy-looking guy with greasy dark hair. He needed a shave. Not a cop, then, just dressed as a cop. He held a new woman by the wrist. She had long dark hair and a split lip, a nasty bruise at the corner of her mouth and chin. The way she gazed around suggested they'd drugged her.

"Please don't hurt her," Allura whispered.

Slade pointed to the dead girl and then the new one as if the choice were Allura's. "These two would have fought each other to death for the opportunity I'm offering you. Care to take me up on it?"

"If she wants it, she can have it. Kill me instead."

Slade frowned, anger suffusing his features and betrayed by a flush. "What would it do to Shaw to see you as my loyal bitch over the centuries? I'm going to enjoy breaking you."

She raised her chin. "Never."

"The response I require is, *I'll do whatever you want, Slade*." He nodded to the second cop, who stabbed the frightened girl in the stomach. She gasped, mouth wide, but no sound emerged. Before Allura could protest, he stabbed her again, and then again.

"You bastard!" Allura yelled impotently as the girl fell forward, blood spreading fast across the cold concrete.

Noah left and brought another woman into the room, this one tall and skinny, her pale strawberry-blonde hair lank. She might have been in her early twenties.

"Please, Mister Mills. I've been good, haven't I?" the girl asked as she stared at the bodies on the ground.

Allura's heart wrenched at the broken tone in the girl's voice. The pleading. She sounded a little like Jenna.

Slade spoke as if the woman were the most important person in the world to him, gently cupping her cheeks with both hands. "Yes, you have, Mitsi. Perfect." He met Allura's eyes. "Choose your response very carefully, Allura. Mitsi needs you."

The young woman's desperate, pleading eyes, reflected Allura's fears.

Slade sighed at the delay. "Do it," he said.

"Wait!" Allura cried, putting her cuffed hands out in

protest. "You win. Turn me into a succubus and I'll give you any promise you want, as long as you don't hurt her or the people I care about."

Mitsi's terrified expression remained, but with a tense sort of relief and hope mixed in.

Slade raised a hand, stopping Noah. "Leave Mitsi here, but drag those two out and send their bodies to the ghouls."

Allura watched in morbid horror as Noah and the other werewolf did as they'd been told, the bodies leaving trails of blood on the concrete as they dragged them out by their ankles.

Slade frowned as he glanced at Mitsi, and then Allura. "Muse, not succubus."

Allura shook her head. "You can't force someone to become a muse any more than you can force them to love you. Shaw told me that."

"I've never made a muse," he whispered. That fact seemed to annoy him, as if he'd tried to make himself a muse before, and failed. "Succubus will do, and then you'll promise me loyalty and obedience."

How had she ever thought he was one of the good guys? "Fine, as long as you promise to leave the people I care about alone. Forever."

A sadistic smile cut his lips wide enough to expose his teeth, and he returned his attention to Mitsi. "I'll need lifeforce to change you. Lots of it. And then we'll have to have sex. Again."

Ignoring the second part, Allura took a single step forward, the heavy chain clinking. "You agreed not to hurt her."

"This won't hurt Mitsi, and she won't die. I don't break deals, Allura. It's bad for business."

Allura wanted to say something, but Slade might have

killed the girl if she had. "It'll be okay," Allura said without confidence to Mitsi, who didn't seem to have the willpower to run.

Slade lifted Mitsi's face. "Perhaps you'll make a good slave for Allura," he said, studying the young woman's face. "Would you like to be Allura's muse?"

Mitsi nodded, clearly having no idea what that meant, but agreeing nevertheless. Slade leaned in and kissed her. Mitsi stiffened, her eyes going wide as Slade drew on her lifeforce, and then she melted into him with a moan of pleasure.

Allura closed her eyes, surprisingly turned on by the unexpected feel of the lifeforce draining from Mitsi's body. Was she really going to let him turn her into a succubus? She began trembling with a different kind of fear now.

Slade eventually pulled away and let Mitsi crumble to the floor, her face so pale she might have been drained of blood instead of lifeforce. She was breathing at least, if shallowly.

"You could have put her down gently," Allura said.

Slade met Allura's eyes. "She'll recover, and when she does, you can make her your bitch, just like I'm going to make you my bitch." He casually stepped through the pools of blood toward Allura. It was all she could do to hold her ground. The wicked smile returned to his lips at her reaction, his teeth showing again.

"Don't worry. It'll be like an orgasm in your mouth. I'm sure you know the feeling." His smile broadened.

"I just vomited in my mouth, actually. I'm sure you recognise the reaction to women seeing you approach." This close, she could feel Mitsi's lifeforce in his body, rapidly corrupting in some indefinable way she didn't understand.

He gripped her chin and forced her face up. "Say please."

She shuddered. "Never."

He forced his lips against hers and lifeforce tore out of her body as if her soul was being ripped out. Panicking, she tried to push him away, struggling as sudden weakness crushed her ability to stand and desire suffused her instead.

Slade broke the kiss with a shudder, a sickly pallor to his skin. "You're his muse!" he said.

Although trembling and barely upright, Allura smiled. "Having an orgasm in your mouth yet? Did you swallow?"

She expected him to wipe his mouth, or maybe to hit her. Instead, he gripped her by the throat. "I'm going to do much worse than kill you now." He lifted her off her feet.

She cried out, gripping his wrist and kicking, wishing for the strength to break his hold. He didn't flinch at her weak attempts to hurt him, so she tried to pry his little finger back like she had with Noah and break it instead. She couldn't even budge one.

"I'm still going to make you my succubus, but you're going to regret not telling me you were Shaw's muse. Do you know what happens to a succubus who's not allowed enough lifeforce? Her body cannibalises itself until she desiccates. Our kind don't die from it, though, not for centuries. You'll suffer, and you'll be conscious the whole time."

Struggling for breath and unable to break his hold, all she had left was her ability to taunt him. "It'll be more enjoyable than sex with you," she croaked.

He snarled, talons extending from his fingertips and threatening to pierce her neck. A little more force and they'd break through her flesh, and he really might turn her into a desiccated corpse.

"Do it," she hissed. Better to die quick, at least. "Punch those talons into my neck and take all my lifeforce."

Anger suffused his features, and it was clear he wanted to.

Certain she was about to die, Allura reached for her only comfort, her bond with Jenna, their connection born from the tiger within Allura that had never been let free. It was all the tiger she'd get, but she welcomed it because it gave her Jenna. Bonding with Jenna was the best thing she'd ever done, and it meant she wouldn't feel alone as she died.

Allura could sense Jenna's distant presence, safe and free, and smiled even as regret pierced her soul. She wouldn't be there for Jenna as she grew into a woman. Although the thought almost broke her, she'd do it again to save the girl.

Jenna wasn't her only bond, however. She had twin bonds now, intertwined and inseparable. Her sense of Shaw was also there, but her bond with Jenna ran deeper.

Allura felt Jenna's warm and fearful presence respond to her, their connection strong. There was something more there, though. Jenna's lifeforce, freely given, rushed through the bond and ignited something vital within Allura, an echo of what could have been if only circumstance had been a little different.

Allura's fingertips tingled and the bones in her fingers itched. Heat scalded her fingernails and then tiger claws erupted from her fingertips, curved and deadly sharp, and all thanks to her connection with Jenna.

Allura smiled and dropped her hands from Slade's wrist and punched her claws deep into his stomach. His eyes widened in pain and his grip on her neck loosened. With all her strength, she ripped her hands upward like a bodybuilder doing curls.

Eight razor-sharp claws tore parallel gashes through his stomach from hips to ribs.

Slade dropped her and staggered back, making choking sounds as if Allura had shoved a hot poker down his throat.

Allura hit the ground awkwardly thanks to the chain, her ankle rolling, and pain was all she knew for long, agonising seconds.

Slade stumbled away from her through the bloody pools on the floor, both hands to his stomach to stop his intestines spilling out.

By the time she recovered enough to sit up, Slade had backed to the door, his shoulder against the frame as he stared at her in shock.

"What are you?" he gasped.

"A mother," Allura said hoarsely, her voice still recovering from his crushing grip.

The window behind her abruptly shattered, glass raining down as the bars and part of the wall tore outward. Allura instinctively curled up as Teddy Bear burst through the hole in the wall like he'd been catapulted. How the hell had he gotten to a window five storeys up?

She'd have hugged him if she wasn't laying in a foetal position.

35

Allura glanced at the door as Teddy Bear helped her up, but Slade was gone.

Teddy Bear froze at the sight of her claws. "What the hell?" He almost dropped her.

"They only disembowel nasty people," Allura said hoarsely, her tone light to hide the pain in her ankle.

"You're human." He stared at her as if she'd grown horns as well. "You smell human." He didn't sound as confident as the statement implied.

"Only on days ending in 'y'," she said. "Hurry. We need to stop Slade."

Another man burst through the hole where the window had been, hitting the ground with booted feet and sliding on shattered glass for a metre. Tony, Teddy Bear's second in command.

"How did you two get up here?" Allura asked as Teddy Bear finished helping her stand. She couldn't put all her weight on her right ankle, but she could stand on it.

"Can you make it to the window, Allura?"

There wasn't a window, only broken bricks.

"She's got claws!" Tony said, jumping back. He glanced from Allura's hands to Teddy Bear as if expecting denial.

"Didn't you know?" Teddy Bear asked with a straight face.

For the first time since arriving here, Allura felt genuine hope. "We've got to stop Slade," Allura said before she could talk herself into taking the win and returning to Jenna. "He won't play this nice next time."

Tony moved to the door, carefully glancing into the corridor. He made a big target, almost as big as Teddy Bear, but nothing happened. "Clear," he said. "Get her out."

Teddy Bear caught Allura by the elbow and began steering her toward the window.

"Hey!" she said at being manhandled, but he didn't let her go. "I'm chained to the floor. Look!"

He glanced down, as if noticing the chain for the first time. He bent and lifted her leg, forcing her to brace her palms against his shoulders or fall. She winced, but endured it as he removed a tool from his belt and used it and brute force to drive it into the lock. A single twist and the cuff fell away.

"Wow," Allura whispered. "Can you do the same for my bracelets?"

It turned out he could, the sound loud as they dropped and struck the concrete.

A rush of wind preceded massive talons slamming hard into the broken bricks as they gripped the damaged window from outside, huge black wings flapping to stop the Creature from falling back.

"Kyle?" It was definitely Kyle, but his arms were wings and his feet talons, even if the rest of him remained the same.

Zannah's husband nodded as heavy gusts slammed into Allura, making her squint.

"So that's how you two got up here?" Allura asked. Teddy Bear nodded as he put a huge meaty hand on Allura's shoulder and guided her toward the broken window.

Kyle remained outside as if something were trying to push him back, wings beating to keep him in place.

"Get Allura to safety," Teddy Bear said. "We're going after Slade. Send the packs in."

Allura pulled her shoulder free. "I'm coming with you and Tony."

Teddy Bear gave her a look full of disagreement. "We can't protect you if we get caught in a brawl."

Allura pointed to the sheathed knife at Teddy Bear's belt. "Is that silver? Give it to me and I can protect myself. Claws and blades, what more could a girl want?"

"Body armour?" Kyle asked from the window. "Maybe a flamethrower too?"

Teddy Bear's lips tightened, but he drew the weapon and handed it to Allura as if he didn't have time to argue. "Shaw is going to kill me," he muttered.

"No, he won't," Allura said. She wasn't sure how she knew, but this was Shaw's choice as much as her own. He wanted this sorted. She knew it. "I don't think I could stay if he wanted me gone."

Allura gripped the knife in her left hand, careful not to curl her fingers too tightly and slice herself open with her own claws. While her claws might be pretty good weapons, silver was deadly to Creatures.

Teddy Bear pulled out his phone and dialled, speaking the moment it connected. "Send in the pack." He hung up. Without asking, he slipped his phone into Allura's hand and stripped off. Tony also began stripping.

"What are you doing?" Allura asked before she realised exactly what they were doing. Transforming. She slipped Teddy Bear's phone into the back pocket of her jeans. "So you can't enter while you're transformed, but you can change if you're already inside?

Teddy Bear nodded.

"Try to kill the human who owns this place," Kyle casually told Allura from the window, his wings still beating to keep him there. "Shaw and I can enter then."

"Kill?" she echoed, somewhat regretting her choice to stay. Killing the person responsible for several millennia of human slavery and suffering was one thing, but the human who owned this place? She had no idea how much they even knew about what was happening here.

Kyle abruptly fell back and twisted, wings spreading wide as he disappeared from view. Her mind went to the massacre in Mitchell a year ago and realised she could very well be about to walk into the middle of something similar.

Teddy Bear gathered his and Tony's clothes and threw them out the window, revealing how buff he was as his muscles moved under his tight skin. Insanely buff. She doubted he had an ounce of fat on him. If he didn't reek of werewolf lifeforce, she might have been far more appreciative. Tony, although a little shorter, wasn't a slouch in the muscles department either.

By the time Allura composed herself, Tony sank to his knees and grunted, his body shifting with a flash of warmth into a huge black-coated wolf. His legs gave way, and he crashed to the floor with a pain-filled whimper.

"I feel ya," Teddy Bear whispered.

"It hurts?" Allura asked.

Teddy Bear nodded. "It kills. Returning to human form is sweet, though."

Tony struggled to his feet, his wolf shoulders almost as high as Allura's waist. His tail had a streak of white down the middle, and there was a tiny patch of white on his snout. If not for the creepy red eyes, he looked kind of cute.

Teddy Bear shifted once Tony could defend them, hitting the ground as a flash of warmth washed over Allura. He released a whining noise she thought might be pain, panting for several seconds, but then he stood and shook, his fur a russet colour and a little shaggier than Tony's.

Tony led the way. They'd have to come back for Mitsi, who remained unconscious near the door.

Allura followed, hobbling to avoid hurting her sore ankle. Tony kept his nose to the ground as he scented Slade's blood trail. The trail was obvious, as the incubus was bleeding profusely.

Allura followed the werewolves with one hand braced on the wall, half hopping, half skipping down the stairs. Her claws scraped paint from the wall where she touched it, and figured she might need a moon boot after this. If she lived.

The blood trail thinned after the second flight of stairs, as did Allura's stamina, probably due to the lifeforce Slade had taken from her.

As she reached the third landing, she could hear a full-on brawl below them, werewolves and god knows what else going at each other. Teddy Bear moved closer to her, shielding her with his body, but nothing entered the stairwell.

Two more painful flights down and they reached ground level, the trail continuing into the basement car park.

Allura jumped as something slammed into the heavy door to the fire stairs, the door rattling but not giving. Beyond it she heard a low snarl, the sound mostly drowned out by shattering glass.

"Keep going," Allura said to herself. Her knife suddenly felt ridiculous in the huge werewolves' presence. She'd be lucky to get a swing in if a beast like Teddy Bear came at her.

The three of them continued down to the last level, the safety lights guiding them, but they did little to illuminate the car park they emerged into. The basement wasn't huge, but it could still house a few dozen vehicles. There were only five though, all of them white vans like the one she'd arrived in. People transporters. The implication sickened her.

The metal roller door to the basement was down, preventing anyone from entering or leaving. Other than another set of stairs on the opposite side of the car park, the basement was empty.

Tony cocked his head, hearing something Allura couldn't. He focused on the van.

"What is it, Lassie?" Allura muttered under her breath.

The rear doors of the second van in the line opened. Slade crouched inside, one forearm pressed hard against his bloody stomach and his free hand around Quicksilver's neck. A desiccated body lay in the van, a girl judging by the long hair and clothes. Slade wasn't fully healed, but he looked a lot better than he had been before.

"Oh crap," Allura whispered. Slade slid out of the van and dragged Quicksilver in front of him to use as a shield.

Quicksilver had been gagged and cuffed. He caught Allura's eyes, his own stare filled with shock and fear. His eyes widened when he saw the werewolves, each impossibly huge and muscled.

The werewolves tensed as Slade shifted his weight, Teddy Bear growling low in his throat.

"Easy," Allura said.

Slade ignored the two enormous wolves, glaring at Allura instead as he forced Quicksilver to stand before him.

The tips of Slade's talons pressed hard against Quicksilver's neck, the threat clear as a trickle of blood ran from each. "I had grand plans for you, Allura. No longer."

"Let Quicksilver go, Slade," Allura said, holding her knife up. It seemed pathetically small.

Quicksilver was trying to appear unafraid, but Allura knew him too well. He wasn't a fighter. Never had been.

Tony and Teddy Bear began moving left and right, leaving Allura directly before Slade with less than ten metres between them. A distraction? Bait? She didn't care if it saved Quicksilver.

Quicksilver tried to look everywhere, probably more scared of the wolves than Slade.

Slade pulled Quicksilver closer. "Call your dogs off Allura, or Quicksilver gets the honour of donating his lifeforce to the task of healing the last of my wounds."

Quicksilver's eyes went wide when he saw Allura's claws. He made a muffled noise through his gag. Allura could imagine what he was thinking. Slade had talons and, at first glance, there wasn't a huge difference between talons and claws.

"If you hurt Quicksilver, you're out of bargaining chips," she countered.

He conceded the point with a nod and a wary glance at Teddy Bear. "Let's make a deal then," Slade replied. "Can you control your dogs?"

Allura had no idea if that were possible, but she nodded. "I'm listening," she said.

The two werewolves moved further from her, drawing a murderous glance from Slade. "Don't test me Allura."

The incubus had nowhere to go but back into the van.

With Quicksilver as his hostage, he had some bargaining power, but she doubted the werewolves factored that in.

"What's your offer?" Allura asked hurriedly, hoping Teddy Bear and Tony didn't do anything before she could make a deal.

Slade kept his back to the van's open doors. "Call off your dogs, let me leave, and when I'm safe, I'll let Quicksilver go. Everyone wins."

Allura shifted her weight, her ankle beginning to hurt more from standing on it. "That requires trust," Allura countered, trying not to let him see she didn't want to put her weight on her damaged ankle. She couldn't afford to look weak now. "You'll kill Quicksilver the moment you get free."

He shook his head. "I told you before, I don't break deals. It's how I survive. You have my word. I'll let him go unharmed. My word's as good as a promise."

That was an opening she couldn't let slide. "So, make it a promise. While you're at it, promise never to harm me, my friends, or my family ever again, and we'll call it a deal."

Slade made a *tsk tsk* sound. "Trust, Allura. If you'd kept your word to me, I'd have left Jenna alone. You've given me no reason to trust that you and Shaw won't come after me."

"That's because you trade in human misery, you asshole," Allura muttered under her breath. The thought of Jenna falling back into this Creature's hands was more than enough to make her want to use her claws on him again.

He smiled a patronising smile, like her bravado amused him. "Let me do you a favour, then. My offer still stands. Quicksilver, Jenna, and all your Menagerie friends safe for as long as you serve me. Last chance."

She stared in disbelief. "Serve you? You creep! You've got

one chip to play, and he's not worth serving you for the rest of my life. Sorry, Quicksilver."

Quicksilver must have seen something in her expression too, because his hopes seemed to die.

"I'll do what I can," she tried to assure him as she glanced at the encroaching werewolves. She hoped they wouldn't attack yet.

Quicksilver glanced at her claws, no doubt coming to all the wrong conclusions. She wasn't a Creature, but she wasn't entirely human anymore, either.

Allura held up her hand as Teddy Bear and Tony moved a little closer, hoping they noticed. They did and paused, bringing her a rush of relief. She didn't want to risk Quicksilver's life, but she might not be able to help him either.

Allura caught movement in the van's side mirror. A driver. That meant Slade had probably only emerged for the chance to nab Allura, but Teddy Bear and Tony had upset that plan.

Slade watched her, and she could clearly see the obsession in his eyes now. She needed a distraction before he decided to fight another day and hauled himself and Quicksilver back into the van. "All this is because a dead woman snubbed you three millennia ago? It's time you grew up, Slade."

There was a good chance the building was in the driver's name. A weakness to exploit, perhaps. Could she kill a potentially innocent person, though? If it meant saving Quicksilver and keeping Jenna safe, she could. Maybe.

The door opposite the fire stairs shattered, bursting off its hinges. The bulk of the door slid several metres across the concrete as two werewolves tumbled through, tearing into each other like they enjoyed the carnage. Two more followed, then several more.

Allura swore while Teddy Bear ran to her side. Tony got between her and the new werewolves, the pair of them like parents protecting a child.

Slade cut his losses and dragged Quicksilver back into the van, pulling the doors shut as the engine started and the roller door to the basement began lifting.

36

"Stop the driver!" Allura yelled. If Slade got away, he'd kill Quicksilver.

Allura sprinted after the van, her ankle screaming at her, but it only took a few seconds. She got to the driver's door as the woman behind the wheel floored it.

Allura punched her claws through the door panel like the sheet metal was cardboard, the vehicle's momentum ripping her off her feet. She cried out and dropped the silver blade to punch her free claws into the steel above the window, her weight ripping jagged lines down the vehicle as she clung on in fear.

The driver turned the wheel hard as a werewolf smashed into the left headlight, the body tumbling aside in a broken heap. Allura desperately clung to the van while the joints of her fingers felt like they were being ripped apart. They probably were.

The driver straightened and drove for the rising roller door.

Struggling to keep her feet off the ground, Allura cried out as her claws cut through metal and she slipped a foot toward the van's rear door, leaving deep gouges in the metal. She desperately wished for talons she could grip with, not claws, and a strange chilling sensation came over her hands. She felt her claws elongate and become longer and thicker, the sharp edges vanishing to allow her to keep her grip.

"Holy shit!" She had claws *and* talons?

The driver hit the brakes and Allura's inertia threw her tumbling forward, talons ripping out of the door. She crashed to the ground and rolled a dozen times before slamming into a concrete wall beside the roller door, bruising half her body. She moaned, but at least she hadn't felt anything break.

The van's side looked like a horror movie effect as the driver gunned the motor again. She could have crushed Allura between the van and the wall, but drove straight through the exit instead, clearly more afraid for her own skin than about damaging Allura's.

Allura winced as she pushed herself up, both elated to be alive and shocked at what she'd done. She glared up the ramp, her hopes sinking as the vehicle disappeared around a corner. She tasted her own blood from a split lip. "Damn."

Fresh adrenaline surged as a massive grey werewolf ran at her. Her fear spiked off the chart at the sight of its red eyes, its teeth showing in a snarl. She braced herself as she raised her taloned hands, wishing for a shotgun instead.

Tony slammed into the beast's side, and they tumbled away, ripping and snarling at each other. Teddy Bear made it to her then, getting between Allura and two more werewolves, doing his best to keep them from her.

One leapt for Teddy Bear while the other, wounded from a gash across its head and blood running profusely into its eyes, circled the fight.

Allura did the only thing she could think of as the

enormous beast came at her. She rolled. The half-blinded werewolf slammed into the concrete wall. Taking her only chance, she plunged her talons into the huge beast's side, crying out in pain from the abuse her fingers had already taken.

Lifeforce bloomed in her consciousness and she drew on it. It rushed into her, laced with toxic lycanthropy. Darkly sensual, it was a delicious rush and a sickening blast at the same time.

The wounded beast howled and tried to pull away, thrashing and dragging Allura several metres, but she clung on and drew out everything it had, its tainted lifeforce filling her body. It tried kicking to dislodge her, but after several attempts, it collapsed, its body desiccating as she watched, horrified at her own power.

Trembling with shock, Allura pulled her aching fingertips free and struggled to her feet before falling back to her knees and vomiting. The tainted lifeforce felt like acid in her veins. Trying to catch her breath, she vomited again, her body trying and failing to get rid of the lifeforce.

Spitting the acrid taste from her mouth, Allura struggled to stand on trembling legs. Her knee must have taken a blow from the fall. It ached and felt badly bruised.

Staggering under the roller-door and out of the carpark, Allura braced herself with one hand on the concrete wall as she limped up the ramp after the van. There was nobody around, and no vehicles, either.

Massive talons slammed down on the concrete a couple of metres away, huge black wings spread wide. Allura screamed in fright.

"Whatcha doing?" Zannah asked with a bright smile. Her arms had transformed into massive wings, her feet into talons for gripping, but like Kyle, she remained the same otherwise.

"Zannah?"

"Who else do you know with wings?"

"Kyle," Allura responded.

Zannah hesitated. "Yeah, okay. How about you sheath those claws and hop on. We need to stop Slade."

How the hell was she supposed to get rid of her claws? Talons? She stared, willing them to disappear. Like liquid metal, they shrank back into her fingertips, disappearing completely.

"Wow." That was easy. By the time they were gone, her fingers felt normal again, too, the ache gone. It should have surprised her more than it did.

Careful to protect her painful knee and ankle, Allura gingerly climbed onto Zannah's back, bracing herself as the shoulder muscles powering Zannah's wings helped launch them into the air.

"Shit!" Allura cried.

Zannah's body blocked the view to the ground, leaving Allura to contemplate the stupidity of what they were doing. A pregnant birdwoman and a mostly human muse going up against a sadistic incubus who was thousands of years old.

Allura had claws at least, but as Slade now knew about them now, she doubted she'd get another chance to use them.

Zannah banked and Allura cried out in fear, wrapping her legs around the woman's hips and struggling not to let her claws reappear and grip the woman's shoulders. That wouldn't end well.

Zannah gained height, lots of it, and then plummeted. Allura squealed as they banked, following streetlights. Allura could barely see thanks to the rushing air and

Zannah's loose hair flicking back into her eyes and mouth, but they seemed to be heading toward Queanbeyan, one of Canberra's satellite cities.

Shaking her head to clear Zannah's hair, she spotted the lights of the airport well to her left, and dark undeveloped areas surrounding it. There were city lights ahead, though. Lots of them.

They didn't fly for long before Zannah banked left and began descending, the rush of air biting with cold.

Allura got a glimpse of the area below as they descended toward a substation on the edge of Queanbeyan, a short drive from the industrial area of Fyshwick. The Molonglo River was maybe half a kilometre ahead when Zannah levelled out and back-winged to land near a dirt road outside the substation.

Allura slid off Zannah's back onto weak legs, almost collapsing from the pain in her ankle and knee. Sick from the tainted lifeforce she'd taken and wind-chilled as well, she didn't think she'd be much help.

"They're just past those trees," Zannah whispered. "Stay here, stay silent, and keep an ear out for traffic while I go for backup. There'll probably be another vehicle on the way to pick Slade up. If I'm not back when it arrives, get the licence plate and stay downwind. Lay down in the grass so you can't be seen. Don't go any closer."

Before Allura could speak, Zannah launched herself into the air again.

Allura glared at the trees ahead. Old-fashioned stake-out it was. Hopefully, she didn't get eaten by a werewolf while she waited.

37

Trembling from her injuries and the corrosive werewolf lifeforce making her nerves feel like they were burning, Allura crept through grass until she got to the trees and shrubs, trying not to break any twigs in the dark. The darkness wouldn't have helped if she made noise, and the entire area was dry. She kept the substation to her right.

She couldn't move fast, but all she needed to do was get into a position and remain hidden. They would be able to use any information she gathered to track Slade down later. She certainly had no intention of letting the bastard terrorise and torment her in future lives, or this one again.

Growing nauseous from the stolen werewolf lifeforce, Allura crawled underneath low branches until she reached tall dry grass. The grass kept her hidden, as did the branches and darkness, but it also broke her line of sight.

Silently cursing her idiotic impulse to get into a better position, she gingerly crawled forward until she got close to a wall about ten metres tall, topped with floodlights. The floodlights threatened to illuminate her if she moved any closer, however.

Peeking above the grass, she could just see the white van facing her way, parking lights on, the door ajar, and the driver messing with her phone. Allura could use that phone. In a rush of inspiration she pulled out Teddy Bear's phone, but the screen was shattered and the phone partly bent, probably from when she'd been thrown from the van. It wouldn't turn on, so she put it away.

She could make out Slade's tall, lean shape against the darker backdrop of distant trees, his phone to his ear. He no longer held his stomach, which didn't bode well for Quicksilver. Hopefully, her friend was still alive. She clung to that hope. He'd been her best and only friend for years, and if he was alive, she'd find a way to help him.

Vehicles approached from behind and to her left, driving off the sealed road and onto the gravel. Allura ducked down as the headlights further illuminated the area. Two 4WDs drove past, the sound of them suggesting turbo diesel engines.

As they circled back and pulled up behind the van, Allura squeezed her eyes shut as their headlights threatened to kill what remained of her night vision.

Realising she was probably too close thanks to all the light, Allura slowly moved backwards on her hands and knees until she was under branches again.

When she dared look again, she could just make out Slade waving at the van driver. The woman put her phone away, started the engine, and left so fast she might have feared for her life. Maybe she did. Hopefully Quicksilver was still alive and in the van. He'd be safer away from Slade.

As Slade turned, Allura pressed herself against the dusty ground again, grass seeds poking through her clothes as she waited uncomfortably for the area's natural quietness to descend once more. The vehicles' lights turned off.

Carefully lifting her head, she found Slade talking to one of the new drivers. She doubted she had long before they left.

"Got her!" called a man's voice from behind her.

Allura cried out as Noah grabbed her ankles and hauled her around in a half circle. She cried out in pain and tried to kick free, but he dragged her face down over grass and dirt toward the cars. Fear and desperation made talons emerge from her fingertips and she dug them into the packed dirt, but the dirt only broke up in into chunks as he dragged her.

"I told you I heard something."

She twisted and kicked, forcing him to drop one ankle, but before she could scramble free he caught her again and dragged her another couple of metres. Dropping both ankles, he put a heavy boot between her shoulder blades and forced her face to the ground.

"Let me go, you nosewipe!" Allura yelled as she kept struggling, but it did no good.

Once Noah had her under control, he grasped her by the back of her shirt and hauled her upright, marching her forward.

She swiped backwards with her talons, but he caught her wrist and twisted her right arm up behind her back until she cried out in pain.

He stopped her before Slade, the incubus clearly annoyed. "How did you get here so fast?"

"I lit a fart and made a makeshift rocket."

Slade backhanded her so hard her legs gave way. Parts of her brain felt like they'd rattled loose.

"How did you get here? Who else is here?"

"Get your hearing checked," she slurred.

He punched her in the stomach.

Her breath vanished in a whoosh and she doubled over

to dry-retch over and over again until she tasted bile. It took her a long while to realise she was lying on dirt, unrestrained, the sickly feeling of tainted werewolf lifeforce keeping her immobile as much as the pain.

Allura eventually got an elbow under herself, spat, and winced. Her right cheekbone felt broken, and she could barely see from her eye. Breathing felt like a bad option. Slade still stood before her.

"You hit like a little girl," Allura muttered, her arms trembling as she tried to support her own weight. She probably looked like she was dying. Maybe she was. There was a good chance she was bleeding internally from the punch to her guts.

Noah caught her by the back of her neck and hauled her upright, the sharp movement making her nauseous again. She struggled to keep her weight on her legs despite his support, her body trembling. She could taste blood too. The inside of her cheek had split against her teeth.

The only bonus was it distracted her from the sickly feel of all the werewolf lifeforce she'd stolen. The moment she thought of it, though, she wanted to be sick again.

Slade pointed to the ground and Noah forced Allura to her knees. She grimaced as a symphony of pain flared all over her body.

"How did you get here? Who's with you?"

Allura forced herself to glare up at Slade. "There're easier ways to get a blow job, you know?" She was as good as dead anyway. Provoking him might save her some pain.

Slade crouched before her, meeting her eyes. "Is that so?" he asked. Slade gripped her jaw, fingers digging painfully into her cheeks. "You look sick," he said as he turned her head left and right, examining her face. He frowned. "Your lifeforce is tainted. What have you done?"

"Snacking on werewolves doesn't agree with me," she said, despite the hold he had on her. She attempted a smile and failed. Her face hurt too much.

He gave a non-committal shrug. "You might survive it, but probably not. Lifeforce from other Creatures is toxic to my kind and you're only a muse, after all. It'll take a few days, but it's like any toxin. Your organs will start shutting down and you'll die slowly, suffering. You should have taken my offer, Allura."

The tainted lifeforce could kill her? "Better than being forced to serve you," she said.

38

Slade released her jaw and stood. "Take her with you. Bound, of course. I doubt she'll offer much resistance. With a little luck, she might live through this, and we can get better acquainted."

"She looks like she's already past it," a third man said, approaching from behind Slade.

Slade's expression darkened. "Then we'll use her carcass creatively. Until then, she comes."

Slade's tone was calm, reasonable even, but the man took two steps back and raised his hands, palms outward. "Of course."

Allura didn't want to contemplate the fate she might expect if she survived. Better to do some damage on her way out, if she could. Maybe they'd reciprocate.

"I'm sorry, Jenna," she whispered. She twisted against Noah's hold, digging talons into his leg and burying them to the bone. Noah yelled in pain and staggered back, twisting and dragging her with him.

She drew on his lifeforce, and it flooded into her. He cried out, stumbled, and fell backwards, trying to break her hold with a kick, but she'd buried her claws too deep. With all her remaining strength, Allura hauled herself forward, pinning his leg to the ground with her weight.

"Help!" Noah cried, still struggling to get away.

"This is for all the people you've hurt and killed," she hissed at him, sickened by the taste of his lifeforce and the corrosive feeling of it as it filled her body.

Allura expected someone to pull her off the werewolf, but neither Slade nor the other man bothered. Seconds passed as she drew every hint of poisonous lifeforce from Noah, his muscles desiccating beneath her body. In a last act of desperation, Noah reached for her, skeletal fingers outstretched in a futile attempt to push her away, but his hand fell limply to the ground before reaching her.

Allura flushed with fever-like heat and collapsed face-down on Noah's desiccated thigh, the poisonous lifeforce from two werewolves far too much.

"Idiot should have been more careful," said the other man.

They could have saved Noah's life, but they'd let her kill him. Sick bastards.

Slade hauled her off Noah by her t-shirt, dumping her onto her back before crouching beside her. "Toxic lifeforce is hard to expunge. The amount you've consumed might even kill me, and that's saying something. It's a pity. I was hoping you'd survive."

Allura tried to speak, but pain wracked her body. All she could do was gasp for air. Dizziness forced her eyes to roll back in her head.

"You've got a day to live at most, I'm guessing, and it won't be pleasant. You'll be suffering and aware the entire time. I think I'll keep you with me just so I can enjoy watching."

She forced in a breath, the air like toxic smoke searing her lungs. "Anything to give you some jollies." Her words were slurred, her voice soft. Allura managed to raise her left hand, talons extended in the hope of trying the same trick on him, but she didn't have the strength to reach him.

He focused on her hand. "That's what I like about you, Allura. You never give up. It's a trait I admire."

Give up? She'd already given up. She only needed to keep him here long enough for Zannah to bring help. Shaw might be able to kill Slade and Jenna would be safe, then. Her own life no longer mattered.

Almost casually, Slade glanced at the other man. "Go. I'll take the other car and Quicksilver."

"Righto boss."

He returned his attention to Allura, smiling wickedly. "Yes, Quicksilver's still alive. Barely. I thought he'd make a good bargaining chip, but with you here, that no longer applies. For you, I'll make sure he suffers for months. Maybe years."

As the man's footsteps retreated, Allura used the distraction to try to bury her claws in Slade's arm. She didn't come close. He caught her left wrist, shaking his head in mock disappointment. He separated her pinky from her other fingers and twisted it sideways until the joint broke.

Allura screamed.

"What? Aren't you going to thank me?" Slade asked. He grasped the next finger. "I mean, the more damage I can do, the shorter the amount of time you'll live. In your state, that's a good thing." He tested the next joint.

"No, no, please," Allura whispered, sweat breaking out all over, the memory of what Noah had done returning.

"A muse with claws and talons. Best to make sure you can't hurt anyone else with them." He broke the finger.

She had no breath to scream this time. All she could do was whimper. It was a long moment before she could even think again.

"Don't you know that even if you got those talons into me, you couldn't take my lifeforce. I'm an incubus, not a werewolf."

"I'd like to try," she said hoarsely.

He broke the next finger.

Allura made a weak, pathetic sound, drawing her knees close to her chest. He gripped her pointer finger and the cold sweats came on again.

"Please don't!"

He forced it back until the joint popped.

She made a mewling sound, tears squeezing from her eyes. "Oh fuck," she eventually hissed, her hand aching and completely useless now.

He dropped her wrist. "You should have stayed a cop, Allura. We were good together as cops."

Allura stared at her broken fingers, all twisted in wrong directions. "You missed the thumb, asshole." Distantly, she was aware of a car starting up and driving off.

He forced her to her other side, gripped her right hand, and squeezed her fist until she opened her hand. She began to sweat again, dread crushing her defiance. "Please don't," she whispered. "Please Slade."

"Or? Will you promise to love me forever?"

"Of course. I'll even sing a Whitney Houston song."

Rather than break another finger, he pressed her palm against his chest. "How about I give you that chance you want so badly? Go on, Allura. Try to suck all the lifeforce from me. Punch those sharp talons into my flesh and give it a red-hot go."

Hatred gave her strength and her talons slowly

appeared, but she barely had enough strength to pierce his shirt and draw tiny drops of blood. His lifeforce was tantalisingly close though, like a cure to all her problems. She curled her fingers, scratching, but whimpered in dismay when her hand slid away, strengthless.

He gave her a disappointed look, put her hand back to his chest and slammed his palm against her fingers, driving her talons home.

She cried out, sure at least one of her fingers had broken.

"There we go," he said, though he winced from the damage. "Give it a go, Allura. Take all you want, if you can."

Gritting her teeth, she reached for his lifeforce, trying and failing to draw it out of him.

"You really are determined, aren't you?" he said with a genuine surprise. "Go on. Try harder," he taunted. "Maybe you'll get lucky."

If she couldn't kill him this way, at least she could think of one other way to do a tiny bit more damage. She leveraged herself to her elbow and used what strength she had left to drive her talons deeper into his chest, feeling them scrape against his ribs.

Slade grimaced. "Go for it, Allura. After you die, I'll make sure to find you in your next life and make you mine. I'll rub it in Shaw's face, too."

She met his eyes, glaring murder. "You said you never had a muse, right?" Allura whispered, a bout of nausea brought on by werewolf lifeforce threatening another round of dry retching.

"True. Why?"

She focused all the poisonous lifeforce in her body and channelled it back through her talons. "Because," she said. "Muses can't use stolen lifeforce. We can only give it away."

His eyes widened as toxic werewolf lifeforce rushed into

him. He fell back, but her talons were embedded so deep he drew her with him.

As the toxic lifeforce rushed into her talons and through them, Allura tightened her grip, her talons already hooked behind his ribs.

Slade gripped her wrist, mouth wide and gasping for air he didn't seem to be able to find as the werewolf lifeforce rushed into him. He succeeded in ripping one talon free, then another, but her thumb and two remaining talons stayed put.

Blood welled from his fresh wounds, but Allura held on, somehow defying his strength as she forced all the poisonous lifeforce from her body and into his.

"Stop," he begged, his grip weakening on her wrist. "Please Allura. Please." His fingers fell away, and he gasped for air like a landed fish.

"How many people said the same thing to you over the centuries?" she asked, the last of the tainted lifeforce finally leaving her body.

Allura focused, turning her talons into claws, and ripped them free, cutting through ribs as they left his body.

Talons formed on his own hands, and he reached for her, but she slashed at them, cutting two fingers free.

"Ahh!" he cried, clutching his hand to his chest.

Allura punched her claws into his chest again, tearing downward with all her strength and ripping through bone and muscle to open both his chest and stomach this time. She might have poisoned him, but he wasn't helpless and she didn't want to risk the chance he might retaliate.

She slashed his throat next, four parallel slashes.

He bucked, and she fell aside, rolling to get clear of his thrashes as blood sprayed and pooled in the dirt. Eventually

Slade lay still, eyes closed, and Allura fell back, her head thumping on the dirt. She barely felt it.

She smiled and closed her eyes, letting the darkness take her. Jenna and everyone at the Menagerie were safe. She could finally die, and welcomed the darkness as it overcame her.

39

Allura awoke to discover heaven existed. Jenna's beautiful face was only inches away, her brown eyes watching with deep concern and her head resting on the same pillow Allura used. A smile spread across Jenna's face and the stress lifted from her youthful forehead.

"How are you doing, Mum? You've been asleep for days."

Allura tried to reply, but her throat felt painfully dry. She swallowed, took a slow breath, and returned the smile. "I'm alive," she whispered. "Why am I alive?"

Jenna impulsively slipped her arms around Allura and hugged her as if she'd never let her go again. "Oh Mum, I was so scared."

"Me too," whispered Allura, hoping not to get crushed to death, but it was still the best hug she'd had in years.

It was a long while before Jenna released her and wiped her own eyes. "Mister Shaw said you won't feel good for a while, maybe a month." That seemed to concern her. "If you were a succubus, you could recover in minutes, though." She sounded hopeful.

Allura smiled, a little overwhelmed. It was as if they'd

always been mother and daughter. "Being a muse with tiger heritage is enough for me."

A flicker if disappointment appeared on Jenna's face, quickly gone. Why would Jenna want Allura to become a succubus? It only took a moment to figure it out. Succubi were immortal, just like Jenna. Muses weren't.

"Is Quicksilver okay?" Allura asked, as much to distract Jenna as from genuine concern.

"Yeah, though Luci said his memories are fading already. If you want him to remember any Creature details, Luci can help out. If not, give it a month and he'll forget the Creature stuff and rationalise the rest."

Allura considered it. "I think he's better off forgetting." She realised she could use her fingers again. They weren't broken.

"Don't ask," Jenna said, as if reading her thoughts.

"But—"

"Please Mum, don't ask. There was a lot of internal damage too, but you're healed now."

"More nectar?"

"Mum, please," Jenna said, the stress in her voice cutting through Allura's desire to know.

"Okay. I won't ask." In truth, she didn't need to. What else could have cured her?

Jenna released a long, slow breath. "Thank you."

"What happened after I passed out? Is Slade dead?" She didn't know if it was possible for a Creature to regenerate after what she'd done to Slade, but she wouldn't put it past the bastard.

Jenna used a gentle fingertip to trace the frown line on Allura's forehead. "Are you hungry? Or thirsty? I could get you something."

"Thirsty," Allura admitted, but she wasn't going to be diverted for long.

Delight crossed Jenna's pretty young face, which no longer seemed so gaunt or pale. It was as if she'd made a full recovery, both mentally and physically, though Allura doubted the emotional scars would heal any time soon. "I'm going to look after you so well, you're going to wonder how you ever coped without me."

Despite whatever they'd given her, it took days for Allura to recover enough to get out of bed without help. Jenna never left her side except to fetch food and drink. The werewolf lifeforce and Slade's abuse had really done a number on her. She must have been close to death.

"I can shower without help," she said to Jenna. "Really. If you hear me collapse, you can come in, but not before."

After showering, Allura examined herself in the mirror, expecting Sparrow to show up and give her some sass. He didn't, and she missed him. She didn't look different, not like the last couple of times she'd been given nectar, but that just told her how bad she must have been.

Her old life, as crappy as it had been, was clearly over now, and Allura smiled her first genuine, easy smile in what felt like years. Shaw had given her a new start with a new home, and she even had a new daughter. This time, Allura wasn't going to let any of it be torn away. She even had powerful friends to help her now. She'd never be alone again.

After she left the bathroom, she found Mia sitting on the couch, Jenna beside her.

"You've got to see this, Allura," Mia said.

Mia held out a computer tablet. They made space and Allura sat between them to watch a news stream showing Slade's operations being raided all across the country. The media called it the biggest international human trafficking bust in history.

Dozens of people had already been arrested and more were being pursued. Quicksilver was getting credit for all of it, too.

"Why Quicksilver?"

"We did the hard work, of course," Mia said. "But we don't need the attention, so we let Quicksilver take the glory. He doesn't know it was us giving him all the intel."

"Where'd he think it came from?" Allura asked.

"You, of course. Sunshine ran interference, saying you'd only keep delivering information as long as he took all the credit. You saved his life even if he doesn't know it. The least he could do was accept all the glory." She said the last part with a smirk.

Allura wasn't sure how to respond. "What about Slade? Is he dead?"

Jenna snaked an arm behind Allura, snuggling up. Allura hugged her back.

"He survived," Mia whispered, sounding disappointed. Upset, even.

"He's far too dangerous to be allowed to live."

Mia pursed her lips in agreement. "He's in the basement. Shaw said he won't escape." She didn't sound convinced.

Given enough time, he might. "I want to see him," Allura said.

"Allura, that's not a good idea," Mia said.

"Yeah Mum," Jenna said in agreement with Mia.

Allura caught Jenna's hand, entwining their fingers together, but she spoke to Mia. "Please."

Mia held Allura's stare a long while before her expression softened. "I'll try to organise it." She glanced at Jenna. "You want to talk your mother out of it while I talk to Shaw?"

Half an hour later, Mia returned and led Allura and Jenna down to the basement. The place, though warm enough, felt cold.

Shaw met them in the corridor outside the werewolf cells. "Are you sure you want to see him?"

Allura nodded.

He took Allura's hand in a way she found comforting and natural, and with Jenna on her other side, she made her way to the last cell in the row.

Slade lay on the bunk, pale and gaunt, but conscious. They'd cuffed his wrists behind his back and he had a silver collar around his throat, his skin red raw and covered and blisters above and below it. They should have spray painted the bastard in silver.

She felt Jenna shudder, the girl's grip tightening, but Allura's stomach turned to acid. "You murdered Piper," Allura said. "And you hurt Jenna for years. How dare you."

A chain prevented Slade from moving more than a few feet from the far wall, but he didn't try. He looked like he was in pain. He glared up at Allura as if she'd betrayed him instead of the other way around. "Come to gloat?" he asked, his voice raspy and broken. The damage she'd done to his neck had healed over, but the tender red scars looked like they could pull apart at any time. She hated to consider what his chest and stomach looked like.

"Yeah," she replied sarcastically. "Or maybe I'd just like to rip your throat out again."

"Had enough?" Shaw asked, clearly keen to leave Slade to rot where he was.

"No. I want him dead," Allura replied coldly, hoping someone would volunteer to do the job.

Slade sat up and strained against the cuffs and chain, no doubt assuming she meant it. He was right. Cold hatred felt like it was suffocating her. She couldn't live while he did.

"Allura," Shaw began.

"Can I have a silver blade? Please," Allura asked.

Jenna gave her a worried look, but Mia, having followed but kept her distance, couldn't contain her thoughts. "Killing in cold blood—"

"Please," Allura asked Shaw again. She drew Jenna close, holding her tight before kissing her forehead, though she had to stand on her toes to do it. "He'll never hurt anyone again, darling. I swear it. Not you, me, or anyone. Not in this lifetime."

Mia tried to protest again, but Allura silenced the tigress with a look. "Please don't, Mia. I have to do this."

"Mia, would you mind getting a silver knife, please?" Shaw asked.

"Don't you carry one?" Allura asked.

"Not in here."

Clearly not happy, Mia left, returning a few minutes later with a long slender blade, single-edged, the tip sharp. She held it out, careful to avoid the metal.

Allura wrapped her fingers around the hilt.

"Please open the door," she said.

Shaw removed a set of old-fashioned keys from a pocket and unlocked the door, sliding the heavy bars open. Slade glanced at Shaw and Mia, as if expecting help. "You're not going to let her do this, are you? We're partners! Brothers!"

"You're not my brother or my partner," Shaw said.

Allura let go of Jenna and walked into the cell. Slade leaned back to the wall as if he could push through to safety.

She met his eyes. "You had everything you could ever want. Even me. I loved you, once," Allura whispered as she placed the tip of the knife under Slade's jaw, forcing his head up until he met her eyes. Courage almost failed her then. "You don't deserve a quick death."

Relief crossed his features, but Allura wasn't doing this for herself. This was for Jenna and all the people Slade had hurt over the centuries, including all the incarnations of herself he'd tortured. She gathered her courage, silenced her fears and doubts, and gripped the knife with both hands.

"Wait!" he whispered as he realised she intended to follow through with her threat. "Lumi—"

She thrust upwards. "This is mercy."

Slade stiffened, eyes surprised, and then the life faded from them.

His weight ripped the blade from her hands as he toppled sideways. She stepped back as his body dropped from the bunk to the floor, dead.

She felt an echo of Sparrow move through her, as if he'd been released from purgatory, the anger and bitterness she'd carried across lifetimes slipping out of her. It was done between them. Slade would never bother her again, not in this life or any other.

Jenna entered the cell and wrapped Allura in a hug, sobbing as she guided Allura out.

"He can't hurt us anymore," Allura said softly as she hugged Jenna back, finally letting her own tears come. Tears for herself. Tears for Piper. Tears for Jenna. "He'll never hurt anyone again."

They cried for a long time.

40

Allura hadn't seen Shaw since she'd killed Slade. If she were honest, she'd been avoiding him. It was time to change that.

Sunshine smiled as Allura stopped before her desk.

"Is Shaw in his office?" Allura asked.

"Can't you tell?" Sunshine asked with a raised eyebrow.

Allura smiled. "Yes," she admitted. "I just... didn't want to presume."

"He sensed you coming. He's waiting for you."

Allura opened the door and walked in, closing it behind herself. Shaw closed his laptop screen.

She turned to the sketches on the opposite wall, the ones Shaw saw every time he looked up. Her own was among them now, and it felt right. She'd earned her place there.

Names came to her as she glanced from face to face, along with tantalising flashes of lives she'd lived, but didn't remember.

Allura turned back to Shaw. "Why didn't you stop me?" she asked. "From killing Slade, I mean? One word from you and I'd have wanted to walk away. I'm your muse now, after all."

He gave her an assessing look. "I've made a lot of mistakes," he said, standing and walking around her to examine the sketches. "These images are here to remind me I'm not perfect, and often wrong, as well. He touched the edge of a portrait, a pretty young woman who looked like she might have been English or French. "I gave Isabeau everything she could ever desire, but having everything made her so unhappy she eventually took her own life."

The name felt familiar, but the words struck no memories within Allura. Perhaps Isabeau had lived a life free of conflict, and consequently nothing stood out.

"You've always been your own person, Allura. I needed to let go enough to allow you to be. Maybe this lifetime I've finally got the balance right." He touched her cheek like he was afraid he might break her.

"I'm not my own person now, though, am I?"

"If you wish to be free, say so, and I'll make you a succubus. Unfortunately, you can't return to what you were. It's not possible."

This close, she could feel his presence like a warm blanket around her. It could protect her, or it could smother her. She wanted to wrap herself in him and never let go. "I'm still only me because you want me to be. I understand that much."

"Let me make you a succubus," he said.

She glanced out his large office windows to the city centre beyond the lake, half expecting to see Sparrow reflected in the glass. He wasn't. It felt like a piece of her soul was missing. Sparrow was made of all the memories and experiences she'd lived across fifty lifetimes. Knowing that made the world feel different.

"I can't risk losing Jenna," Allura said. "As your muse, I'm still mostly human. If I became a Creature, I might lose my bond with her. I can't risk it," she said.

Shaw sighed and returned to his desk, sitting on the edge with his hands out to her. She didn't know whether she wanted to go to him because he wanted it, or because she genuinely wanted to feel his touch and the connection they shared.

Allura went to him. "It's hard to distinguish between your desires and my emotions," she said. "I understand it logically, but... I've never felt a part of something like the Menagerie before, even as a cop. I don't want to lose that."

"What do you want then, Allura? Ask, and I'll give it to you. Anything at all."

She smiled. "I've got everything I want."

He drew her in close, his arms slipping around her shoulders.

Allura hugged back, feeling the comfort and warmth, and taking in the musky scent of him. "Luci would kill me if she saw us like this."

He shook his head. "She's envious, not jealous. There's a difference. Luci and I can't be together, and we both understand that. It's just the way things are."

"I'm sorry. I know you love her. I can feel it. You love me, too."

Shaw gently moved Allura away and smiled. "We don't all get what we want, do we? You've got Jenna though, but I can sense she's not enough, either. What else do you want?"

She stared at him, realising he knew her better than she knew herself. There was only one other thing Allura desperately wanted, but she didn't have the courage to voice it.

He held out a hand and guided her to one of the black

leather chairs near the window, and sat after she did. "I have money and resources. They're yours now. Use them. Tell me what you want."

She hesitated. "I want my children back in my life. Max and Clarie. I want to know they're safe and happy. I want to be a good mother to them. I..." She began to tear up and had to pause to wipe her eyes.

"Whatever you want, I'll support you."

She melted into him and closed her eyes. "Thank you."

***

ALLURA FOUND Quicksilver as she walked through The Atrium Bar later that day. He looked a little pale and moved as if sore, but seemed fine otherwise. She'd called him an hour ago, asking to talk, but hadn't expected him to come this quickly.

She didn't know what to say, but was certain they needed to put a few things behind them.

"You look great," he said after taking a moment to study her face. "Like you've spent a month at a retreat with cucumber slices on your eyes."

That was something she'd never tried. "Thanks. I hear you've been in the news. Congratulations."

"Yeah. We're cleaning up Slade's operation, but the man himself has disappeared. You wouldn't know anything about it, would you?"

Allura felt herself flush, but tried not to let anything show in her expression. "I heard."

Quicksilver narrowed his eyes, clearly not buying her feigned ignorance. God, she couldn't get away with anything.

This close, his lifeforce was beguiling, and she found

herself contemplating taking some of it for Shaw before shutting the thought down.

He cleared his throat. "We found your fingerprints in a room with a smashed window. Wanna explain that?" Quicksilver asked.

Allura swallowed and shook her head. "What did you do about it?"

He gave her a long, steady look. "What did you expect? They disappeared," he replied. "Unofficially, what happened Allura? You know you can trust me."

She wasn't sure how much to say. "I can," she agreed. "You remember Slade taking me from here, don't you?"

Quicksilver looked around as if expecting to find people listening attentively. Some probably were, but they'd be of the friendly werewolf variety. Probably.

"Yeah," he finally admitted. "It's all a bit fuzzy thanks to a couple of concussions over several days. To be honest, I don't remember much of anything between the car crash and waking up in a van. I remember seeing you being led out of the Menagerie in cuffs, though."

"Slade locked me up in that room, but I got away." Hopefully that was enough and he wouldn't pursue it. "Don't ask how."

He gave her a hard look, but eventually nodded. "Do you know where Slade is now? If you do, I'll keep you out of the investigation. I swear."

Allura shook her head. "Sorry." The less involved he got in the Creature world, the better.

"Allura—"

"You won't find him," she whispered, trying to keep her emotions under control. She hated lying to him and hated the fact he could tell. "Please don't look." Slade's body was probably at Tammy's crematorium. He might even be ash on the wind by now.

"You realise I'm the only person on the planet you can genuinely trust, don't you?" There was an edge to his voice, as if he could sense she was holding back crucial information, and it cut him.

Allura glanced around the Atrium, feeling oddly at peace for the first time in years, despite Quicksilver's hurt. This was her home now. Quicksilver lived in a different world to her, and it wasn't something she could escape, or wanted to. Protecting him meant keeping him out of her world. "Did you know it was Shaw who gave you the intel to take down Slade's network, not me?"

Quicksilver stood a little straighter. "Bullshit. There's no way that asshole would help me."

Now it was her turn to be hurt. Thanks to her bond, Shaw meant everything to her. Almost everything. Jenna still came first. "Do you remember seeing me in the basement of Slade's building? Do you remember the wolves? Anything?"

He began to speak. "I... not really."

"Then trust me when I say Slade's not coming back, not ever," Allura said a little too tersely. "Leave it alone. Please." The last part sounded more like an order than a request.

Quicksilver looked her over, coming to some conclusion Allura couldn't guess at. He glanced around suspiciously once more before leaning in close. "I know you're scared—"

Allura laughed, only schooling her expression when she saw his surprise and hurt at her reaction. "I'm not scared, Quicksilver, but thank you," she said quickly.

He glared back as if she'd intentionally hurt him.

Allura tried to console him with a hand on his shoulder. "You looked after me for the longest time, and I owe you a debt I can never repay, but you have to let me go now. I'm good. I really am."

He pulled away, irritation furrowing his brow. "I'm going to find out what happened. Either you help me, or—"

"Quicksilver—"

"No, Allura. Slade's part in this is too important to bury, even if you were involved somehow. I can't look away. You know I can't."

Allura let out a long sigh, wishing she could find a way to put a lid on the situation. The only thing she was sure he'd settle for would be the truth. A version of it, at least. "Remember how I couldn't pull the trigger when we caught up with Piper's killers?" she asked, not wanting to mention it, but unable to think of another way to get past the issue.

"Of course." His tone was cold. Cautious. A little bit hopeful.

Allura met his eyes, her stomach churning. She had to stop him from investigating Slade's disappearance before it led him back to the Menagerie. "I'm stronger now. Trust me when I say Slade will never hurt anyone again. You. Won't. Find. Him. Ever. Understand? I took care of it. He's gone."

He stared back at her as if seeing a stranger. He opened his mouth to speak, but then closed it again, studying her for a long time. "The Allura I know could never do that. You're covering for Shaw, and I'm going to prove it." He turned and walked away.

Fighting deep hurt and an unexpected sense of betrayal, Allura watched his retreating back, and couldn't convince herself she'd said the right thing. She wanted him out of the Creature world, but it seemed as if she'd drawn him closer to it.

Someone put a hand on Allura's shoulder and she spun to find Mia by her side, Jenna with her.

"He's going to be trouble," Mia said. There was a subtle undertone to her voice, a hint that something might need to be done before long.

"Don't," Allura said coldly.

"Allura—"

Allura pulled away from Mia's hand and reached for Jenna, slipping an arm around her daughter's back. "I need a hug," Allura said.

Jenna smiled, and the world felt right again. "I have hugs, lots of hugs. So many I doubt I could give them all to you."

That was all Allura needed to hear. "I think you should try. I'll need as many as you can find for the next few days."

REVIEWS

Thank you for reading A Soul Incarnate. I hope you enjoyed
the story as much as I loved writing it.

If you enjoyed it, I would consider it a personal favour if you
left a review wherever you buy good books.

Reviews are the best way to spread the word about stories
you like.

Thank you,
Chris

ABOUT THE AUTHOR

Chris Andrews is an author of fantasy, science fiction, horror, and non-fiction.

Find him at http://chrisandrews.me

Stay in Touch
Subscribe to Chris's Newsletter

facebook.com/chrisandrewsau
instagram.com/chrisandrews.me
amazon.com/author/chrisandrews

ALSO BY CHRIS ANDREWS

FANTASY

Divine Prey

Epicentre

Moonlit Genesis

Urban Magic and Other Tales

NON-FICTION

Character and Structure: The Foundations of Fiction

Use the QR code to go to Chris's website: